# ROSEN

D1547654

*A Novel By*

**Michelle Hall**

*For anyone who ever listened to me when I declared that I had an idea to share. Thank you for your time and patience.*

# Contents

# How It Ended

**ROSEN**

MICHELLE HALL

# November 23rd, 2021

What went wrong? The dreaded question that had plagued Leonard dozens of times every day over the last six years. He tried to combat it whenever the thought entered his mind, but the fight was a losing battle to this problem, where the answer never revealed itself. The only way to mute the struggle would be to simply go to sleep. The upcoming week would be challenging, as Leonard already knew what date approached on the horizon, but tonight, he refused to be distracted. This evening, he wanted to enjoy breakfast for dinner with Jackie.

On Tuesday nights, Leonard guzzled pancakes with ample toppings, not caring if this meal sent his blood pressure into the moon's orbit. There was not enough syrup fathomable to quench his desire for the sweet flavor tickling his tongue. Pats of butter melted and dripped off the golden stack and onto the white knife-scratched plates. Two scrambled eggs sat on a bread plate in the middle of the table, perfect for sharing. Leonard's grandson, Jackie, sat across from him, eating the food but not enjoying it like he usually did.

The boy did not touch his orange juice, something unusual Leonard noticed right away. At this point in the meal, Jackie usually indulged in a second glass of juice. He loved OJ, but tonight, he drank water only. Leonard's latest ex-wife always begged him to drink anything other than soda and attempted to incorporate water into his diet, but he always won the battle. Life was too short, right?

"Jackie, how about some blueberry French toast? Last time, we said we'd try it."

Leonard stared at his lanky boy with sandy surfer hair. He wondered when the last time Jackie showered as his hair sported a greased sheen.

The boy's sapphire eyes failed to make eye contact as he plopped the tiniest morsel of food into his mouth. Leonard was unsure if he had even heard the question.

"Earth to Jackie?"

"We already ordered, though." Jackie's prepubescent voice screeched. His eyes searched the barely touched plates before casting them down onto his clean linen napkin.

Leonard wasn't sure if anger or anxiety coursed through his bones from Jackie's nonchalant answer, but it didn't sit well in his gut.

After the meal, Leonard noted to add 'Eat a Tums or maybe several' to the list of exciting activities to do within the lonely walls of his home. Uncertainties drove him to the point of mental collapse.

"Doesn't mean we can't still order. And who said there are any rules here? Let's have some fun. That's what our nights together are about, right?" Leonard watched Jackie for a reaction, awaiting any muscle movement from him but got nothing. Something was wrong tonight. Leonard wondered if it had to do with the deadbeat father, Jesse, the biological one. You could be a parent by DNA, but that didn't mean anyone can claim the title with any right. "Everything okay, Jackie? You've barely touched your food tonight. Is it your stomach? Did you want something else? You know you can always ask to go somewhere else, right?"

"I thought that wasn't allowed." Jackie swallowed, struggling. "No, it's not that." He put his metal fork down for good and brought the orange juice to his lips but never swallowed a sip. "I'm fine."

"Nuh-uh. Something is up. I know I'm not your old man, but I am your oldest man. Talk to me. What's up?"

"It's nothing." Jackie forced his barely audible words out of his quivering mouth.

Leonard hissed air through his nostrils, upset at himself for not being able to solve whatever transpired at the table. Leonard would flip the table if this sudden issue had anything to do with Jackie's parents, who shared half a brain combined.

"Did something happen at school?"

"Everything is fine, Grandpa. It's just that sometimes I wish I could see you more. Maybe even live with you for a few weeks here, a few weeks there. Or spend a summer together?" Jackie didn't make eye contact once Leonard fixed his gaze on the boy's dirty fingernails. "I'm full." He pushed his plate away.

"You know, Jackie, I know we don't talk about this too often because I never want to upset you, but this week it's your...." Leonard searched for the word. "Your other mom's anniversary. Is that what's bothering you?"

"I know what's coming up this week. But it's not that." Jackie stared back with dead eyes.

"Is something going on at home?" Leonard leaned forward. "You can tell me anything, and I promise I will always protect you. You know that, right? What you say stays at this table."

Jackie shook his head, not confirming or denying anything Leonard just offered, but his mind was closed for the night. The boy crossed his arms, blinking tears away as his eyes glossed over.

Leonard shifted in his seat. A sudden queasiness slammed into him, almost triggering a loud gag. He squashed it by downing a glass of iced water. *Water.* Leonard just drank a glass of water. Something was wrong.

They drove home in silence, save for the moment Jackie told Leonard to go when the light turned green. Leonard detested backseat drivers, and Jackie had once corrected Leonard's driving about two years ago. The moment the criticism flew out of Jackie's mouth, the boy instantly regretted it when Leonard shot him the infamous Rosen death stare. Jackie hadn't done it again, but a moment before, he simply didn't care, as if nothing mattered anymore.

Leonard zoomed his yellow BMW M3 down a lit main road in a residential area. Jackie's behavior had Leonard torn between wanting the night to end and wishing it could continue. He looked forward to these nights as they were the only constant he maintained with Jackie. All the other occasions together warranted a fight and a bargain. A stupid, frustrating dance Leonard needed to perform with the deadbeat dad, Jesse, and his bitch wife, Margot.

At least in two days, he got to see Jackie again for Thanksgiving. According to Margot's rules, not for the whole meal. Just for the dessert portion. Leonard planned to go to the cemetery in the morning, to his brother's house for the main dinner, and then to Jackie's for pie. He just cared about seeing Jackie. Thanksgiving fell on his daughter Millie's death this year.

Leonard held Jackie's heavy black backpack while walking a still sullen Jackie to the front door. Most of the lights in the house were off. The doorbell produced a dreadful science fiction horror buzz. Jesse's white rusted pickup truck was parked in front of the house, and the black tarnished motorcycle was laying sideways on the weed-filled front lawn. This neighborhood undoubtedly harbored decent people, but it was not Leonard's crowd.

"Your dad's home, right?" Leonard eyed the messy lawn, shifting his gaze from Jackie to the peeled front door.

"Yeah. Mom likes to keep the lights off now. Says it saves money," said Jackie, staring at a moth banging into the dimmed yellow porch light.

*Mom.* Jackie believed Margot was his mom. But she was not the real one in Leonard's eyes. Millie was his mom. Leonard's daughter, his beautiful girl, whose life he shouldn't have to remember and hold as a distant memory, she should still be here. It should be Millie who Leonard dropped off Jackie to. He wouldn't need to drop Jackie off from dinner because Leonard would be welcomed into Jackie's home any night if Millie was alive. But this was everyone's reality. Leonard awoke to a partial nightmare each morning, needing to piece himself together to get out of bed. In Leonard's lifetime, he had lost a lot. Broken marriages, failed engagements, millions lost in the stock market, and attorneys from poor business deals and life choices. But the most significant loss of them all was losing Millie.

The door creaked open, revealing Jesse's lean silhouette in the door frame. His overgrown nicotine-stained fingernails adorned his hand as he switched on the light.

"Hey, Margot? I'm turning on a light, but only for a minute. Jackie's home," Jesse said. Sleeves of tattoos and Jesse's raccoon-eyed face were bathed in a dim glow. Leonard caught the aroma of beer the instant Jesse took another step forward. "Hey, Leonard. How was dinner for breakfast?"

Leonard grimaced over the apparent mistake but decided not to correct him. "Always a good time." Leonard patted Jackie twice on the back.

"Right-o. Okay, Jacks. Say goodbye," said Jesse.

Jackie gave Leonard a cold limp hug while Leonard held the boy for an extra second longer than usual. Once Leonard broke his hold, Jackie bolted into the tiny house for the night. Jesse turned back to Leonard, offering a weak smile but not retreating.

"Hey, Jesse? Tonight, at dinner, Jackie seemed off. Is everything okay? I got the impression Jackie wanted to tell me what was bothering him but couldn't."

Jesse looked at the dark sky for an answer then dipped half a knee down as if he just remembered. "Ah, yeah. Ha, it's kind of funny."

Leonard just stared, bracing himself for what would come next.

"Leonard. We're going to Thailand. I told Jackie about it this morning, and yeah. I guess he's not taking it good."

"What do you mean? Are you taking a vacation there? I hear JFK is beyond crowded lately, " Leonard said, trying not to lose footing on the splintered porch.

"Nah, we don't vacation. We're not fancy like that. We're moving to Thailand. We're done with New York." Jesse's eyes had grown heavier since he last spoke. His sockets sank into his bony face, resembling black, empty orbs.

"What do you mean you're moving to Thailand?" Leonard thought he would only experience his blood run cold when he found out about Millie's death.

"Margot, she's an artist. And she's got some Thailand gig lined up or something she wants to explore? Same difference. So, Thailand it is."

Leonard stepped back, running his hands through his thick, now frizzing, silver-fox hair. He breathed through his nose, trying not to collapse. "What about you? Aren't you working now? I thought you just started at a new garage?"

Jesse must have changed jobs at least a dozen times every year since Leonard knew him, and it wasn't because Jesse found better opportunities. Jesse fooled Leonard when they first met, playing first impressions like the number one seed in tennis at the Wimbledon finals. But once day two arrived of knowing Jesse, the truth showed its jagged teeth, and the only way to get rid of the sharp edges was to toss Jesse out fast. Leonard never experienced that privilege.

"Oh, that place?" Jesse laughed, rolling his eyes.

Yes, that place. Any place that paid, rather than crying poverty to Leonard for some food money.

"Yeah, it didn't work out. I'll find something better. I always do, am I right?" As if anything better would present itself to him. Jesse wasn't worth half a penny better. "But doesn't matter now. I can't commit myself to anything long-term because of the move. It's time to keep my options open."

"Hold on." Leonard held up a hand, losing patience fast. "Have you ever been to Thailand? Speak the language? How do you know you'll even like it there?"

Jesse waved a hand in the air, dismissing the questions. "It'll be an adventure. Ever seen House Hunters International? People move to some pretty wild places. Plus, I love Chinese food. It shouldn't be that different in Thailand. I like Pad Thai. Had it for lunch the other day."

Metallic blood dribbled into Leonard's mouth as he bit his tongue. He stepped forward until the stench of beer mixed with some other odor was unmistakable. "Just two months ago, you asked for money because of a rough patch. And that's not even counting what I give you for groceries every month. Moving is expensive, and this isn't moving to another state or city. Have you ever even been out of the country?"

"I assure you, Leonard, I will pay back every penny I owe you. And I appreciate all your other concerns, but we're pretty excited about it. Except Jackie, but he'll come around."

Yeah, right. Jesse was the worst bullshitter once you got to know him. And then it dawned on Leonard. "Jesse? Have you taken the money I've given you and put it away for this Thailand move? How long have you known about this?"

Jesse threw his hand over his heart, feigning dramatics on an amateur level. "Really, Leonard? Are you serious right now? Are you insulting me on my front porch right before a holiday?"

The mere idea of Leonard overstepping his boundaries caused him to stand back and regroup his tumbling array of fraying emotions. He held no rights to see Jackie, except for the cooperation of Jesse and Margot, the tyrant. Margot's influence when Leonard saw Jackie grew increasingly under her aura. Caution was vital, even if it meant relenting to the wrong. "I'm just shocked. I'm sorry.

Jackie doesn't seem happy about this at all. I'm worried about him. He barely spoke or ate tonight."

"Aw yeah, well…" Jesse released a thick exhale. There was more than just beer mixed into that humid breath. "The other kids can't wait. Like one big permanent vacation."

Those other kids were Margot's kids, the only children treated equally well by both parents, while Jackie was the constant bystander. Leonard wanted to vomit. His boy deserved more and didn't belong here. He belonged with Leonard in his home, a genuine home with no favoritism and an open space for dialogue and respect. This wasn't the life he envisioned for Jackie. Leonard had so many plans for his grandson, but Jesse and Margot continued to stifle the efforts he pursued. It wasn't fair.

"Jesse! I thought you said this would be a minute! Turn the damn light off!" Margot called from some distant place within the cramped house. Leonard noticed each word she spoke melted into the next one. Jesse rolled his eyes and gave a half-laugh while Leonard remained frozen, trying to keep his legs from collapsing.

"When is the move happening?"

"Probably three to six months. Aiming for three months."

"Three months?" Leonard's mouth went dry, his tongue as bristly as fresh sandpaper scratched against the roof of his mouth. He longed for any kind of drink to bring him back to earth, even water.

"We're trying for sooner."

Leonard's eardrums vibrated with the word.

"Yeah. Well, thanks again for tonight, Leonard. Same time next week? Oh, about Thanksgiving. Let's cancel the dessert. We're having family over. Probably will get too hectic. We don't live in a big house like you, am I right? You can see Jackie next week for the usual dinner-for-breakfast gig."

"Wait, what?" Leonard believed he would collapse any minute.

"This is what Margot decided."

"And you too?" Leonard asked.

Jesse shrugged, not caring either way. "Goodnight, Leonard."

The door creaked closed as Leonard swung out a hand to stop its movement, almost falling over from his forward force, as he unintentionally flung the storm door back off its hinges.

"Wait a minute now. No one has thought this through. How about school for Jackie or all the kids? I know you said Margot might have a thing, but there needs to be something solid for money. What will you do once you're there? It's not like flying to Florida. Why don't you move to a cheaper state here?" Leonard was desperate, but he saw his life trickling down a drain, with no hopes of returning. "Are you sure this is something you can handle?"

Jesse stepped out from under the yellow buzzing light. The moon's light cascaded onto his face like a dirty waterfall. "We'll manage."

Leonard's blood ran cold. Those two words throttled his world six years ago and now threatened to do worse this time.

# *November 24th, 2021*

Leonard sat in the legendary Greg Cohen's office. He was a notorious matrimonial attorney who had aided Leonard in escaping all six of his marriages with little to no financial harm. Besides the prenups, postnups, and divorce cases Greg handled for Leonard, he also served as attorney extraordinaire for all Leonard's legal real estate closings.

Leonard canceled all his Wednesday plans after the Thailand bomb had been dropped directly on his head, producing a massive post-dinner headache, incurable with any amount of aspirin. He made a surprise visit to Greg's office. Since Leonard was one of the firm's best clients, Greg squeezed him in without issue. Leonard wanted to believe they held a relationship of higher substance than just lawyer to client, but he didn't assume something sentimental could exist. Leonard mainly did whatever worked for him and sometimes questioned if he was innately flawed in this manner. Greg had known Leonard longer than most people in his life, probably even better than most family members, too. So there, Leonard, who barely slept last night, maybe three hours at most, collapsed in a brown leather chair across from Greg and his many law books.

"I need to know what rights I have."

"Oh, no. What now, Leo?" Greg didn't flinch, though. He was always prepared to handle the curveballs Leonard threw in this office.

Greg was the only person Leonard permitted to call him Leo.

"It's that bum, Jesse. Are you ready for this?"

"Ready whenever you are." Greg held his hands wide open, ready to receive the ball.

Leonard took a drink of diet soda, always a fresh glass furnished whenever he entered Greg's office. He wasn't kidding when he told people his attorney's office knew him better than any of his ex-wives. He indulged Greg in the latest Tuesday night breakfast for dinner ritual with Jackie and told him how the meal turned sour when the twelve-year-old was not acting like his usual happy self and then dropped the giant bomb from Jesse.

"Thailand?" asked Greg, sounding like a parrot repeating something obscene.

"Thailand. The move could be even sooner. Who the fuck knows?"

"Isn't the guy a deadbeat? How can he afford to move to Thailand? What is in Thailand? Have you ever watched the HGTV show *House Hunters International?* These people up and leave to take a job in some foreign country to knit." Greg began his line of lawyer questions to check off the list. "How can anyone plan for this without money?"

"Exactly. How can this be a plan, period?" Leonard curled his hands into the tightest of fists. His nails dug into each palm, leaving dents.

"Fucking weird." Greg snorted, swiveling back and forth in his well-earned executive chair.

"I'm here because I need you to tell me what I can do." Leonard reached into his front pocket, feeling the blank check he packed just in case.

Greg's eyes shifted, lost. "I don't quite understand what you're asking, Leo. What do you mean, what can you do?"

Here it was, Leonard's big reveal.

"I want my boy, Jackie. There must be a way, and I know you can find one."

Greg was already shaking his head the moment Leonard's confession started. He was a fantastic attorney who always figured out a way to win, but he seemed stumped with this. "This is a slippery, losing slope you're asking about here. You're talking about full custody of your grandson?" Greg leaned forward, clasping both hands on his desk, raising a single bushy eyebrow.

"Yes, I want full custody." Leonard didn't flinch, and Greg looked completely surprised with his seriousness. Did Greg think this was all for fun? "Greg, I'm serious. I want Jackie."

Greg reclined in his chair, befuddled. It was the first time Leonard doubted if his attorney and confidante could help him. He hated the uncertainty.

"I feel like you once wanted to do this, but a long time ago. Am I wrong?"

No, he was not.

"When Millie first passed, I approached you about the idea. You said to wait and see if the father could handle fatherhood and go from there. I tried to believe he could, but he can't, Greg. He just has the title of Dad and nothing else."

"I'm not arguing with you."

"I've sent Jackie to camp, swim lessons, signed him up for sports, bought him clothes..." Leonard held up each finger to validate his point of how he's the actual caregiver, not Jesse.

Greg remained silent.

"Jackie needs me in his life. If I'm not there, who knows if he would have any quality of life."

"I believe you, Leo. I do."

"Then why aren't you saying what papers we need to draw up to get the ball rolling? You're just sitting there listening. You never just sit there."

Greg cleared his throat and adjusted his yellow power tie. "So far, from what you've told me, you sound like a very generous and excellent grandfather. These are all things you've chosen to do for Jackie. You're not obligated to do any of those things, right?"

"You're missing the point. They do nothing for him. He wouldn't have anything new if it weren't for me. When Jackie speaks, I listen. We genuinely laugh together. And I remember as a kid, the only person I ever did that with was the person I loved and knew loved me back."

"Not everyone can afford to do these things for their kids as you've chosen to do for Jackie. It's very noble what you've done for him over the years." Greg shrugged, still not offering any hope of stopping Thailand from happening.

"I want him, Greg. There must be a way." Leonard's shoulders hunched down to the carpet.

"Then give me something to work with. Any abuse? Drugs? Alcohol? Any of that stuff going on you've witnessed?" Greg pulled out a black pen with a yellow legal pad, ready to work.

"Yes. Last night when I dropped Jackie off, Jesse reeked of booze." Leonard watched Greg jot down the notes, getting into it.

"His fingernails are never cut. Sometimes Jackie smells like he hasn't showered."

Greg twisted his face, doubting every word. "Give me something better. Those are vanity things. Alcohol is something we can play with. What about drugs?"

"He's a young boy, though. Shouldn't his nails be trimmed?"

"Look, I know you're passionate about the nails, but it doesn't cut it in this situation you're gunning for." Greg noted one last thing before pushing the pad away.

"They're even dirty underneath. Anyone can see that." Leonard refused to give up on the nails.

"Leonard."

Greg never called him Leonard.

"What, Greg?"

"Ya gotta give up the nails." Greg showcased his own perfectly manicured fingernails to drive home the point.

Leonard didn't like this at all. Greg was usually so agreeable. Didn't he want to earn his fee today? Leonard was ready to write him a fat fucking retainer fee. Any number, Leonard came prepared to write and sign on the line. Leonard released a long exhale, feeling like he was slipping. He slipped away from the reason and confidence he carried into this office a few minutes ago. The arrogance had rippled under his skin on the drive over, so sure of himself and everything about today. Believing this custody situation would be solved in a single afternoon, the day before Thanksgiving, giving him something to be thankful for. But now, all Leonard saw himself doing was grieving the loss of his daughter, precious Millie, alone.

Greg frowned, watching the fading energy across from him leak onto the floor. He edged to the front of his seat. "Would you like another Diet Coke?"

"Fuck the Diet Coke, Greg. Give me what I want." Leonard never considered himself the type of legal client who put pressure on his attorney for unreasonable actions until today. Yes, his first out of many divorces proved the messiest. But Leonard never pushed Greg to the edge because Greg always knew what to do and how to handle things. That's why he was the magician, the David Copperfield of attorneys. But today, on this shitty Wednesday, Greg was failing. Leonard never considered seeking another attorney's opinion until this afternoon.

"I know what you're thinking, too," Greg said. "Ask another attorney. Go for a second opinion. Be my guest. After all these years, I never lied to you and always delivered. You know I'm right, Leonard."

"You're telling me to walk away, Greg. And if I walk away, that fuckhead takes my grandson with him. And I'll be the putz to fly to Thailand, only to be told when I do show up on their doorstep, to try again tomorrow." Leonard watched the spit fly out of his mouth. "If Jackie goes there, that's it. I'll never see him again, and I can't allow that to happen."

Greg sat there in silence, unsure what to say to the tirade. He breathed in deeply, staring at the ceiling for an answer.

"This will be the messiest of things if we pursue this. Forget about my legal bill. Everyone knows you can afford that. Psychologically, I'm talking about," said Greg, tapping his tan, creased forehead. "And I'm not worried about you. My concern rests with Jackie. Remember what we went through with your kids, Leo? You chose not to put them on the stand. You did that for them. I know you remember."

Leonard did remember like it was yesterday and didn't want to put his children through that misery, so why do it to Jackie? But it was different this time. Millie was gone, and the only part of her Leonard had left was her son. He couldn't lose both.

"What about the alcohol? He was drinking when I dropped Jackie off last night."

Greg shook his head, disappointed. "Drinking on a Tuesday night. Could signal a problem."

But Leonard wasn't convinced and knew Greg didn't believe it to be strong enough, either.

"If you were me, what would you do?" Leonard asked, leaning back.

"I'd find a way to figure this out away from the court system. Remember, even if we got Jackie pulled from his house, there's no guarantee he'd instantly move in with you that minute."

"I don't follow," Leonard said.

"He could end up in CPS, foster care before they decide to hand him to you."

Leonard grimaced at the imaginary knife in his gut, twisting harder and harder. There was no way he'd be able to eat a holiday meal tomorrow.

"This makes no sense. None, Greg."

"Nobody said the system was fair, my friend. But it's the one we live in."

"So, now what?" Leonard stared at the most unhelpful attorney in the room.

"If this father is the true and ultimate deadbeat you say he is, just pay the guy off."

Leonard threw his hands in the air, like batting a crazed hawk away, disgusted.

"I'm being serious, Leonard. Pay the prick off."

"Oh, yeah? What's the magic number?"

"That's for you to decide."

Leonard considered it for a moment. Yes, he had the money, but that wasn't the problem. It could become a trap he had set up, only to be the one who gets caught in it. He made up his mind.

"No. Hell fucking no," Leonard said.

Greg shrugged. "Only a suggestion."

"You know as much as I do, I'll say one number, and next thing I know, Jesse will come back asking for double, and it'll keep going up and up. Do you know how many times he has duped me? And I consider myself a pretty savvy guy. But Jesse somehow always found a way to screw me."

"It can't hurt to throw a number out there."

Jesse always knew how to pull another fifty bucks from Leonard whenever there was an opportunity, but Margot? She was worse than Jesse with her monetary demands, and while Leonard never asked for any acknowledgment, he never received a nod of appreciation from any adult in that house. But all this time, Leonard agreed to pay up because he wanted to keep seeing Jackie. Leonard extracted a blank check from his pocket and penned a five-thousand-dollar number made out to Greg. He slid it across the table onto the calendar blotter.

Greg eyed the check. "What's this?" He wouldn't touch the paper yet. A dark fear entered Greg's eyes at the check's sight.

"That's for your help today and for the research you're going to do once I leave this office. We're going to figure this out."

"It's one o'clock the day before Thanksgiving. How late do you expect me to stay?" Greg asked, but he took the check anyway.

"You decide. I'm not saying anything else."

Greg already endorsed the back with his bank stamp before tossing the paper into a growing pile.

"Well, always a pleasure, Leo." Greg extended his hand. The men shook. "I hope you know the advice I give to you is the advice I would give to my brother."

"I thought you hated your brother."

"Not that brother. The other brother."

Leonard nodded to say, of course. He pushed himself out of the chair, his sixty-five-year-old bones fighting him, despite most days holding a thirty-five-year-old's stamina.

"Wait, wait! I almost forgot." Greg reached into his bottom desk drawer, pulling out a hefty legal-size manila folder. He held it up in victory, drumming his fingers against the file. "The appraisals are in." Greg beamed like a kid about to eat the most decadent chocolate cake.

"Oh, shit. Let me see." Leonard fell into his chair without thinking, nearly grabbing the folder from Greg's slippery hands. Leonard thumbed through the documents. A few weeks ago, Leonard summoned Greg to order appraisals on four properties he owned in

Brooklyn. Leonard's lip caught the pooling saliva pouring out of his mouth onto the documents. He looked at Greg's unwavering smile after looking at the values. "Did you read through them?"

Greg nodded silently but never dropped his grin.

Leonard sat there stunned with only one thought in mind: time to sell. "Unbelievable. Can you believe this?"

"After we sell these properties, we'll all retire and live happily ever after." Greg held up a multi-gold ringed hand. "We didn't discuss a fee for this, but you can pay me another time. Or if you have an extra check in your jeans, it can be now. Whatever works."

Leonard stared in awe at Greg, the shark attorney, always hunting for the kill. "Next time. And hopefully, you'll have an answer about Jackie for me." Leonard sprinkled a quick reminder.

"I'm going to research and don't you worry. But it's the day before the holiday. We don't have to decide what we will do right this minute."

Leonard already decided he couldn't lose Jackie. He stood up with the thick stack of appraisals under his arm as Greg mimicked the stance, watching Leonard walk out of his comfortable office.

"Oh, and Leonard?"

"Yes?"

"Happy Thanksgiving. Doing anything for it?"

"Tomorrow is Millie's anniversary. So, I'll probably think about her the whole day, like I do every year. I often go from the day she was born to what her last day might've been like. I like to torture myself, I guess."

"How about you take a break and enjoy the day with the family?" said Greg.

"There are no breaks with kids, especially when they're not here."

"Try something different if you can. Maybe go from the most recent memories to the earliest ones?"

If Greg only knew what he asked, but then again, Leonard was happy Greg had no idea about the pain he carried with Millie gone. He didn't wish that on his worst enemy.

# September 24<sup>th</sup>, 2020

Today, Jackie turned eleven. Leonard knew he wasn't invited to the birthday party today as it was explained to him by Margot. This was a celebration with the other side of the family, her side. Jesse and Margot assured Leonard that it wasn't even their idea to throw anything for Jackie today. How nice, it was Jackie's idea. He wanted to see his cousins and eat hot dogs fresh off the grill—the American dream of a young boy. Fine, an invite did not exist for Leonard, and he swallowed the bullshit excuses as to why he couldn't attend, but it didn't mean he couldn't stop by in the morning hours before celebrations with the other side commenced.

For months, Leonard had researched what to buy Jackie for the big day. He wanted it to be spectacular, something he would use daily, and something he could enjoy for hours. And, of course, it had to be neat. No, make that awesome. Leonard believed in giving Jackie nothing but the best, and he certainly would not fall short today. Leonard knew what Jackie had and didn't own because, honestly, Jackie wouldn't possess anything without Leonard in the picture. Jesse and Margot realized Leonard was the pot for serving Jackie, not even his spoils, but anything the boy needed. From school supplies to toys, Leonard sourced the well. He didn't mind, as long as it granted him the active role Leonard had carefully carved for himself since Millie's death.

He roared down Jackie's street in his stick shift BMW he had just picked up from the dealership a week ago. Yellow was his grandson's favorite color. He specifically picked the shade to impress Jackie. Leonard thought one day he would be the one to teach Jackie how to drive a stick. Leonard learned how to drive manual from his grandfather when he was sixteen, and he wanted nothing more than to pass down that tradition to his boy.

Leonard whipped into the driveway that needed to be sealed and maneuvered the car over the craters with expert precision, not wanting to damage his Perelli summer tires.

Leonard couldn't wait to present Jackie with his gift, the excitement skipping through his blue veins. He opened his trunk and stared at the black box in awe, spotting an old grey stuffed bunny sitting in the corner next to the gift. A brand-new Sony PlayStation 5 sat in the black trunk, waiting to be played by the birthday boy. He had hinted to Leonard months ago that it was a dream to play on the console. Jackie had no clue Leonard listened and noted to research the device for hours because that's what Leonard did when he started a new quest to find the best for someone he cared about.

He lifted the one-thousand-dollar box out of his trunk, securing it under his armpit, and marched to the front door. Of course, he forgot to attach the card to the gift, but something told Leonard that Jackie wouldn't mind once he saw the box. His dream birthday gift. Leonard fought to sleep last night. He was so excited about today and the reveal. He bought ten video games to go along with the console to ensure Jackie had enough game variety to get him off to a good start. Obviously, more would come by next week.

Leonard pressed the struggling buzzer without a sound resonating throughout the tiny cape. He tried again until the buzzer sizzled under the touch, so he resorted to the old fashion way, pounding three times on the door with a tightened fist.

Heavy footsteps neared the stained white peeling door with splashes of mustard patches. Margot appeared in the doorway seconds later, her hair in a messy bun, her cheeks a blushing, unflattering rose. It was only noon, but Leonard swore he caught a whiff of wine. Her face twisted at the surprise of Leonard on her unwelcome mat at this hour of the budding day.

"This is unexpected," said Margot. "What's wrong?"

"Hi Margot, how are you?" Leonard needed to stay pleasant, even though he despised this sloppy bitch three feet away from him.

"I'm trying to get ready for the party today, Leonard. I thought you knew."

Oh, he knew. After all these years, Leonard never received an invite to come into their humble house. He was never permitted inside, and when he strongly hinted he wanted to go in, someone always shunned him away. Again, he never wanted to push anything because he didn't want to lose Jackie.

"Oh, yes. Yes, I'm sorry." Leonard tapped his forehead. "I guess I'm getting old." No one in the vicinity believed his bullshit line.

"Is there something you wanted?" Margot crossed her arms over her fat, unattractive, sagging breasts, supported by a flimsy sling.

Leonard assumed she wanted to cover up with small kids in the house. "I wanted to give Jackie his birthday present on his birthday." Leonard held up the shiny black box in front of his stomach for Margot to see.

She didn't budge while her eyes danced around the box's corners as air hissed from her nostrils.

"What's in the box?"

"The latest PlayStation 5 console. It's what Jackie wanted."

When she remained silent, Leonard, for whatever reason, decided to give some homeownership advice.

"I didn't mean to pound on your door before. Is your doorbell working?"

"Nah. Had Jesse snip those wires a few weeks ago. Waste of electricity and money."

"Anyway, would it be okay if I gave Jackie his present today? I wanted him to have it on his birthday." Leonard tapped on the box, noticing his finger pads developed a sheen of sweat.

"He's in his room. I think."

Of course, Margot didn't know Jackie's whereabouts. She didn't fool anyone into believing she cared an ounce for Jackie compared to her children. No one expected her to favor him over her kids, but at least she could make a small effort.

"Can I go in and give it to him? I'll be in and out fast. I promise." Leonard showed Margot the box one last time to prove to her this was the only reason he wanted to see Jackie. It was his birthday, goddammit.

"Leonard, I'm sorry, but I don't think that's a good idea today." Margot tightened her arms across her chest, accentuating her cleavage in an unflattering, bone-grinding fashion.

"I see." Leonard dropped his eyes to the ground. "May I ask why?"

"Well, for starters, his room is a mess. I always tell the boy to clean up after himself, but he doesn't listen."

Leonard bit his tongue and grasped the box tighter to stop himself from slapping her across her pimple-pocked face. Give his grandson a break. It was his birthday.

"And if he sees that game now, he'll just want to play it all day and miss the afternoon."

It was his birthday. What the fuck was happening?

"Also, if my kids see Jackie has such a fancy gaming thing, they'll want to play or fight over it. I don't need fighting in my house, right, Leonard? You had little kids. Who wants to hear the fighting?"

"I don't want to cause any trouble."

"Or my kids will want us to go out and buy something like that thing you've got there. I can't afford something like that now. And I'd never ask you to go out and buy a second PlayStation?"

Oh, you wouldn't? Leonard thought. Of course, she fucking would. Just last month, she asked for some money to buy clothes for Jackie that Leonard had yet to see his boy sport.

"Now that I think about it, maybe just keep it at your house, and when he sees you, he can play it then?"

"If I keep it at my house, Jackie will never get to play with it. C'mon, Margot. Let him have it. It's his birthday." Leonard signaled with his hand inside the cluttered house. It wasn't just Jackie's alleged messy room that prevented Leonard from entering, but the entire house, from Leonard's view, resembled a tornado that had barged its way through. "Also, I only see Jackie at night on Tuesdays. We eat dinner and then come back here, not that there's anything wrong with that. But there's never enough time."

"I know what day it is, Leonard, but these are my rules and what I think is best."

"Can I at least wish him a happy birthday? I'll put the present back in my car, so he doesn't see it."

Margot shook her head, no. "He's busy now, Leonard. I think he's in the backyard."

"You said room before." It was Leonard's one challenge to Margot he permitted for this exchange.

"Whatever. He's busy. How about you call later? My guests aren't arriving until three."

Leonard staggered a few steps away from the door as a sick knot formed in his stomach. He thought about standing his ground, but what did he have to stand on? What were his rights here? Instead, he bent. He bent so far backward and forwards that he swore his bones cracked.

"Okay, I'll be sure to call him when I get home." Leonard's voice croaked each word from his parched mouth.

He left and called Jackie later that day, but he never gave him the gift and was only granted the promise that Jackie would pick out whatever sports gear he wanted when they saw each other next. And so, the once sparkling game console sat in the back of his junk closet, collecting dust.

# June 24<sup>th</sup>, 2019 – Camp

The engine's roar almost deterred conversation from happening during the four-hour car ride to upstate New York. Leonard tried to keep the engine noise at a minimum, but it proved impossible with all of its modifications. They soared through open, windy roads as limitless plush green trees lined the highway. Leonard loved a solid drive as it tested all gears in the car, and he showed off his true driving skills to Jackie. It was time to teach him what real driving entailed, where you controlled the car's response time to the engine and not some automatic machine.

"You excited, my boy?"

"Yeah. Thanks for taking me, Grandpa," said Jackie, staring at the trees whipping by.

Leonard's downshift caught Jackie's attention.

"Don't worry. I'll teach you how to drive one day." Leonard tapped the boy's skinny knee.

"My dad says he'll take me to a parking lot when it's time."

"Oh, yeah. He can do that, except I'm talking about driving a stick. That's real driving." Leonard winked. "Everyone drives an automatic these days. Not everyone can drive a manual car. That's something only I can teach you. Plus, it makes you sound tough. Also, your car will never get stolen."

"Why did you learn to drive stick if everyone drove automatics?"

"When I learned how to drive, manual transmissions were much more common. Automatic cars were on the rise and fast. Do you know why?"

Jackie stared at him with his wide eyes, waiting.

"Because it was easy. Real driving always was and always will be a stick shift." Leonard dumped the clutch and launched the car like a hot pocket rocket.

Every time Leonard threw the car into a swooping turn, it produced the brightest smile from Jackie as he braced himself from the force. It was a smile Leonard waited for during their moments together.

"Who taught you how to drive a stick shift?"

"My grandfather." Leonard shifted his eyes to the open dusty road.

"And now my grandpa will teach me." Jackie flashed a smile, showing his charcoal-braced teeth.

They drove a few minutes in silence, admiring the trees and highway carved through mountains. There wasn't a cloud in the sky, shaping a blue canvas that welcomed them on the open road ahead. Only a handful of cars had passed them on their trip up so far, which made the drive more eventful for Leonard to display his driving skills to an amazed Jackie.

"Aren't you glad you'll be up here for the full six weeks?" Leonard motioned to the foliage, nothing but green surrounding them. "This will be your landscape for the summer."

"Yeah, I'm so stoked. I'm happy Mom let me stay longer."

Leonard swallowed a mouthful of bitter saliva from Jackie's last admission. Jackie's mom, what a horrible joke. She was a placeholder for the real mother who would never be. Leonard's stomach ached from the reality.

"Four weeks would have gone too quickly. I'm glad Margot... I mean, your mom... changed her mind."

"Will you come to visit?" He hugged his knees, tucking them under his chin on the leather seat.

Leonard winced from the sight of Jackie's sneakers on his leather Alcantara sports seats, special order for this model car. He stopped himself from correcting Jackie's stance. This ride was close to perfect and had no room for criticism. Everything today was for the boy.

"Of course, I will. I already cleared my schedule, kiddo. And when I come up, you better not pretend you don't know me."

"Nah, you're a cool grandpa." Jackie dropped his feet back onto the racing mats, kicking them under his seat.

Leonard breathed easier, revving the engine for no reason, but still bewildered how Jackie couldn't keep his legs entirely away from his prized seats. "Anyway, you're gonna love this place. They have every imaginable sports activity. Air-conditioned bunks. Even the food looks awesome." Leonard wasn't lying about the food. He had never seen meals plated at camp to resemble a five-star restaurant. A camp that offered air-conditioned bunks was another selling point and wallet-bending decision Leonard couldn't ignore for Jackie's sake. This was his first taste of a Tiffany-tiered sleep-away camp, and Leonard wanted him to love it.

"When it's time to leave, will you drive me home?"

"We need to check with your parents first."

"They won't care. My brother and sister keep them busy."

"I'll double-check with them first. But I will be more than happy to drive you back."

Jackie popped up in his seat and fist pounded Leonard.

"Cool," said Jackie.

"Cool," repeated Leonard.

# *March 25th, 2016*

Leonard popped open a crisp bottle of Diet Coke. He decided that if he sat in one more office and was offered one more glass of tepid water, he'd scream and throw the cup against the wall. Leonard stayed ahead of the curve this time and brought his own damn beverage of choice with him. He didn't want to be there, but after Greg praised therapist Doctor Levine, saying this chick could cure anything in one session, Leonard hoped she'd pull the gnawing ache from his belly.

This month marked four months since she passed, and the tears would just fall every night when Leonard sat down on his bed, and he didn't even expect to cry, but it happened. He chalked it up to his grieving process, but lately, the tears stung more. For the last three weeks, Leonard had been truly alone. Amy was gone, but that was Leonard's doing. He needed to be away from her and everyone he didn't want present in his life. The only person he bothered was Greg daily.

Leonard drummed his fingers at a maddening pace on his knees. He was almost sure there would be quarter-sized bruise marks on his skin from the constant finger motion later tonight. He couldn't sit still. Squirming morphed into as regular a need as it was to breathe. The chair Leonard sat in cost a fortune. He knew this chair well because he had owned one with his ex, Becky. Leonard forgot to ask the price of this session, but if the furniture was any sign of this therapist's taste, then today's forty-five-minute visit would be anything but reasonable.

Dr. Levine swung the door open, throwing back her cherry brown hair, shiny as a perfect sun's rays during the height of the day. Her skin didn't display a single blemish, containing the ideal amount of tan, and was spotless. Her figure matched the tan. She was perfect, and there was no way Leonard could ever concentrate on healing from this woman. He wanted other things from her, and forty-five minutes were not enough to get them.

"Leonard?" said Dr. Levine, gliding across the room, sitting down a perfect six feet away from Leonard's stance. Six feet too far, he thought.

"Hi. Hello." Leonard shifted from one hip to the other. "How are you?" So lame. So fucking lame, Leonard, he scolded himself.

"I'm doing well. Loving this weather."

"Right, it feels like spring." Leonard forgot what season it was until Dr. Levine mentioned anything relating to her perfect skin tone. "I haven't really been outside that much the last few months. I'm usually a beach bum."

"Usually? Meaning you haven't been one recently?" Dr. Levine craned her neck, offering a slight grin.

"It's been a weird time in my life." Leonard cleared his throat, ready to open up. This is why he was here, to dish and tell things to a complete stranger. "I just told my wife... well, yeah. My soon-to-be ex-wife that I want a divorce."

"Oh, I'm sorry to hear that."

"Nah, it's fine. I'm used to it."

Dr. Levine squinted, trying to understand Leonard. He thought he'd help her comprehend.

"I lost my only daughter four months ago to a drug overdose. She's why I'm here today. Her name is... *was* Millie." Leonard's leg shake commenced at a stirring speed, enough to produce slight vibrations throughout the room.

"Oh, I'm so sorry for your loss." Dr. Levine uncrossed her legs but kept them pressed together. She clasped her hands in front of her body, ready to listen without offering verbal feedback.

"Thanks. It's funny. I can't tell you how often I've heard people say that to me. I guess it's just part of it right now, right?"

Dr. Levine swung her sandal-covered foot counterclockwise. The gold straps on the footwear complemented her olive complexion.

"I keep asking myself if I did something wrong. Did I mess up somewhere along the way to lead me where I am now?

"That's very general. You've lived a lot of life to ask such a vast question. Unless you're referring to something specific?"

"My biggest regret is not fighting for my kids when my first ex and I were battling it out in our custody case." Leonard crossed his arms, attempting to mute his pounding heart. The instant he thought of his ex-wife, rage that started as a burn and transcended into a vicious cold coursed throughout his body. "I don't blame myself for Millie's death if that's what you were asking."

"I wasn't asking that."

Leonard held up his hands. "I just wanted to make it known that I do not blame myself for Millie's death. The mother should blame herself." He pointed to the open air.

"What did she do?"

"Everything wrong. No discipline. No rules. Pitted them against me when money was needed. She lied. She was a master manipulator. Just a terrible, terrible person. Oh, and she finally abandoned them when they were both teenagers." Leonard rubbed his temple, fighting away a headache. "That's how I finally got them."

"How many children do you have?"

"Just Millie and a son, Steven. So, I guess one now. Steven's younger. He doesn't talk much about Millie and what happened."

"How old is Steven?"

"Twenty-nine. I got him just in time. Steven was thirteen; Millie was fifteen, going on sixteen. She wasn't bad when she first moved in with me, but the signs were there. The seeds were planted. She already had her group of high school friends, and they weren't the best. With Steven, I had time to set him right."

"If your ex was this awful, how come she got custody of your children?"

Leonard shook his head, running his hands through his thick hair. He clapped his hands together, rubbing them for heat. "I ran into hard financial times during the divorce. Made a few bad decisions with business deals. I lost almost all my money and couldn't afford to hire child psychologists and all those other specialists required. But the court still favored the mothers usually. It had to be a terrible situation to pull kids from their mothers back then. Things are different now, I think." Leonard raised his eyebrows, shrugging. "Now, I've made all my money back. At least I had the money to send her to the best rehab facilities. Whatever good that did."

"So, she tried to get clean."

"Oh, yeah. First, we tried those detox centers that aren't very intense. But then, after she broke into my house with a bunch of her junkie friends, that was the final straw. I sent her down to Georgia. You should've seen this place's brochure. It looked like a five-star resort."

"Did she get clean?"

"Yeah. Yeah, she did. And then she lived in a halfway house down there for some time. And I guess things fell apart one day. All it takes is one bad day where you fall off the wagon, right?"

Dr. Levin offered a half smile with heavy eyelids.

"I think about that one bad day a lot. I often wonder what happened to her to make her go overboard."

"And she was completely clean until that moment?"

Leonard squinted, recalling the details he didn't want to acknowledge. "I think she started to slip a few weeks before then. She started to act erratically. She wasn't answering my phone calls and texts. She lost twenty pounds suddenly."

Dr. Levine threw her head back, nodding as if understanding what the weight loss signified, and it wasn't anything pure. The drugs won once the weight started to melt away.

"So yeah. I think about her last day a lot," said Leonard, registering his sudden need to have a partner. He knew who he would call later.

"When you think about that day, what is it that runs through your mind since you weren't physically there?"

"I just hope she didn't feel lonely. Like she didn't have anyone." Leonard rubbed the back of his aching neck, his skin hot to the touch. "See, she called me up, begging to come back home several times leading up to the day it all happened, when they found her dead. But I just couldn't say yes to her whenever she asked."

"Why couldn't you?"

"I knew she wasn't clean. I wasn't particularly happy with my wife. I knew we weren't going to last. But really, I didn't want to deal with Millie when I knew she wasn't straight."

"It must have been a challenging situation to deal with at the time."

"Everyone told me to cut her off before she hit rock bottom. I could never do it. But this was the first time I told her she couldn't come home. I thought she was better off staying down there to get clean."

"Of course. You probably registered rehab as being the only place to stay sober."

Leonard shook his head. "That was the only time I rejected her pleas to come home. And then look what happened."

"So, do you blame yourself for that? Telling Millie she couldn't come home when she asked?"

"No. No, I don't. After she broke into my house that day, that was it. She crossed a line. But the thing is..." Leonard fought the ball settling in his throat. "She has a son. My grandson." Leonard's voice cracked. He slapped his hand over his lips, stopping a weakness from spilling out of his mouth. Rosen men didn't cry. They were tough.

"It's okay. Take your time." Dr. Levine nudged a grey box of tissues on the glass table toward Leonard.

He scowled at the tissues. There was no way he'd break down in this overpriced leather chair and cry in front of a stranger he wished to court outside this room.

Leonard cleared the rattle in his throat. "My grandson, Jackie. He's five. He hadn't seen his mother, my Millie, in months. She lost custody of him over a year ago. Anyway, he lives with his father now. He's not a great guy by any means. I'm not even sure what kind of father he is."

"Do you believe Jackie is safe with the father?"

"I think he'd be better off with me, actually. After Amy, my soon-to-be ex-wife left, it got me thinking. I could be a better father figure to Jackie than his own dad. The night I saw the father come to the hospital to get Jackie from Millie..."

Dr. Levine raised a suspicious eyebrow.

"There was an incident. But I just knew I could do better. Hell, that night, I gave the father money to thank him for taking Jackie back to his house. Imagine having to give a father money to take his own son home." Leonard ground his molars, fighting off a mad leg shake. "That piece of shit."

"Do you believe money can solve problems?"

Leonard didn't speak. He only craned his head to understand.

"I hear what you're saying about wanting to take in your grandson. But so far from what I've listened to, it sounds like you've equated your problem-solving to what you can afford. Please, tell me if I'm completely off course."

Leonard shifted in his chair, adjusting to the sweat stains forming behind his knees.

"Money has allowed me to do things more freely than others. Hell, I sent Millie to the top-notch rehab center in the country. That just bought time and didn't change the outcome everyone else and I dreaded."

"And money has also failed you," said Dr. Levine, raising her pointy chin.

Leonard considered the thought for a second before continuing. "Yeah, sure. Yeah. I couldn't afford the child psychologist that time to put the kids on the stand during my custody battle."

Dr. Levine nodded.

"Sorry, but I don't understand what's happening here." Leonard leaned forward, ready to do battle.

"Why do you want to have your grandson live with you?

"I can provide a better life for him. Give him all the things I gave to my kids once I got custody of them and all the things I would have given them if I had them all along." Leonard pulled at his collar with a sweaty finger. What temperature was the thermostat set to?

"Things." Dr. Levine let the word hang off her tongue like a thorn.

"I remember Steven was fourteen. There was this baseball hat with these rips and, I think, a chain. Something like that. The thing looked like a piece of crap, but it was the hat to wear if you wanted to look like someone in school. I must have devoted an entire day tracking down that hat. And when I gave it to Steven, he was so happy." Leonard welcomed the smile spreading across his face. "Once I got my kids, I wanted them to have nothing but the best and know they could have it and know they will be taken care of. That's what I want to give my grandson, Jackie. I want him to know he'll always be safe."

"Why does he need to live with you to get those things from you?"

"You're not understanding. His dad is a deadbeat and difficult. God knows if he'll even let me see him regularly after everything that's happened."

"I see."

"No, you don't. No offense, but you don't know the father. You don't know the whole situation. We've only just met and have spoken for ten minutes, so no. You don't see. I see what needs to be done. It's obvious to me." Leonard banged his chest.

Dr. Levine's eyes clung to Leonard's still fist, frozen solid against his chest. She lifted her eyes once to meet Leonard's but didn't speak.

"Why are you fighting me on this?" asked Leonard.

"I just think you wanting to pull a child who's suffered a lot so far in his short life from his father just because he can't spoil him the way you would..." Dr. Levine trailed off, shaking her head. "I don't know. I just disagree."

"You're not seeing it the way I do."

"I see you equating money with love. You reward those you care for with expensive things. Or if they're behaving, you buy them something shiny."

"Is that a bad thing?"

Dr. Levine pursed her lips. "What happens if you get Jackie, but he starts acting up? Then what? You stop rewarding him. Give him the cold shoulder?"

Leonard slumped into his chair, realizing something about this session if Dr. Levine hadn't already.

"I think we're done here. I don't think this is going to work out."

Dr. Levine stood up, flattening out the pinstripe skirt that hugged her hips, and walked to the door, pulling it open for Leonard's premature exit.

Leonard frowned but proceeded to the door with the best posture of his life. He paused mid-step, pulling out three hundred dollars in crisp bills and tossing them onto the water-stained glass table. He walked to the exit, stopping to peer at Dr. Levine for the last time.

"Look, I know this didn't work out, but would you like to grab dinner sometime? Maybe we'd have better luck at a nice steakhouse?" asked Leonard, running his eyes the length of her body.

She retreated a step away from Leonard, not returning his roaming gaze.

"Good luck, Leonard."

About an hour later, after raging on the expressway to Greg's office, Leonard sat stewing in the chair across from his attorney. He had already downed a cold glass of Diet Coke within the first minute of arriving at Greg's building.

"She was the worst fucking therapist. How could you vouch for a bitch like that?"

Greg cocked an eyebrow as he circled around his desk like a shark marking his prey. He popped down into his executive's chair, ready to do business.

"Slow down. I know she's a shit therapist."

"Then why? Why did you vouch for her like you did?" asked Leonard.

"She's an attractive woman, and I thought the two of you would get along well." Greg's eye caught his college twenty-four-carat gold ring. He stopped to huff on its center, polishing it off with the corner of his suit jacket.

"Three hundred dollars, Greg. I just wasted three hundred dollars to be told I'm wrong about how I fundamentally operate as a person."

"Really." Greg's voice climbed an octave higher. "I thought the two of you might have hit it off."

"Well, I did ask her to go to dinner after deciding the therapy wasn't going to work."

Greg threw his body back into his chair, clutching his belly as the laughter roared out of his black hole mouth. He gasped for breath, slapping his mahogany wood desk.

"And of course, she said no. So, it really didn't work out with this chick."

"Oh, Leo," said Greg, regrouping, smoothing his greasy hair back. "Don't change. Don't you ever change. You are a legend, my friend, you know that?"

"I'm here for another reason." Leonard shifted in his seat, finishing off his second glass of diet soda.

Greg straightened himself, adopting his lawyer stance, pulling out a yellow legal pad and uncapping a black felt-tipped pen.

"If this is about Amy, I haven't heard anything from a divorce attorney," said Greg.

"She's shopping around for one. I told her to take her time. I'm not worried about her, though. She's going to be an easy one."

"Fair enough. I like easy. So, what's up?"

"I think I want to pursue custody of Jackie. Millie's son. My grandson."

Greg dropped his pen on his desk, frowning. He clasped his hands, resting them on his rotund belly. "Why?"

"I can provide a better life for Jackie." Leonard's pulse quickened. "C'mon, Greg. You've met Jesse. He's not the ideal person to raise a kid."

"But he's been raising Jackie while Millie's been away."

Millie's death, Greg could have just said her death. Leonard's hand wiped away the sweat beads forming on his brow.

"I know me raising Jackie will give him a chance. Jesse steered Millie in the wrong direction. God knows what he'll do to Jackie if he did that to my daughter."

"This all sounds very speculative. Would it hold up in front of a judge? Probably not. Does Jesse do drugs?"

"What's the definition of a drug these days?"

"How are you doing?"

"What do you mean? I'm fine. Things are moving along. Don't worry about me. I'm not divorcing Amy because of what happened. I had planned to before anything with Millie."

"I worry about you. I consider you more than just a fantastic client."

"You must say this to all your best paying clients."

"I'm telling you this idea you have with Jackie right now. Raising him and all? It'll be very tough to achieve right now. Unless you have concrete proof he's being abused, or it's an unfit living situation for him, you're facing a very steep and slippery slope. Would I love to charge you for this work? Sure. But it would be the equivalent of me stealing your money. You're my friend, and I can't do it."

Leonard clutched his heart with both hands, throwing his head back.

"Oh, Greg, don't make me cry over here."

"You wanted my advice. Here it is."

Leonard leaned forward, catching his breath. It was the first time since the night of Millie's death that he experienced several waves of complete failure. He wasn't going to get Jackie today, tomorrow, or anytime soon. So, now he needed to do the dreaded work of figuring out what to do about it.

"Now, what do I do?" Leonard's eyes darted about the room, landing everywhere except for Greg's face.

"Have you seen Jackie since everything that's happened?"

"Of course."

"And the father allows you to see him?"

Leonard's throat tightened. "Yes."

"So, continue doing what you're doing. I know it's not what you want. But sometimes, we need to make the best out of the situation. I know you're not used to the idea of settling." Greg signaled around his office, reminding everyone where they were. "Sometimes, we have no choice."

Leonard fought a wave of dizziness, realizing today marked the first time he acknowledged the idea of settling over any situation. But if it meant doing what was best, for now, by his grandson, he had no choice.

Leonard dragged his eyes from the floor to the diploma at head level on the wall behind Greg. Leonard nodded, understanding today was over. He extended his hand to Greg's side, and the men shook.

"Hey, do you want to come over for dinner? My wife's meatloaf is to die for." Greg stood up, matching Leonard's stance.

Leonard laughed. "We both know your wife doesn't like me."

"You're right. She doesn't. But I like you. That's all that matters."

Leonard waved his final goodbye for the day and closed the door.

# November 29th, 2015

His fingertips ran along the wood's smooth finish, not spotting a single dust particle. A chestnut lacquered coating for this expensive box was what he would call it, for now, a box. He couldn't bring himself to use the proper label, not yet. He flattened his palms against the cover's shiny surface. The box rested on a platform, closed. They decided not to have the box open. The rabbi reassured Leonard that it was customary in the Jewish tradition to keep the box closed, and it was the correct decision. Leonard really wasn't familiar with anything having to do with the day's happenings. He just wanted it to be over with. Then again, it meant saying goodbye. And he wasn't ready to say goodbye to Millie. Only thirty-one. She was only thirty-one. And then it hit him: what this box's finish reminded him of, his piano at home, a once prized possession, no longer prized. His Steinway baby grand piano at home by the bay window had this exact finish. He knew what his next project entailed: to get rid of the fucking piano that reminded him of his daughter's coffin.

That day sucked. It absolutely sucked as if lemons were being squeezed into your eyes. The day Leonard buried his daughter was proof nightmares existed in this life. His life. It was ruined, tarnished for the decades to come. He was only fifty-nine and knew he had years to live with this pain, this void. But Millie had so much ahead. Her life was a blank canvas with the blackest of paints thrown against the white surface that ruined everything. Her life was cut short by what they say was an accidental overdose. Accidental. Of course, it was. She never meant to harm herself. She had a problem. There was only a five percent chance of her conquering that addiction. She never had a chance. That was the line he kept repeating to everyone who attended the funeral. She never had a chance. Only five percent. She wasn't here; she was there, getting better. But clearly, she lost. It took one day. One bad day and within a moment, she was gone.

A palm landed on Leonard's shoulder. He turned to see it belonged to his son, Steven. He offered a weak smile to his dad. The rims of Steven's eyes appeared like red vines wrapped around multiple times over.

"The director said they'll take her into the hearse soon. We should probably get to our cars," said Steven, his voice rattling with phlegm.

Leonard forced a nod. He didn't want to leave her side. Not yet. He even brought her favorite stuffed animal and intended to place it with her when they lowered her into the ground. It was a bunny. A plain blush bunny with a faded pink nose. She named it Pinky Rose when she was four. No one knew where Millie got the name, but Leonard thought it the most brilliant and creative thing to exit a toddler's mouth. His beautiful girl was intelligent, creative, and full of light. And now, things were the complete opposite. She was gone.

He would put Pinky Rose with Millie right before they said goodbye. But not yet. He would wait for the cemetery.

"Are you sure you don't want to come in my car? I don't mind driving us," said Steven.

Leonard shook his head no, half chuckling. He didn't think he could create any sound resembling happiness other than the sobs he had fought over the last three days. Only in private would he release everything he bottled up inside. He patted Steven's shoulder.

"No, that's okay. I want to drive," said Leonard. He did not permit anyone to drive him around, not for the longest time, and he certainly was not going to turn over a new leaf and begin today. He needed to maintain any sense of normalcy, some sort of control. It wasn't like he'd be driving alone since Amy, his umpteenth wife, insisted on riding shotgun with him in every direction. He yearned for space, not needing to share any oxygen with anyone, but she didn't get it and never would.

At the gravesite, the rabbi waited for the mourners to congregate. Leonard hoped this speech proved better than the one at the funeral home that was sprinkled with inaccuracies. Rather than focusing on his daughter's last moments above ground, Leonard had corrected the rabbi's mistakes like some heckler at a cheap comedy club.

"Glasses, now," Leonard said to Amy through gritted teeth.

She fished out a new pair of ultra-black darkened Ray Bans. He grabbed them from her, forcing them on. Amy had a continual stream of tears falling behind her aviator-covered face. When Leonard peered around at everyone there for Millie, there wasn't a dry face in the vicinity, filling him with an eerie warmth.

Leonard glanced at his charcoal grey sharkskin suit, white shirt, and black tie. He couldn't fit into this suit for months, and it took a full year of slow and steady eating to lose twenty-five pounds. He finally did it and had better plans for this attire, never expecting to wear it first at his new svelte weight for his daughter's funeral. He hated this suit and had every intention to toss it the instant he returned home.

The rabbi locked eyes with Leonard, silently communicating this part of today's procession was about to commence. Millie would be buried in the family plot and the first relative of the clan under seventy to join all of their lost loved ones. Leonard massaged his aching temple, preparing himself for what came next. At some point, Amy slipped her cold hand around Leonard's arm, but he didn't notice. His entire body had reached a new level of putty numbness.

"Friends, I want everyone to look up at the sky," said the rabbi.

Everyone listened and peered at the bluest of skies. Not a single cloud blemished the day's ceiling.

"It's perfect, today's sky. The weather. Some might say it's the most beautiful day of the year. Saying goodbye to Millie, a woman who should be here with her family, her parents, her siblings, and her son. But Hashem made other plans that we'll never be able to fathom, agree with, or come to terms with for Millie. But at least he gave us a beautiful day to say goodbye to an equally beautiful soul."

Leonard even surprised himself as he hadn't begun to cry yet. He clutched Pinky Rose close to his hip, unsure when to place her with Millie or if he should let go of the cherished stuffed animal.

The rabbi extracted the silver shovel from the mound of clay-colored dirt and held it in both hands. Leonard had requested a brand-new shovel for the ceremony, the first request of its kind, the funeral director told Amy. He wanted everything immaculate and shiny for Millie today, nothing but the best.

"In the Jewish tradition, we conclude this part with various prayers and then pass a shovel to the mourners present today. No one must participate, but those who do, think of it as a brave mitzvah. Covering our lost loved ones in the final blanket, they will ever know. With each shovel full of dirt, you give something back. A part of you goes with them, and Millie will never be alone."

Leonard spotted two other shovels in the mound but knew only the shovel in the rabbi's hand would be used. The rabbi peered at the somber group until his eyes landed on Leonard. He silently extended the shovel in Leonard's direction.

He cleared his throat, nodded, and accepted the shovel. He expected it to have a substantial weight, but it felt like tin in his strong hands. He shoved the head of the shovel into the dirt, triggering a brown dust cloud to penetrate the perfect day's air.

Leonard dropped the first heap onto her coffin, onto Millie, and began his long and final goodbye. From the first thud, he had to stop. He stopped to shake his head and fight the tears. He paused for what felt like forever and only produced another handful of powdery dirt onto her grave until he believed he would fall into the six-foot-deep hole to join Millie. Leonard buried his daughter. He offered the shovel to Steven, who shook his head, declining, and then forgot who had taken the tool from him. All he recalled after was Amy steering him by the elbow away from the plot.

"I thought you wanted to give the bunny to Millie?" said Steven.

They walked away from the site and back to their cars. Leonard peered at his left hand that still grasped onto Pinky Rose.

"I decided to have her stay with me."

# November 25th, 2021

Leonard awoke to an odor, a hint of smoke. Was something fucking burning in his house? This is how it would happen. He always feared fire and even prohibited using space heaters in his home. Fire. He feared the idea of one, especially being caught in a blazing inferno alone. It was only nine in the morning, but he already felt like the walls were closing around him. He jumped out of bed in a half jog, chasing the smell of something nefarious. As he skipped steps, the odor grew stronger. He landed in the kitchen and instantly spotted the source.

Wax dripped from Millie's Yahrzeit candle onto the blue marble countertop. He forgot to place foil under the candle, but these candles were never supposed to leak.

"Shit."

Leonard grabbed the glass encasing, only to drop it from the heat it emitted. He swore he heard a crackling pop upon skin contact.

"Fuck."

He pulled his hand away to suck on the bruised, sizzled fingers. Without thinking, Leonard blew out the mourner's candle. He had lit it last night before passing out with the aid of an Ambien. Since Millie's death, he had found an Ambien to be his friend on the eve of the date that had changed his life forever and whatever it took to get through the one night, Leonard accepted the aid. It was the single exception he made during the year to his aversion to pills. Upon further scrutiny, Leonard discovered a hairline crack down the side of the candle's cup that had grown overnight once the wick burned and its liquid pooled. The candle was ruined, a piece of junk. The one actual symbolic image of Millie's passing for Leonard to honor, he couldn't even deliver in full.

He called the Judaica store where he bought the candle a few weeks ago, but no one answered. And then he remembered, it was Thanksgiving. On Monday, he would tell off the owner and demand a refund, maybe even call the credit card company in advance to challenge the charge.

Leonard hobbled over to the breakfast nook with a cup of black coffee, not waiting long enough. The skin on the roof of his mouth bubbled, and the raw, icy hot sensation of damaged skin settled. It was going great so far.

The reality sucked. Everything sucked. Millie not here sucked. Leonard choosing to remember and re-live life with Millie on one of the biggest family holidays today sucked. At noon today, he planned to go over to his brother's house for an early Thanksgiving dinner. The reminder that he could not enjoy dessert with Jackie pained him further on a day where anguish acted as the worst thorn-filled blanket. He wasn't even sure if he would go to his brother's. His only real plan, after that, was to head to the cemetery at some point. Every year, he visited Millie and brought her favorite flowers, a bouquet of the brightest sunflowers.

This was the first year that Leonard wasn't entangled in a relationship with a woman in a long time. He couldn't pinpoint the last time he was thoroughly single. No side pieces, no full-blown romances, nothing. It was a strange and odd cocoon to inhabit, and he was unsure if he wanted it to be this way next year. He could change his relationship status in a week if he called upon the correct woman from his past. He had a navy leather book of females he stayed connected to, just in case. He took another sip of his coffee and started to think about Amy. She was with him when everything with Millie fell apart. The more he wondered about Amy, the more he wanted to remember what was it about her, about their relationship, he didn't want to deal with anymore? He suddenly wanted to call her, so fuck it, he would. Leonard was sure she wouldn't mind a drop-in call. They didn't end on bad terms necessarily. They just ended. Sometimes things didn't work out. The more he considered it, he believed he actually said that line to Amy when he broke up with her. Yes, she cried, but from Leonard's experiences, they all cried. Life was too short, so why waste it? Why settle? He wanted to be happy and didn't want to drag the other person down from his unhappiness being with them. In his mind, everybody won when the breakup occurred. So, yes, he would call Amy.

On the third ring, she answered.

"Happy Thanksgiving, Leonard."

"Hey, you. I had a feeling you would answer. Happy Thanksgiving, Amy. How are you?"

"Leonard, is everything okay?" Amy cleared her voice.

"Everything is great. It couldn't be better. How about you?"

A man's voice muffled in the background jolted Leonard as a reminder that Amy had probably moved on. They broke up years ago, and she was pretty attractive, despite her shortcomings within Leonard's vision. But why did they break up? Think, fucking Leonard, think.

"We haven't spoken in years, Leonard. Why are you calling? Is everything okay? Are you okay?"

"Why do you keep asking me that? Can't an old friend call to say hi?"

"You're my ex-husband. Not just a friend."

"Yes, I am aware." Leonard bit his bottom lip.

Amy breathed into the phone as Leonard pulled away. A scowl grew across his face. He wanted to enjoy a light conversation with his ex-wife. Suddenly, he doubted this idea and wanted to escape.

"Leonard, just tell me you're okay."

"Why do you keep asking me if I'm okay?"

"Are you single now? Is that why you called?"

"I might be, and no, it is not." Leonard breathed. "Are you single?"

Now, Leonard regretted his decision. Why was he still talking to her? Anything having to do with Millie always threw his judgment and better instincts out the window, always opening the door to him and falling into duped terms, like his reasoning for calling Amy today. He shouldn't be talking to her, mainly because he ended it with her, and she didn't want things to end. She wanted to continue to be his wife, she claimed, six years ago.

"No, I'm not."

"Well, that's great. I'm happy for you, Amy. I really am."

"I keep asking if you're okay because we both know what day it is. I don't want to say it. But I do think about Millie all the time. How's Jackie? Does he remember Millie?"

And then Leonard hung up on her because he remembered why he divorced Amy. She was so fucking stupid.

# *November 25ᵗʰ, 2015*

On the way home from an uneventful dinner, the clutch to his car acted up tonight. Whenever Leonard shifted, something about the clutch's grab point seemed off. Like it didn't... grab? He didn't feel one with the car as he usually did driving the blue M3. Although, his driving technique, lately, one might deem as aggressive? If anything was wrong with the clutch, it was Leonard's fault, not the device's. Oh, well, he could always take it to the shop the following week. What's another thing to fix? He shifted into third when he sensed the car slipping out of gear.

"Shit, fuck," said Leonard. He didn't mean to swear. It just spilled out.

"Ugh, really?" said Amy, riding in the passenger's seat.

Leonard ignored the comment and her, wanting to pretend she wasn't there. He didn't want to be here either, with her. Their third wedding anniversary passed last month, and while Leonard still bought her an expensive piece of jewelry as a present, he didn't mean the sentiment behind the diamond necklace. If anyone saw what he spent on her gift and the beauty of its design, anyone would assume their relationship rested on solid ground. His true intentions behind the gift were to follow through on the basic motions he believed were needed to be fulfilled in a marriage. It was their anniversary, so buy the wife a gift. He had money to spend, so, of course, the gift would be pricey. But at this point in their marriage, a partner was missing with Amy that Leonard yearned for. He wanted to be cared for, but

Amy could only do so much. She wasn't home in time to cook him dinner. She worked full-time in the city and didn't get home until seven or later. During her downtime, she insisted on decompressing. What puzzled him most about his desire to burn the marriage was that she didn't change. He realized this wasn't what he wanted in a partner. It was a funny thing with Leonard's perception of the perfect woman. They often started as a ten in his head, but once they lived together, the latest woman dwindled to a measly three, far below his standards and needs. Whatever went wrong between him and Amy, Leonard knew he couldn't continue the charade and, even worse, Amy would not see it coming. Leonard planned to celebrate his fifty-ninth birthday in a month, and he was almost sure that by the time his sixtieth arrived, Amy wouldn't be by his side, and he was okay with the idea. Almost relieved, actually. It sounded heartless to admit knowing they wouldn't be together in a year. It brought him a strange joy, a freeing solace.

"Maybe we can plan a trip to Aruba soon? I was thinking February? I can call the travel agent," said Amy, gazing out the window.

She really had no clue how her life steered towards a new path, a path where she would have the option to change her name from Rosen back to her maiden name.

"Why does it always have to be someplace hot and with a beach? What about a ski resort?"

"You don't ski." Amy rolled her eyes while studying her freshly polished red nails.

She was correct, but he hated being ridiculed. True, he did not care for skiing, but his point was just to try something new.

"I think trying something new would be nice."

"But I really wanted to go someplace warm where I can just collapse on the beach with a cocktail. Doesn't that sound nice?"

Sure, except Leonard didn't drink. Maybe the last time he sipped any form of alcohol was at his Bar Mitzvah, and he hated it. Once he made up his mind on something, especially for flavor, there was no going back, similar to how Leonard viewed their marriage.

Leonard bit his lip and said, "We have time to decide."

He caught Amy rolling her eyes as she looked out the window, and at that moment, he wondered if she found herself unsatisfied with their relationship. Something must tug at her. They hadn't been intimate in three months at least. A rarity for them and for Leonard. Even stranger, he didn't look for a new woman. Usually, he would only fully break off whatever current failing relationship he was in with a new female persuasion. He didn't consider it cheating. He rationalized this was his way of extracting himself from the current relationship.

"Do you even want to go away?" Amy asked, facing Leonard full on.

"Jesus, Amy. Don't you know when to stop? I said we can talk about it later, goddammit."

Leonard made a sharp turn into their long driveway, not caring how the back of his car kicked out from behind. Indeed, Amy was not a fan of his technique as a medium yelp escaped her mouth, and she grabbed onto the door's handle for dear life.

And then, there was a set of flashing lights from a police car. He knew. Leonard had zero troubles or ghosts in his life, except for one person. His daughter Millie. She lived in Georgia in another attempt to get clean from her rampant addiction. But this was the first time he ever came home to cop lights. These colorful lights never existed, even with his nastiest divorces and combative exes. Leonard stopped his car six feet away from the cop's vehicle. He got out, leaving the engine running. Amy stood by his side, clutching his arm before Leonard protested. He couldn't feel his body. Something terrible had happened. Life-changing, maybe.

Two cops stood outside of their car. One was the silent partner, Leonard could tell from his broad stature and blank stare, while the other was the face of the duo.

"Are you Leonard Rosen?" the face asked.

Leonard wondered if he denied the question, would whatever they were about to tell him just disappear? He didn't decide further because Amy chose to function as his voice.

"Yes, and I'm his wife. Is everything okay, officer?" said Amy.

"Do you have a daughter named Millie Rosen? Living in Georgia?" The face asked.

Leonard forced a swallow. "Yes."

"I'm sorry, Mr. Rosen, but your daughter was found earlier today unconscious on a park bench," the face said but then paused.

"What time was this?" asked Leonard.

"At two in the afternoon," said the face.

Okay, six hours. Hopefully, she would be awake by now. She probably had a bad day. All it took was one bad day to slip back into dangerous ways.

"Where is she now?"

The officers exchanged a quick glance as Amy squeezed Leonard's arm tighter.

"Mr. Rosen, I'm sorry, but your daughter didn't make it. She was pronounced dead when she arrived at the hospital," said the face, removing his hat as he spoke.

Time fell silent, and the words weighed on his heart like a spiked blanket, squeezing his blood source to a pathetic puddle of pulp. Leonard swore his heart ceased beating, and his blood ran cold. The first thing he heard was Amy's sobs when he returned to himself. Millie didn't make it? But this wasn't the first time something like this had happened, so why should the end be different? Did the hospital make a mistake or cause a terrible misunderstanding? This couldn't be his Millie, his precious Millie, who brought him loads of happiness years ago before flooding his mind with constant, unwavering anguish. He needed to call his attorney, Greg, to find out what he could do. His mind raced while nothing else moved. Nothing else made sense. Ten minutes before, he would have called himself the luckiest man on earth. Ten minutes before, he was a father of two. And now down to a father of one. Or was he still a father to two children? How does this change? It changed everything.

"Mr. Rosen, would you like us to escort you inside? Do you need any medical assistance?" the face asked, taking one step closer.

The only thing Leonard wanted to do besides process the idea of Millie gone from this earth was to see Jackie.

# November 25th, 2021

A green shirt seemed appropriate for the holiday meal. Pairing it with jeans, a brown belt, and loafers, Leonard deemed himself good to go. He had already showered, styled his hair, and shaved. There really wasn't much more to do than wait until it was time to leave for his brother's house. He would probably spend an hour, at most, at his brother's. Dine and ditch. Leonard didn't care. He stopped caring a long time ago. Leonard popped on the television to see if anything worthy played today. He switched to the news as the broadcasters recapped the parade from the city earlier this morning. It was the usual array of floats. One float appeared to be a superhero with a red flowing cape that gave the character's identity away with the centered logo on his chest. The cape seemed to be huge on the screen. It dominated the size of the eighty-two-inch display.

Leonard cleared his throat several times as a sudden itch crept up and down his esophagus. As the itching worsened, he couldn't rip his eyes from the red cape. And then the tingling followed and sensational face numbness. He took the remote and did the only thing he could think of. He flung the device full force until it hit the screen. He didn't know the TV would shut off from the collision, but miraculously, it did. Leonard needed to get a Diet Coke and fast. He just hoped he didn't forget how to swallow. Of all days to have an episode. He needed to quell the anxiety, this body-controlling tug that threatened to topple him. A cold, clammy sweat coated every pore of his body. Great, he would need to take another shower if this continued much longer. Leonard reached for a glass cup but forgot how to lift his arm. The panting quickened, and his chest muscles twisted. Was he losing it because of Millie? Or was it because Leonard could possibly lose Jackie in a mere three months? He couldn't figure out anything until he drank something crisp, but he was losing this battle and fast.

Leonard slid down the side of his kitchen island, now gasping for breath. He was going to die. This was how they would find him. The police? His son, Steven? He wasn't sure. But someone would find him dead in a puddle of his misery on Thanksgiving. Think of your happy place, Leonard. His previous therapist advised him to do this whenever these random episodes commenced. They weren't often, but they occurred enough that he sought the help of a professional to teach him tools to utilize, avoiding the medication route he resisted with every fiber of his body.

The only problem? He forgot what happy place he had chosen. It had been at least a year since he had an attack. Think Leonard, time to fucking think. What was your goddamn happy place? Failing to recall his happy place only produced anger. It wasn't the beach. Amy ruined all the sandy escapes for him with her incessant whining about needing to go to a beach to unwind from her stressful job. Screw the beach. It was not his happy place. But it was too late to recall now. Leonard slumped further down on the floor as the light penetrating his pupils faded, his eyes fighting to stay open. They pushed and struggled until everything went black.

"Dad? Dad, wake up!" A voice called out, producing an echo.

Leonard's body shook from a force produced not by his own strength. He pried his eyes open. Someone found him. But he wasn't dead. He came back from an episode. A panic attack. Still, on the kitchen floor, Steven, Leonard's only child, cradled his father like a baby.

"Dad. You're going to be okay." Steven cooed to his dad like he did to one of his dogs. Steven had no kids, just animals. Steven positioned Leonard to a half-sitting position, bringing a glass of cold water to his father's lips.

Leonard welcomed the cold sip. He finally opened his eyes to see Steven's face inches from his own.

"Dad, what happened?"

"What do you mean? Nothing. I fell, that's all."

Steven frowned, unconvinced, as he refreshed the glass with more water. He returned to Leonard's side, kneeling next to his shaky father.

"Do you think it was a panic attack?"

Leonard scowled and grabbed the glass from his son's hand, pushing him away. "Watch your tone. Don't look at me that way, either." Leonard once heard his therapist throw around the term panic attack. And even if Leonard did experience a few sporadically throughout his life, what was the big deal? It wasn't like he suffered from them regularly. Still, he detested the expression that glued itself to Steven's or anyone else's face who realized Leonard might have suffered through one. He wasn't a fucking invalid. He experienced emotions; sometimes, they played out more physically than others who processed them. Leonard wasn't even sure what set off his panic attacks. They just happened, and he moved on, only to expect another one to occur in the future.

"Are you still up to going to Uncle Robby's?" Steven asked.

"Yeah. Of course, I am. I'm fine. Jesus, Steven."

"I just want to make sure you're okay."

"I am fine. Everyone needs to relax." Leonard wrangled his arm free from Steven's hand and clawed his way up to a standing position. He took one last gulp of water before sliding onto a barstool. He caught his breath, finally.

"Are you prescribed anything for when you have one?" Steven asked, taking the seat opposite Leonard's.

"Steven, drop it now. I'm fine." What a ridiculous inquiry. Anyone who knew Leonard understood his rejection of medications. He'd rather suffer than take pills. What if he became addicted?

Steven shook his head at his father's impossibly stubborn ways. "Sorry, Dad. I know today isn't just Thanksgiving."

"Does this mean you'll come with me to visit Millie today?" Leonard eyed his son, studying him from his choice of wearing a baseball cap to his brown Sperry moccasins. He never understood why Steven abstained from going to Millie's grave after a certain number of years and acted like Jackie didn't exist. Steven was never rude to Jackie when they seldom saw each other, but his son made no effort as an uncle. It bothered Leonard, and he once tried to poke Steven over the topic but quickly abandoned it when he saw an argument was about to erupt. Everyone dealt with loss in their own fashion, Leonard surmised, himself included.

"I'll see. It's a busy day, you know? Theresa is meeting me there later. She needs to stop into her family's feast first." Theresa and Steven got engaged about six months ago after Leonard pressed Steven to ask her for marriage. They dated for years, and Leonard never comprehended the need to make sure two people were meant for each other before making the marital commitment. Of course, Leonard couldn't comment too much given his track record, but life was short.

"Theresa didn't make you go with her to her family's thing?"

"Nah, we're not like that. There's no pressure to show face with either side."

"That's good, I guess."

"I know you think it's weird, but it works."

"Clearly, I'm not a relationship expert, so keep doing what you're doing. Did you pick a date?"

"Looking to lock down a date in June and just bang everything out from there," Steven said as if he recited a play-by-play to a baseball game.

"That's good."

"We're going to get a dog soon, too." Steven perked up at the mention of buying a pet. "We decided to hold off on kids for a while. The dog should keep us plenty busy."

Leonard craned his head off center, staring at Steven, unsure what to say or this conversation's direction.

"We're not even sure if we'll have kids. This world is a nasty place. Why bring another innocent child into the world to see the ugly?"

Leonard wanted to scream and call Steven a fucking fool, but it was a holiday. There was always tomorrow to persuade him to reconsider his views on having children. How could Steven simplify the idea of parenting into a small bottle of clouded misunderstandings when he never ventured into the territory? It was an excuse to not have kids, and that was okay. Leonard would respect the choice more if Steven just came out and said they didn't want to have kids and not how ugly and vile this world they lived in became.

"I never thought of it that way." But then Leonard did think of something else. If Steven ruled out kids, that would make Jackie his only grandchild who was about to be ripped away from him. The mere idea pushed Leonard to call Greg, but he stopped himself only because of Thanksgiving. He hoped Greg came up with something from their meeting the day before. Silence equated to no news, like waiting for a doctor to call about test results.

"I saw Jesse yesterday when I dropped Jackie off from dinner. They're thinking of moving to Thailand." Leonard shook his head. "Not even thinking of doing it. Jesse made it sound like it's a done deal. In three to six months, he told me."

Steven's jaw dropped, leaving him speechless. "Get the fuck out."

"I know. All of them in that house are real pieces of shit, especially Margot. She holds the strings." If only Leonard found a way to appeal to her. The day she permitted Leonard into their house would be when he conquered her and won.

"Shit. And what about Jackie?" Steven asked.

This was the first time Steven said Jackie's name aloud, catching Leonard off guard. "Jackie goes to Thailand as well. I just can't believe this is happening. I'm going to lose him." Leonard ran his hands into his eyes, rubbing away he didn't know what.

"I'm sorry, Dad." Steven reached his hand across the kitchen island, but Leonard didn't return the gesture. The Rosen men weren't wired to display their emotions or coddle other men's feelings in their families.

"Nah, don't worry. I'll figure it out." Leonard batted Steven's hand away.

"Figure out what, exactly?"

"I met with my attorney, Greg, yesterday. You remember Greg?"

"Dad, everyone knows Greg."

It was true.

"Very funny. Anyway, I asked him to research ways I can seek full custody of Jackie to stop him from being kidnapped to Thailand."

Steven began shaking his head, silently protesting the notion of Leonard's statement.

"I know what you're thinking, but I've bounced around this idea for a long time, Steven. And this Thailand move was the final straw. It was what pushed me to decide." Leonard found his strength and walked away from the island into the massive living room with floor-to-ceiling windows. He sat down at the black Baldwin piano, tickling the white keys only.

"Dad, you know this idea sounds nuts, right?"

Leonard kept his back turned to Steven. He wasn't even sure why he mentioned anything. He knew Steven would never approve, especially when he pretended Jackie didn't exist to a certain extent. "I don't think it does. Jackie is miserable, they don't treat him well, and you think his life will get better once he's in some foreign country with deadbeat parents? Let alone I'll be out of his life."

"These are all valid points, but you really want to restart your life again like that? Be a parent again? You even once said parenting is for the young."

"Steven. I am a parent. I will always be a parent, and no, I'm not afraid to restart this clock, as you allude to with Jackie." Leonard struck a chord on the piano, extracting a fierce thunder from the percussion instrument.

"What did Greg say?"

"He'll figure it out." Leonard waved Steven's comment away as he continued to play jazzy gibberish on the piano.

"That's never a good sign when Greg doesn't have an answer."

Leonard spun around to face a miserable-looking Steven. He was unsure if he appeared this way when Leonard regained consciousness or upon confessing his desire to get custody of Jackie. When did Steven morph into a tepid human?

"Discourage me all you want, but I've made up my mind. I will find a way to get Jackie."

"You make it sound like Jackie is a piece of land you want to buy."

"He's a part of Millie, which means he's a part of me. Plus, I love the kid. I won't make the same mistake." Leonard began toying with the piano again, pumping its pedals without striking a single note.

"And what mistake is that?" Steven asked.

Leonard knew the exact mistake he referred to but couldn't say it to Steven's face. He didn't want to disappoint his actual son and rehash elements from Steven's unstable childhood. Also, the Rosen men didn't mull over regrets or mistakes. They continued business like any other day.

"I know you think having Jackie under your roof will be enough. But do you really think you can be there for him?" said Steven, waiting for Leonard to return his gaze.

Be there for Jackie? Did Steven believe Leonard wasn't there for him and Millie? Is that how Leonard was viewed? Some absentee father while in their physical presence? He would not hear it, would not accept it. He lived his life and provided a life for his children the best he could.

"Do you want to drive together to Uncle Robby's house?" Leonard asked, quickly changing the subject.

"How about I drive us?" Steven said.

"Not a chance. I'll see you there."

# February 20<sup>th</sup>, 2015

All Leonard heard coming from Millie were uninhibited sobs, and the problem was he didn't care. He didn't have a bone of pity left in his liquid jelly body. He blamed her for the lack of empathy. At one point, she was his girl, his rising athletic star, but that was a long time ago before she threw it all away and now begged him for something he refused to give her right now, at least not until she proved herself trustworthy and clean, neither of which she was on this particular call.

The other week, a counselor for the halfway house Millie lived in called Leonard to inform him of Millie's constant skipping out on meetings. They even caught her sneaking in a Mike's Hard Lemonade. It wasn't the deadliest cocktail but went against sober living rules. He thanked the counselor for giving him the heads up, and then he had it out with Millie since fighting was the avenue they chose to communicate with each other lately. It wasn't intentional. It was just the way the magnet drew them together.

"Please. I'm begging you. Let me come up. I missed the holiday, so let me come up now," said Millie, struggling to catch her breath, on the brink of hyperventilating.

Leonard didn't buy it as he let too much slide in the past. He should have been tougher on her. Maybe cut her off, throw her out of his house, but all of that was too late to consider now. He focused on keeping her in Georgia and getting her clean for good.

"No. I'm sorry, but you can't. You have to stay down there to get better."

"I am better, Dad. Please don't do this. You have to believe me." Millie's voice cracked.

"I believe you are better than you were a few months ago, but it's still not enough. You have to stay there."

"I've been gone for four months. That's a long fucking time." Her voice adopted new hoarseness that remained.

"I'm not buying you a ticket. I don't know what else to say," said Leonard.

"I miss Jackie." Millie sobbed into the phone.

"I know you do. But you owe it to him to get clean. Call him tonight. I'm sure he'd love to talk to you before he goes to sleep."

"That's if Jesse lets him pick up the phone when I call. Or better yet, just ignore my calls completely."

Leonard pulled the phone away from his ear as she wailed her words to a new, deafening level. Lights flashed in his face. He'd almost forgotten he carried on this conversation within the confines of his car. He planned to go straight home from his parking garage in the city, but he sensed a detour from his original goal.

"What do you mean he doesn't let Jackie talk to you? Jesse promised it wouldn't be a problem." Even as Leonard spoke the words, he realized how foolish and duped he sounded.

"Oh, come on. Wake up. Jesse thinks I'm a fuck up, just like the rest of you." Millie was an inch from collapsing and losing it altogether. "What's the point of getting clean if I can't even speak to Jackie?"

Leonard ground his teeth, fighting a tightening in his gut. Thinking about that fucking prick, Jesse, sent him into a spiral, wanting to kill. Leonard cracked his knuckles against his taut leather steering wheel, knowing where he needed to head next.

Leonard pulled up in front of Jesse's new residence, pretty sure he left tire marks on the residential streets he just traversed. He reached the address in record time, maneuvering the back roads as if he had driven down those streets thousands of times. Jesse had moved there with Jackie about two weeks before from the dump of a studio apartment they'd inhabited for over a year. To live in a real house with separate rooms must have been a relief for Jesse and Jackie, but the area was very common. That's all Leonard surmised from his foreign surroundings, the parked cars on the front lawns, the beach chairs on the poorly maintained front yards. Nothing about Jesse was Leonard's scene. The only thing of interest to Leonard was Jackie, so he would accept wherever his boy lived if it meant being able to see him in a more appropriate and comfortable environment.

Leonard jumped out of his sparkling blue Porsche, bolting up the broken brick path. He almost tripped on a cracked planter on his way up. He remembered Jesse briefly saying how he moved into this new house because of the latest girl he dated. Leonard forgot her name, but she probably wasn't a prize. Leonard still fought a chill rippling down his spine, knowing how he would forever be connected to this deadbeat bum through his precious grandson caught in the crossfire. He sometimes wondered how Jackie even had a shot with two losing parents, one being his daughter.

Leonard tried the flickering buzzer to no avail. He then pounded on the door. First trying with one fist and then with both simultaneously.

Fat heavy stomps charged towards the front door. It swung open, revealing a chubby, sizeable chested woman, clearly in her thirties but looking older because of poor nutritional choices. Her hair rested in mismatched rollers on the top of her head. Even though she was fresh from a shower, she still carried an odor that made Leonard take a half step backward.

She stared at him like walking venom. "Who the fuck are you?"

"Hi. I'm Leonard." The words caught in his throat.

She thought about his name for a moment before a light flickered in her dull eyes. "Oh. You're the grandfather."

Yes, the grand-fucking-father.

Leonard cleared his throat, pushing the anger from his mind for a moment of clarity and to remember why he sped here. "Is Jesse here? I really need to talk to him."

"He's showering." The lack of intonation in this woman's voice buzzed louder than the struggling fly light on the splintered front porch.

"Can you check to see if he's done? I'll wait."

She crossed her arms over her unevenly tan chest. Leonard guessed she was a fan of tanning beds at this time of year. It was close to frigid temperatures as his hands fought the numbing chill.

"I really need to speak to Jesse. Can I come in, please? I'm begging you." Leonard watched his breath cloud in front of his face. "Is Jackie awake? I know he goes to bed usually in about an hour."

"No, it's not a good idea for you to come in."

Leonard's heart dropped. "Can I at least say hello to Jackie?"

"Just give me the message, and I'll tell it to Jesse."

Wet flip-flop steps approached the door, revealing Jesse fresh from a shower as his hair still dripped onto his army green shirt.

"Hey, Leonard. What a surprise," said Jesse, wrapping an arm around the still mystery woman. "Have you met Margot? She's my new fiancé."

Margot flashed a smile. Leonard was quite surprised to see she had all of her front teeth intact.

"Jesse, can I talk to you in private? Maybe it would be easier if I came inside?" Leonard shot a quick glance over to Margot's disapproving stance.

"Nah, better to do it out here," Jesse said before turning his attention to Margot. "You go inside, tell him Grandpa is here. He can say hello after."

Leonard shot Margot a quick grin of triumph as she turned back into the house, retreating silently. Jesse shut the door behind him with an unsettling thud. Jesse's smile faded from a grin into a scowl.

"What's this about tonight?" said Jesse, not amused by Leonard's presence.

"When did you get engaged?"

"Oh, what? You came here to congratulate me?" said Jesse.

"No. I'm here for a different reason."

Jesse rolled his eyes.

"It's Millie. Look. I think she's doing much better, but not there yet. I was talking to her earlier, and she was pretty upset. Said something like sometimes she has trouble talking to Jackie when she calls?" said Leonard, wiping away the beads of sweat forming on his brow despite the freezing temperature.

Jesse crossed his arms, releasing a white air stream through his nostrils, piercing the midnight navy atmosphere.

"Do you know what she's talking about?"

Jesse shrugged, clicking his jaw.

"Jesse. We need Millie to get better. I need her to. You need her to. Jackie needs her to," said Leonard, pointing to the space between them.

Something came alive in Jesse at the mention of Jackie. He dropped his arms to his slender, narrow hips and moved toward Leonard.

"Yeah, you got that fucking right. Jackie needs his mom. And you know why? A judge said she needs to pay up each month. Lately, the kid eats so much. All he wants is snacks. Do you know how much groceries add up to?" Jesse jabbed his finger towards Leonard's sinking chest. "So, while Millie's down in Georgia doing God-knows-what, I'm here struggling to feed our son. Make sure he grows. Do you know how hard that is? Where's my help in all of this?"

Leonard put both hands in front of him, trying to air brake Jesse's rant.

"I hear you, I hear you," said Leonard, softening his voice.

"I don't think you do," said Jesse, his voice cracking. "I just lost my job again. But it wasn't my fault. The moron there didn't see my creative vision with bike paint jobs."

Leonard hadn't a clue what Jesse meant. All he heard was that Jesse had lost his job again. But he played the part and nodded, coaxing Jesse to continue.

"So, now, I'm trying to look for more work. I can't even do unemployment. Do you see where I'm coming from, Leonard?"

Leonard swallowed his pride. "I do."

"So, where's my money from Millie? Doesn't she care about Jackie at all?"

Leonard wanted to scream that Jesse's talk was about money. He missed the point. Leonard saw right through his transparent argument.

"Millie can't work right now. We know this."

Jesse stomped his foot in successive beats, not having the excuses for Millie's non-assistance.

"But I'll help you. Whenever you need help, all you have to do is ask."

"It's not always that easy to ask, Leonard."

"But I'll make it easy, okay?" Leonard whipped out his Gucci wallet, pulling out sixty dollars. He held the twenties out to Jesse, but no one budged. Leonard fished back into his wallet, increasing the total to one hundred.

Jesse crossed his arms, letting out another hiss of cold air. Leonard frowned before finding the light to an idea.

"Here, take this." Leonard clearly placed one hundred and fifty into Jesse's hand. "You get this each week, which should cover groceries for Jackie. And how about this? Starting tonight, I get to take Jackie out for dinner."

Jesse craned his head, considering the offer while not taking his eyes off the fresh money in his hand.

"It'll be a Tuesday night tradition. I can send him home with leftovers that'll spill into the next day. If you want something, we'll order it and bring it home. But let me have Tuesday nights with him."

Jesse kept switching his eyes from his palm back to Leonard. His hand trembled a tad.

"Starting tonight," said Leonard. "I want to take Jackie to a diner. Something simple. I promise not too much sugar."

Jesse stepped backward, half into the house. "Hey, Jackie! Get your shoes on. Your grandfather is here!" said Jesse. He jammed the money into his back-ripped jean pocket. "Just so you know, it's not like Millie calls every day."

Leonard closed his eyes and breathed. "I know, but please don't give her a hard time when she does. Let her talk to Jackie."

Jesse nodded.

"I have a car seat still in the back, so don't worry."

Jesse threw a careless hand in the air. "Five-year-olds don't need car seats. Everyone is too careful these days."

Jackie appeared, running into Leonard's arms before he had a chance to prepare himself for impact. For a skinny kid, Jackie packed a solid tackle. Instantly, Leonard thought of football. Jackie, the football star. He was barely of age to play, and already Leonard had mapped out his grandson's sport's path.

"Hey, Grandpa!"

"Hey, kiddo," said Leonard, scooping Jackie into his arms like a feather. He hugged his grandson, letting their energies join in full force. Leonard put Jackie back onto the ground, looking up at Jesse, who stood frozen a foot away. "I'll have him home by eight."

"Have fun." Jesse waved. "Hey, Jackie? Bring home some extra French toast, if they have it?"

Leonard noted to order two extra portions of French toast to send home.

Jackie gave his dad a thumbs up, grabbing Leonard's hand for the walk to his Porsche. Jesse slammed or allowed the door to close behind him. Probably the latter. The hinges on the door appeared to have rusted and died.

Leonard held Jackie's hand, swinging it in a pendulum motion. "So, Jackie. Every week, you and I are going to have dinner together. How does that sound?"

"I think it sounds great." Jackie shot a sharp thumbs up with his free hand. "Your car is so cool." Jackie's eyes widened as Leonard unlocked the sports car.

"What are we having for dinner?" said Jackie.

Leonard thought about it for a second before a grin spread across his face. "Have you ever had breakfast for dinner?"

# How It Unraveled

**ROSEN**

MICHELLE HALL

# August 15<sup>th</sup>, 2014

"If you need more clothes or more of anything, I can always pack up more and send it to you," Leonard said to Millie, who sat on the bed puffy and red-eyed. She never believed his bluff when saying she'd be sent to a full-blown rehab facility. However, the notorious break-in proved his words valid after the most recent events.

"But when will I see Jackie? Can I even tell him I'm leaving?" A fresh round of sobs exploded out of her mouth, heaving her body forward. She shook like her bones would crack from the pressure. He wasn't sure if it was from the genuine tragedy of not being able to see her son for the next few months or that she hadn't had a hit in over twelve hours.

"At the rate you're going, you won't get to see Jackie at all. Do you understand?"

Death. Leonard meant death. But he couldn't bring himself to say it to Millie's face, his daughter. The worst part was that this was Millie at her lowest, and he couldn't comfort her. He couldn't even put a hand on her shoulder, let alone a single finger. He called Amy earlier to tell her about the arrangements for Millie over the next three months, and even Amy couldn't hide her excitement. Everyone needed to witness Millie get clean for real.

"Will you visit me?" said Millie.

"Let's just get you down there and clean. I don't know the rules or protocols this place has. It seems beautiful, though. The director sounded nice on the phone. Almost looks like a resort, actually."

"Oh, I see. Resorts are fun." Millie scratched blindly at her track-filled, bruised forearm. At one point, she had concealed the evidence from Leonard, but not anymore. All her secrets were present for a damaging reveal. He caught a glimpse of the blotchy skin and shuddered.

"The weather is nice down there. Pleasant breezes. I checked weather.com." Leonard tossed Millie a white cotton long-sleeved cardigan. "Put this on. Sometimes it's chilly on the plane."

Millie obeyed without question. "What time is the flight?"

"Ten o'clock tonight." A sweat broke out onto Leonard's brow. He had to get her packed. This had to be done right this time. They'd never done this before, sending Millie away for a prolonged period.

"What if I hate it there?"

"You'll be fine."

"What if no one likes me there?"

Leonard laughed. "People have always liked you."

"What if I change my mind about leaving tonight?"

Leonard frowned, throwing a mismatched pair of socks on top of the neatly folded clothes in the luggage. He sat next to Millie on her bed. They hadn't been this close to each other in months, and the first thought entering his mind was that she needed a shower.

"Millie, I'm unsure what we can do from here if you don't go tonight. You can't stay at my house anymore, and I don't want to throw you out either."

Millie scrunched and rubbed her pasty skin on her forehead as new tears streamed down her face. It shocked Leonard to witness any more tears dispense from Millie's eyes after the amount of crying already achieved today.

Leonard placed a shaky hand on Millie's knee. In the past, this sort of gesture would be natural. It would be a need to comfort his daughter. But, today, he forced his hand there to show Millie he cared and that he was sorry. She wouldn't see Leonard sending her to the most expensive and exclusive rehab facilities as his way of caring. She needed to witness the physical act.

"Will you miss me?" asked Millie. She leaned onto Leonard's shoulder like she had the night before she left for college, asking the same question.

Leonard fought back hot tears, rubbing his face, pulling his lower lip down with his palm. "Lately, I've been waiting to get a call from the police about you, serving some bad news, the worst news for a parent. You know?" He patted her knee twice and cleared his throat. "I'm glad I won't need to worry about that anymore."

"I'm sorry you had to live that way." Millie stared at her torn sneakers.

Leonard nodded and resumed packing up her life. "Go wash up. Afterward, we'll say bye to Jackie and head to the airport."

Millie walked into the bathroom, not making eye contact with Leonard. He held his breath until he heard her turn on the shower.

"Dad?"

Leonard whipped his head up, hearing a snap in his neck.

"Thanks," said Millie smiling before disappearing into the bathroom to take her needed shower.

Leonard nodded to himself as his heart quickened and realized the one part of Millie that remained undamaged was the teeth implants that Leonard had paid for. The thudding pulse traveled to his ears, where it thundered, blocking out all the surrounding noise. He staggered onto Millie's bed from her teenage years. He caught his breath when he mustered the strength to sit up.

He didn't have much time before Millie reemerged. So, Leonard took the next three minutes for himself. He cried—cried for everything he lost, everything he missed, everything that Millie wasn't anymore.

# August 1ˢᵗ, 2014

The worst thing to catch during the summer months was a cold, and not just a regular sickness, but one that clogs your head and seeps into your chest. The slightest breath traveling too quickly down your windpipe could set off a series of body aching, muscle-twisting spasms, ending in a severe coughing fit. Leonard suffered from not only a summer cold but a man cold. He was the worst person when he felt unwell. No one wanted to be around him. Not even Amy. This was supposed to be their honeymoon phase when no one could do any wrong, and everything was fresh. He didn't expect to catch the world's worst cold at the end of their vacation in Italy, but it happened.

Leonard left his office early to venture to the drugstore to buy another round of cough and cold syrups. He was over swallowing pill-form decongestants. He wanted something sweet to treat this sickness, so he opted for over-the-counter medicinal drinks to ease his persistent symptoms. And Leonard rarely left work early. He considered himself a workhorse but continuously operated as a fair boss. Just because he stayed at work until seven every night, he did not expect his employees to. He managed several buildings. The last time he spoke to his accountant, he remembered the number of properties held steady at twenty-seven. In a year, he planned to sell a third of them. Maybe even slow down and enjoy life with Amy. Time would dictate his actions. Leonard always pictured these grand plans and assumed his life would venture down a specific path, but his plans never panned out the way he imagined.

He pulled into his empty circular driveway, bleary-eyed. The sun even irritated his eyes. This congestion and cough were winning, and all he wanted to do was collapse onto his mounds of pillows, thanks to Amy's latest decorating episode. He didn't mind the decor, but the pillows annoyed him. The copious items on the bed slowed him down from his goal—to just lay down. Today, he didn't care. He just wanted to kick this ailment and return to normal. He decided to park in the multi-level garage. Leonard was a car nut, so when he purchased this house years ago, he had lifts installed in the driveway as one of the first projects.

The heat from the day won over the air-conditioning as the mechanism battled against the attic's poor insulation. Leonard checked the thermostat, and while it was set to seventy-two, the house held steady at a mild seventy-five. If he wanted to feel like he was in Florida, then he would live in fucking Florida. Leonard was inside his comfortable home, edging onto a hot, humid path. He knew what he had to do but dreaded it. He needed to go into the attic to examine the air-conditioner and see if it needed to be fixed. This shouldn't be happening with a top-of-the-line equipment. He eyed the cold medicines he left on the kitchen counter. Just as he walked over to the brown bag to unload them, he spotted a drip out of the corner of his eye. He waited to see if it appeared again. Leonard inhaled, only to set off a series of hacks. He caught himself against the refrigerator, and then it happened again. The drip came from an air-conditioning vent above the breakfast nook. Just fucking great. Now he needed to go into the attic and maybe bring some towels. On one of the hottest days of the year, with one of the worst colds, Leonard had no choice but to head into the hottest part of the house, the attic. He unloaded and lined up all the cough syrups on the counter before heading upstairs.

He grabbed a few paper and terry cloth towels. Oh, well. He hoped these weren't the good towels Amy splurged on, but they all looked identical to Leonard. He considered calling Amy to double-check which towels he could use, but he decided to save his voice. Earlier in the day, his vocal cords lost a battle to all the phlegm dripping from his nose into his throat.

Leonard trudged up the wooden steps into the hot, hazy, dust-filled attic, but at least the space appeared clean. No signs of rodents, no vile odors of any sorts arising from the dry wood. Just a bunch of dust, an enormous failing air conditioning unit, and off to one side, pink insulation lining the attic's perimeter. If Leonard wasn't careful, he could easily fall through the pink stuffing. It was a trap.

Leonard examined the AC unit, and just as he suspected, the drip pan wasn't draining, overflowing, and triggered the leak into the kitchen, meaning this fix equated to a tiny fortune. He threw down the towels to soak up the slight flood when he swore he heard a sudden crashing. A sneeze shot out of his nose, almost causing him to fall back and through the insulation when he heard more clacks and foreign sounds coming from a part of the house.

His pulse thundered in his chest when he started to assume his house was being burglarized. The attic was the one room in the house that did not contain any weapon to defend himself. Just his fucking luck. Then he heard he heard muffled voices. This was quickly racing to a new level of reality. People were in his house. Leonard dropped onto his rear and pulled his sweaty legs into his chest. His forehead dripped with perspiration. His hair clung to his head. He was about to call the cops when a familiar female voice penetrated his eardrums. If his hunch proved accurate, then maybe he wasn't being robbed. And then he remembered the cameras. Yes, there were cameras installed all over the house. Just look at the fucking cameras, and he would get the answer.

All fifteen cameras appeared on a single screen on his iPhone, mocking him. Three of the cameras showed activity in the house. There were two people in the living room. Both guys, Leonard assumed from their attire and haircuts. He never saw them, but they searched bookshelves, under pillows, in the cracks of couch cushions. On the camera facing the ajar door to the guest bathroom, a singular male, pale as snow, searched in the drawers for something but only found linens and extra soap. And then, Leonard saw his answer to his living nightmare in the kitchen.

*Millie.*

It was her voice he heard moments ago that prompted him to check the cameras. About two weeks before, he had driven her to a detox center in upstate New York, where she promised this would be the trip where she got clean and sober. A new beginning. Every trip to a detox facility, she always declared as a fresh start, but Leonard knew better. He did not know when she would be released from her latest stint there. They hadn't spoken in over a week, and no one called him from the center, but he didn't call either. Their relationship over the last two years had soured over her choices and his hopelessness. There were too many open and oozing wounds for Leonard to drop the damage caused by Millie's addiction and character to go back to how things used to be and converse like a father and daughter should.

Leonard watched Millie rummage through the refrigerator and the freezer, only grabbing food with ample sugar. Lately, she despised anything healthy and ate junk. Although, one would never know Millie consumed a diet of garbage food based on her skinny frame.

Leonard could spot when Millie's addiction ramped up by watching her weight. When Millie sported an emaciated figure, Leonard knew she would crawl to him and ask him for help getting her clean. That would be Leonard's cue to call a detox center or the best rehab facility on the east coast. When she did get clean, granted, not for long, her weight shot up, and her face filled with light, and he had the old Millie back. He wanted to freeze those moments because, so far, they never lasted long.

But now he watched his daughter, who must have escaped the latest detox stint early, and brought buddies from the same place to ransack his house for drugs and money. Millie opened every drawer, only closing half of them, looking for something to smooth her itch. She even looked under the kitchen sink. It almost made Leonard laugh as more sweat dripped like an open faucet off his forehead. Millie knew the only items under there were cleaning fluids, Clorox, and dishwasher soap. What was she hoping to find? Leonard knew what Millie wanted, but he washed himself of those thoughts to laugh about the ludicrous search under the sink for a minute. She backed away from the sink, leaving those cabinet doors ajar. Leonard thought about calling the cops, but he figured if these asses and Millie found nothing in his house to steal, which they wouldn't, then they would leave, and he could get into bed and think about how to deal with Millie later. He just wanted to kick this cold. It consumed him, and he had already stifled a new tickle in his throat that would set off a series of coughs.

Millie wandered around the kitchen, almost in a daze, when she spotted the camera mounted in the ceiling's corner. She stared at it, and Leonard stared back through his phone. Unsure she was being watched, Millie took a few steps closer to the device. She craned her neck to peer out of the kitchen, maybe to check on her friends? Leonard zoomed in on her face; at that moment, her eyes shot back to the camera's lens. Her eyes were dark circles, the skin under her sockets sporting a raccoon mask. Her skin had adopted a waxy texture, and her cheeks had sunk into her skeletal frame. He understood he was looking at Millie, but this was not his daughter. The drugs ruled her body, her mind, and her thoughts. He understood she acted under the need to fulfill an addiction she hadn't conquered and wasn't ready to eliminate. She was strong, she was smart, she was his daughter, and she had to find a way to survive and beat this. But not today. His closest friends and family kept advising Leonard to cut Millie off. Throw her onto the streets. Let her hit rock bottom alone, but he couldn't do that to her. Not to his Millie. He knew that lately he acted with an open disdainful approach to her antics rather than the encouraging parent filled with hope. He couldn't turn his back and let her rot on the streets because he knew that would happen. It wasn't in him. Nausea seized his belly as he watched Millie stare blankly at the camera. He knew the queasiness wasn't from his cold, either.

She backed away from the camera and spotted his cold medicine. Wait, the cough syrup? Not the cough syrup, Leonard's mind screamed. He sucked in a sharp breath as he witnessed Millie down the only red syrup that coated his lungs and eased his hacking. It was the only medicine that would grant him a peaceful sleep tonight. It was the only syrup left on the shelf out of the four pharmacies he ventured to today. Because, apparently, a horrible summer cold circulated, and everyone bought this one cough syrup. Millie downed the bottle in three manageable gulps. When Leonard saw her tip the empty bottle upside down to reveal no liquid remained, the sharp breath from a second ago caught up with him.

The coughing started. It wouldn't stop. He gasped for breath, for air, for something to control his body from fighting to breathe. The moment he found an inch of oxygen, all Leonard thought to do was scream.

"*Goddammit!*" Leonard forced the words out of his burning throat.

He brought his left hand down, assuming his fist would meet the hard unfinished wood floor, but it pummeled through the pink insulation. And then it all happened so quickly. He lost his balance. Leonard pulled his body to lean to the right a half second too late. As his body fell to the left and through the insulation, crashing through the ceiling, landing on some couch in an unknown room, he heard screams mixed with his own.

# *November 25th, 2021*

As Leonard parked his yellow sports car a block away from his brother's house, not by choice, he regretted saying yes to Robert's invite for today's holiday festivities. Seven years younger than Leonard, Robert swore today would be an intimate holiday gathering. Leonard had already counted ten cars, not including his BMW. He spotted Steven's navy Ford Explorer parked in the driveway. At least Leonard wasn't trapped or boxed in by one of the foreign cars he had spied during his walk to his brother's front door. Something hinted to Leonard that he wouldn't last this meal. He didn't have to ring the bell, either. The door rested ajar as if waiting for dozens of more guests to arrive. Leonard let himself in.

The house smelled like home. Warm turkey and roasted brisket filled the structure with the decadent aroma of home cooking. Leonard recognized only half the faces as he wandered through Robert's house. There were at least twenty people there. Leonard followed the sound of Robert's rich laugh and Steven's locker room mouth. He smiled and nodded to the unfamiliar faces. He hadn't taken off his coat and, as of then, had no plans to. He thought about leaving. He could do it. No one of substance saw him enter. The premature plan faded when stocky cousin Frank hobbled over to Leonard, stopping short of engulfing him in an uninvited hug.

"Leonard, is that you?" asked Frank.

"Happy Thanksgiving, Frank." Leonard half laughed as he studied his balding, short cousin. The epitome of a doomed nerd,

Leonard observed. He also caught a whiff of Frank's sour breath, instantly triggering Leonard to take two steps backward. Leonard spotted an iron coat rack and chucked his coat and scarf onto it, noting its position in the house, just in case.

"How have ya been, Leonard? Last I heard, you've done real good in the real estate world." Frank never shied away from pointing out someone's success. He always found Leonard fascinating and wanted to know his secrets. "Ya gotta tell me what to invest in. Where can I buy, so I can make a killing like you?"

Leonard considered popping Frank's balloon of real estate hope by pointing out the evident missing funds from Frank's bank account to make any kind of real estate killing. But Leonard chose a softer approach because it was a holiday. "I'd say, head to the Carolinas."

"The Carolinas?"

"Yup. The Carolinas." Leonard spotted the whiskey in Frank's hand.

"North or South?" Frank rubbed his pocked chin. Time had not been kind to this poor man's complexion.

Leonard threw his head back and sucked in a breath, bringing on the theatrics for Frank. "I'd say... South. Definitely South Carolina, Frank."

"Like Myrtle Beach?" Frank smiled, showing off his crooked, yellowed teeth.

"Myrtle Beach." Leonard nodded his head, flashing his perfect smile. Frank slapped Leonard's shoulder while releasing a wheezing laugh as if Leonard had uncovered the jackpot and handed it to Frank. This poor simpleton, Leonard mused. Every family had that idiot cousin, and Frank was the Rosen's. Leonard shifted away from

Frank, rubbing his shoulder from the light tap. "Hey, have you seen my brother?"

"Who?" Frank asked, taking a chug of whiskey.

"Robert." Leonard rolled his eyes.

"In the kitchen." Frank snapped his fingers, remembering the answer.

Leonard nodded a thank you salute before being stopped again by Frank's greasy, cheese-smelling hand.

"What about short sales?"

"Oh, I would stay far away from short sales, Frank. Perilous and little promise in the long run."

"You think?"

"I know." Leonard wasted no additional seconds with his hopeless cousin as he left him to think about short sales, despite Leonard wrapping up three short-sale transactions of his own recently. Frank might be clueless, but even Leonard wouldn't give up his business tactics to morons.

Leonard discovered all the action in the kitchen. Mounds of food lined the counters, not quite ready to be exposed to the gigantic gathering as Robert's wife Patty basted the turkey, easily a thirty-pounder. He gave Robert credit for finding his one wife, and she could cook. Leonard had always wanted a woman who cooked. Maybe this would be the year he grabbed his at-home chef and everything else under his umbrella of perfection.

"Leonard, hot damn!" Robert threw his long, strong arms in the air and got up so fast from the kitchen table he almost knocked his chair and Steven over. Despite Robert being Leonard's baby brother, his stature towered over the general population, Leonard included.

Robert inherited their father's stature and physique. Leonard was everything his mother embodied, not that it mattered, but it was never a bragging point. Robert pulled Leonard in for a hug before anyone had time to protest.

"Happy Thanksgiving, Robert," Leonard said, stiff as a board.

Robert dropped Leonard down like a rag doll and slapped him in the stomach. "Listen to this guy. You sound like a fucking greeter at a steakhouse." Robert pulled Leonard in again with one powerful arm. "How are you doing, brother? Are you okay?" Despite Robert's jovial character, he knew what today marked. Anyone close and in the family knew. Well, maybe not Frank.

"I'm fine. It's been a few years now, Robert." Leonard patted his baby brother's arm to reassure him to not ask again.

"I worry about you, that's all."

"Well, don't. I'm fine." Leonard saw his opportunity to escape Robert's vice grip, and he did. "Intimate gathering, huh?" Leonard gestured to the throngs of people, and Steven, who remained at the kitchen table with his fiancée, Theresa, while they chatted away with people, Leonard couldn't name for the life of him.

"You know we love hosting the holidays. It's not that many people. You get used to it once the food and booze get going." Robert chased his last words with a swig of beer. "Do you want?"

Leonard held up a singular hand, declining the offer. It was known Leonard did not drink, but maybe Robert forgot in the haze of hosting.

"See anyone yet?" Robert asked.

"Frank. Already gave him real estate advice of the century."

"Ah, I'm sorry. Of all the fucking people to greet you. Shit," Robert said, finishing his beer.

Leonard only laughed at his brother's love for a good ale.

"Yeah, yeah. Don't worry. We've got your Diet Coke coming. Or is it Pepsi you prefer?"

"Coke is fine."

"Good, because we ain't got Pepsi in this house. Hey, Patty! A Coke for Leonard." Robert pointed to Leonard's mussed hair.

Patty, donning a turkey bird embroidered apron and braided hair, waved to Leonard from the other end of the kitchen as she manned all the food. She fished him out his beverage like a good wife and host, certainly not like any of Leonard's past wives.

"Holy shit. Leonard, no date this year?"

"Very funny." Leonard waved a finger in Robert's face, who wasn't smiling or joking. This was the first year Leonard showed up to a major holiday without a woman on his arm. "That could always change. There's always tomorrow."

"But what about today? Are you seeing anyone?"

"No, not at the moment." And it was true. This dry spell was new for Leonard and had nothing to do with age. He simply hadn't connected with anyone recently, but it was not like he didn't know how lonely his nights felt without company. The companionship of a woman. Did he miss it? Sure. Did he feel like settling? No.

"Bullshit. You've got that black book that's navy. Hey, Stevie! Is your dad engaged yet?"

Steven shook his head, burying his forehead in his hands. Theresa exchanged an innocent smile with Leonard as she tugged Steven's hands away from his face. Everyone knew about Leonard's love life.

It wasn't a secret, and he had nothing to be ashamed about. The only regret he held today was Millie's absence, but at least Robert didn't poke that subject.

At some point, they strolled to the table where Steven and Theresa sat. Robert popped a fresh beer while Leonard sipped his crisp Diet Coke with sliced lemon.

"How many beers have you had?" Leonard asked Robert, watching him in wonder as he guzzled down half of his new bottle.

"Not nearly enough for today. I didn't expect this many people to show up. Patty kept saying, invite this one, tell that one to come. We didn't think they would show." Robert threw a hand in the air over his head. "Plus, Patty loves to host. So, this is more of her thing, but hey. I can show support."

"By getting drunk while she does all the work?" Leonard nudged his brother, enjoying the coolness of the soda sliding down his throat.

"So, someone tells me you're going to become a dad again?" Robert raised a questioning eyebrow in Leonard's direction. Leonard shot a death stare in Steven's direction that his son happened to catch.

"Uncle Robert, don't," said Steven.

"No, it's fine, Steven. Just tell me when you became the gossip column?" Leonard asked his son, who couldn't make eye contact anymore. When did Steven grow this scared that he couldn't face reality with any backbone or poise, Leonard wondered?

"Forget I said anything. I'm sorry," said Robert, holding up two hands to surrender, letting go of his beer.

"We can talk about it. It's no secret I've wanted to raise Jackie for a long time. Everyone knows Jesse and Margot are terrible. So now, I'm going to act on it," said Leonard.

"But why now?" asked Robert.

Leonard turned to Steven. "Oh, you didn't tell Uncle Bobby why?"

"No, I didn't. Let's drop this now," said Steven.

"Maybe I want to talk about it. You're the one who opened the door on this subject," said Leonard, suddenly wanting to piss his son off, to make him squirm. Steven would shut down whenever anything about Millie was ever mentioned. Well, not that day. It was a day to talk about her, to honor her memory. No one told Leonard what to do regarding Millie on her anniversary.

"I'm going to go watch the game. Babe, you wanna come with me?" said Steven to Theresa, not really leaving her a choice. She silently agreed and followed Steven out of the kitchen like a fresh puppy.

"What's his deal?" Robert asked Leonard, finishing another beer and belching half a second later.

Leonard scowled at the bodily eruption.

"Anything having to do with Millie, Steven wants nothing of it."

"I wonder why?" Robert stroked his gray-stubbled chin. "Maybe his way of dealing with everything?"

"Maybe, but I disagree with it. And I don't need him running around talking about my plan for Jackie, either. He's still the kid's uncle but struggles to acknowledge him, too." Leonard chased his anger down with a fizzling gulp of Coke. He grimaced at the stinging bubbles hitting his tongue like pellets.

"What's going on with Jackie? Steven only told me the bare minimum."

"Are you going to laugh? Because if you do, I'm leaving."

"You have my word, Leonard." Robert held up his left hand and placed the other palm over his heart. Leonard studied his brother, unconvinced. Robert, always the ultimate ball-buster, took particular aim at Leonard. But he never won. Leonard wore the ultimate thick skin until now.

"I'm going to seek custody of Jackie. Already contacted my attorney about it yesterday." Leonard waited for a reaction, word missiles fired his way. He got nothing. "You're probably wondering why?"

Robert nodded.

"Well, this is something I've always toyed with. But now things have changed." Leonard rubbed his hands together, preparing to drop the bomb. "Tuesday, I found out that Jesse and the whole crew are planning to move to Thailand within the next few months."

"Thailand? What the fuck is in Thailand?" Robert's voice silenced the kitchen for a minute before everyone returned to regular conversations. "Shit, Leonard. I'm sorry."

"Nothing to be sorry about." Leonard patted the air to calm a visibly distressed Robert down. He probably should have waited to unload this news to Robert when he wasn't on his way to being inebriated. Robert had three grandchildren of his own, a set of twins and a newborn.

"So, what are you going to do? Go through the system? Are there any rights in your favor, even?"

"My attorney is trying to find that out. I'd prefer to not drag this through the system, but I'm not sure. I made a mistake with my own kids by not fighting. And look where it landed me." Leonard ground his teeth whenever he recalled the custody debate with Greg over two decades ago.

"Nah, don't say that. Don't put that load on you. When you finally got your kids, you did everything possible to turn it around. You're a good father, Leonard."

Leonard wondered if he had gotten full custody of Millie and Steven even a year sooner than he had, would it have made enough difference to reverse the damage of their terrible mother and her neglectful parenting? His kids knew no rules or discipline until they lived under his roof.

"I can't lose Jackie. Thailand. It sounds so ridiculous whenever I repeat the story and the circumstances. They can't even afford anything. How the hell are they going to pack up and move to the other side of the world?" The thought of Jackie leaving for good left Leonard swirling with sickness and a touch of phantom vertigo.

"Leonard, if it were me, and I had your money..." Robert began, only to be met with vehement negative head shakes from Leonard. "I would pay the assholes off."

"I won't do that."

"Why not?"

"Whatever number I say will never be enough."

"Offer them a million dollars. Yeah, offer them a fucking million bucks, and I bet you they take it."

"If I offer a million, they'll come back asking for two million, and it'll keep climbing from there."

Robert rubbed his mouth, absorbing the fake offer on the table. "You really think they'd turn down a million?"

"Jesse loves his son. I don't doubt that. But he would want more. Margot would want way more. And after a while, it doesn't feel right."

"But you say you really want Jackie." Robert tapped Leonard on the shoulder.

Every point thrown in Leonard's direction, his heart quickened, and his appetite for today's buffet evaporated.

"I'd be willing to write a check for a million. But I also know it wouldn't be enough."

"Is there a number you would go up to?" Robert leaned in, ready to hear the magic number that Leonard didn't have.

"It just feels strangely awkward to buy back my grandson. I can't explain it."

"Well, you're dealing with bad fucking people." Robert banged on the table with solid knuckles. He huffed a few breaths before capturing enough oxygen to calm down. "You're a smart guy. Always have been and a heck of a big brother to look up to." And then Robert considered. "Maybe not the best in the marriage department..."

"I knew I had that coming." Leonard cracked a smile.

"You're going to figure this out. I know you will." Robert landed his catcher's mitt hand on top of Leonard's.

He placed his ordinary palm over his baby brother's hand and enjoyed this rare moment of tenderness he probably wouldn't speak about again.

A crash reverberated from the stove side of the kitchen. Leonard and Robert's moment subsided as they charged over to assess the damage. Patty must have lost her grip on a few empty China platters, and shards of ruined dishes scattered the tile floor. Robert grabbed chunks off the ground, shucking them into black contractor bags. Patty emerged from the mess holding a red, jagged broken plate in her hand, almost too stunned to move from the havoc she accidentally caused. Leonard forced himself to take another step towards helping but found himself fixated on the broken plate in Patty's hand. He froze and forgot how to breathe, how to move. No one noticed Leonard's fog yet, but it would only be a few more seconds until his anxiety-ridden stance revealed itself. He wanted to swallow but couldn't force down a gulp of any size. The skin on his left cheek tingled. He saw black spots out of the corner of his right eye. A split second of lucidity burst through the harsh light spilling into his pupils, where he found the hidden strength to bolt to the guest bathroom.

Leonard splashed frigid water over his face under the brass faucet in the tiny powder room. He wasn't sure if anyone noticed his disappearance, but at least he didn't collapse like earlier. That would have been disastrous. There was no way he could eat, let alone sit at this not-so-intimate Thanksgiving dinner with hundreds of people. He needed to get out of there and drive. Speed. He wanted to gun it and not care for the few minutes on his way to see Millie. Yes, that was his plan for the rest of the day. He would go to Millie's grave and stay there until sunset. Maybe even call Greg on his way.

Whatever he decided to do, all Leonard knew was that he couldn't remain there. He grabbed for a disposable hand towel only to come up empty-handed. He opened the drawer immediately under the sink and found plenty of extras. But in the back of the drawer sat an ornate wooden box with an engraved army star in the center of the lid. He remembered this box. It had rested on top of their fireplace mantle while growing up. This belonged to his father and housed all of his wartime medals, and while his mother swore it was lost, Leonard never believed her. To say Leonard shared a warm relationship with his mother was a gross overstatement because they despised one another. Leonard attended her funeral when his mother died, but that's where the mourning ended. So, in the end, she gave the box to Robert, her baby, who brought her so much joy while she tossed Leonard to the side, always eyeing him as a nuisance. Leonard opened the box, and the medals rested there, collecting dust. He peered around, ensuring no one was in view, even though he had locked himself in the restroom for at least ten minutes, and took three medals, pocketing them. Feeling the weight of the treasures pressed against his thigh in his jean pocket produced a sudden calm, sucking the crippling anxiety away. It was as if Leonard's father placed his arm around his shoulder, reassuring his boy that it would be okay. He would make it through that day, and Leonard believed it was possible for the first time.

# July 2013 – Family Court

For once, Leonard wasn't in court fighting over his children or an ex-wife wanting to serve him hell. Instead, he watched his daughter Millie fight for and lose custody over her almost-four-year-old son, Jackie. He stared across the hallway as his daughter melted in her chair, weeping. Leonard was shocked but had somewhat expected the judgment after Jesse demanded an emergency custody hearing. He had volunteered to go with Millie to the hearing today after she begged for his company, and Leonard had a relationship with Greg, and so they waited for him to emerge from the judge's chambers to find out the exact details of visitation rights and the new custody agreement. Leonard knew things weren't ideal with Millie and her parenting. It would be a lie if Leonard said Millie was a fit parent because she wasn't even close to one for a long time now. Her problems had spiraled after Jackie turned two. Leonard was unsure what drugs she ingested, and Millie always denied it whenever confronted about the obvious. If she were a good mother, Millie would tell the truth. But she was so far gone past knowing right from wrong within her addiction, whatever degree it had reached at this point. Leonard always viewed Jesse as the catalyst. The bad guy who ruined Millie. Now he questioned everything. Who exactly ruined Millie? Leonard may never know, but it certainly wasn't his fault. He reasoned that he received custody of Millie a year too late to guide her onto a better path and that her mother had screwed Millie up.

Her sobs grew louder, enough for random strangers in the hallways to notice and frown. Leonard walked over to her but couldn't bring himself physically to lay a hand on her shoulder for comfort. She'd put him through a lot as a father, and today he thoroughly resented her wreckage.

"It's not the end of the world, Millie. It'll be all right."

"I've lost Jackie. I can't believe it. How did this happen?" Millie wiped away the droves of tears spilling down her cheeks.

Leonard rolled his eyes, reaching into his jacket pocket for anything to serve as a tissue. He found a crumpled-up napkin that appeared clean, so he handed it to Millie.

"This could be a temporary arrangement, so try to stay positive." Leonard's words dripped with the lies everyone knew to be true. Jackie's new home now shifted to Jesse's for the unknown future.

"I thought you said Greg was good?" Millie stared at Leonard.

Greg was Leonard's prize and the only one who didn't falter or disappoint Leonard throughout their relationship. Greg possessed a gusto, a specific energy that was unmatched in Leonard's life.

"Greg is good."

Leonard couldn't hide his disgust as his lip curled. Why couldn't Millie ever take responsibility for anything? Not even for her child? This wasn't the first time she lacked utter awareness as a sloppy parent. He didn't want to think about her inability to parent the first time she stepped blindly into the ugly light.

"Then how did this happen?" Millie sat there, drowning in her own befuddled cloud. She really had no clue.

"Let's just focus on the future." Leonard took a step back from Millie, craving some necessary and substantial distance.

"What's the future?" Millie asked.

"Let's wait for Greg to find out." Leonard sat in a chair facing Millie. He didn't want to look at the crying puddle she had morphed into, so he texted Amy. He needed comfort, someone to remind him he was a king, a winner. He typed out, 'I miss you,' but didn't get to hit send because Greg busted out from the chambers, killing Leonard's mood.

Greg huffed over to Millie and Leonard, having difficulty catching his breath. Leonard warned Greg to lose weight, but the stubborn attorney refused to listen and ate his way into each day, thoroughly enjoying himself.

"Tell us some good news," said Leonard.

Millie didn't budge or lift her head from her blue plastic chair. Greg cast his eyes at Millie's slumped posture and shook his head. "Millie, are you up to talking?" Greg bowed his head down in her direction.

"I guess I have no choice, huh?" Milled asked. Leonard stared at her like a little parasite shit. She had just lost custody of her baby and didn't want to know about the plan?

"Greg, you can talk to me. Feel free to chime in, Millie," Leonard said, his voice thick with sarcastic disdain. Leonard obviously paid for Greg's representation for this predicament, and Greg charged by the hour, so by no means did Leonard plan to wait for Millie to lift herself out of this funk in the courthouse. Greg shot Leonard a warning gaze to be gentle. If only Greg knew how long Leonard had exercised great restraint with Millie.

"It's not what we hoped for," Greg said, addressing everyone.

"What does that mean, Greg?" Leonard asked.

"Millie can only have supervised visits with Jackie. And if she wants to take Jackie outside of Jesse's house, either you or Steven need to be present." Greg took a white handkerchief and dabbed his sweat-bubbled brow.

Leonard's eyes almost popped out of his face. "Wait, what? How the fuck did this happen, Greg?"

"Dad, don't," Millie said, suddenly waking up.

"You agree with this?" Leonard asked Millie, pointing a bent finger at her forehead and empty eyes.

"What do you want me to do? The judge or whoever decided," Millie said, shrugging as if this wasn't a big deal. Losing her child to the deadbeat dad.

Leonard wanted to shake her awake. Send her somewhere to get clean. But he knew neither option was possible right now. So, instead, he turned to Greg, fighting for an answer. Someone needed to fight today.

"Greg, what's going on? What was said in the chambers?" Leonard asked.

Greg peered over to Millie, who floundered in her own shrinking world. Leonard even wondered if she had gotten high before the hearing today. It wouldn't have surprised him. Nothing did with Millie lately. It was a sad reality they both settled into, and he hated it.

"It wasn't good in there," said Greg, leaning into Leonard's ear, discounting Millie's participation in the conversation.

"What does that mean, Greg?" Leonard asked.

"From what was gathered against Millie, it's pretty bad. A lot of uncouth details, Leonard."

"Greg, just tell me. I'm paying for this." Leonard steered Greg away from Millie, who still showed zero interest. She sat there like a statue, completely stuck.

Greg frowned, knowing he spared little choice with Leonard's demands.

"Greg, tell me. I can handle it." Leonard pressed, laying a hand on Greg's shoulder for light persuasion.

"She exposed him, Leonard. To things. A lot of things."

"Greg, just say it."

"Drugs. Jesse told the judge he once found Jackie playing with a needle but got to it in time. And apparently, Millie didn't deny it either."

The men stared at each other, and Leonard believed he would lose balance. His ears rang as his pulse pounded in his throat. A cold sweat coated the back of his neck, the type that starts hot then runs frigid. Leonard turned to Millie and glared. Of course, she didn't notice. She didn't care about anything except chasing the next hit, the next high. Whatever she called it. His daughter was a junkie. How did this happen to him? He never did drugs. He never stuck a goddamn needle in his arm. He never picked up a drink. But forget about him. How did this happen to his Millie?

"There's more, Leonard."

"What now?"

"The judge ruled that child support be paid to Jesse." Greg swallowed, bracing himself for something.

"Millie pays Jesse? How? She barely works. How is this possible?" Leonard took a few steps back, jamming his hands through his hair. He couldn't hold back anymore and stormed over to Millie. He shook her shoulder, rougher than he intended. Her eyes shot to the affected shoulder like hot lava poured onto it. "Hey, wake up. You've got even bigger problems than you think."

"Don't you think I know?" said Millie, an inch away from slurring her words.

"Not only are you limited in seeing your son, but now you need to pay Jesse child support every month. Did you know about this?" Leonard spat.

Millie's eyes darted from Greg to her father, lost. "Is this true?" she asked Greg.

"I'm afraid so, Millie. You do have a job, so a number is being worked up that's viable, but you will pay child support. And it's not something to mess around with either. They can garnish your wages if you don't pay," Greg said.

"You better pay, Millie. Got it?" Leonard said.

"The court will take my pay before I decide what to do with it? How does that make sense?" said Millie.

"I'm about to fucking lose it. I can't fucking take this," said Leonard to Greg.

Millie's leg shook as her eyes danced around the floor. After a minute, she cast her gaze in Leonard's direction. "I thought you said Greg would fix this?"

Leonard threw his arms in the air, tossing on his jacket, deciding he was done with today's fiasco of results. "Nothing is your fault, right? It's always someone else's fault. My fault, his fault, the fucking judge's fault, but never yours, huh? What happened to you? When did you get like this, unmindful, ungrateful... always out of it? Be honest, Millie. You can't get much lower than you are right now."

Leonard waited for Millie to prove him wrong, but she stared at him with her dark, hollow eyes filling with fresh thick tears, her bottom lip trembling, and yet she offered not a single word to Leonard.

"I've had it. Greg, thank you for your help today. I'll call you later in the week to settle up." Leonard shook Greg's hand before focusing on Millie. "And you have a lot of thinking to do. Don't call me over the next few days unless you want to see Jackie. So, I better get a call soon, got it?"

Millie nodded, only because she was expected to, not because she knew seeing her son was the right thing to do.

"Where are you going?" asked Millie.

But Leonard didn't answer. All he wanted to do was get away from her, far away from this building and everything sour between its walls.

# *November 25th, 2021*

At ninety-five miles per hour, he believed the road and his tires would morph into one, but it wasn't happening, and a taste of unsatisfactory road rage sat in the pit of his stomach. Leonard needed to go faster on the highway as he downshifted into third, throttling the engine to explode through a loop of cars. Hoping his mood would improve once he spoke with Millie, he made impeccable time on the way to the cemetery from Robert's house. He didn't even say goodbye to his brother or son, all because he needed to escape after battling a second panic attack in one day. Leonard was so close now, only five minutes away, with the odometer holding steady at ninety-seven.

Four minutes away. He saw the signs alerting the drivers who searched for the cemetery on the highway as helpful hints. So close. And then the flashing lights and whining sirens emerged in his rearview mirror.

"Fuck," Leonard said. His car self-braked to seventy and then fifty as he searched for a shoulder to pull onto. Of all days to get pulled over for reckless driving, it had to be that one. Although he was driving like an asshole, Leonard couldn't sit in complete denial. This just wrinkled his plan to reach his destination in record time.

Leonard pulled to a complete stop. He reached for his glove compartment, where he owned numerous PBA cards from years of real estate dealings and barter agreements. This was a ticket he could easily escape, but something in him stopped from opening the compartment. It was like he wanted the full punishment of a ticket and nothing to be sugar-coated today because of the raw moments he needed to remember. Millie suffered, and so could Leonard from a beefed-up moving violation. The officer, no older than thirty, wearing blackout gold-rimmed aviators, sauntered to the parked car and tapped Leonard's window.

Leonard whipped his head in the officer's direction, finalizing his decision to not use a PBA card, and rolled down the window.

"License and registration," the cop said.

Leonard exhaled a hiss of oxygen through his nostrils, reached into his wallet, and pulled out the requested documents. He handed them over, neither of them exchanging a singular syllable or glance. The cop studied the paperwork and then stared at Leonard. He shifted in his seat as the cop's eyes stung his face. Finally, Leonard made eye contact with the officer.

"Do you know how fucking fast you were going? You could have killed someone."

The cop was pissed as Leonard thought, reconsidering his choice of not grabbing a PBA card from the waiting black canvas bag in the glove compartment. He said nothing, though. The cop leaned closer to Leonard, getting a thorough look at him.

"Have you been drinking today? Coming from a relative's house?"

"Drinking?" Leonard half laughed, shaking his head. "Nah, I don't drink."

"Are you high?" The officer sniffed Leonard twice, not that he would have caught anything from that distance besides his Kenneth Cole cologne. A weak form of intimidation and a rookie move.

"You've got the wrong guy."

"You're driving like you've got some fucking death wish. I ought to arrest you for how you drove."

The cop wasn't wholly wrong, Leonard thought. He didn't say anything, only irritating the cop more.

"Where are you heading to?" The cop peered into Leonard's speed demon vehicle.

"To visit my daughter." Leonard sucked in a breath.

The officer jotted something down. "Might want to text her saying you're going to be late."

Leonard bit his tongue and ran his eyes over the officer's pathetic macho guy stance. The officer grinned at Leonard and marched away from the car, probably to write up that award-winning speeding ticket, filling his quota for the end of the month. Leonard whipped out his phone and dialed Greg's number. He needed to fight this ticket, and Greg was his guy for every legal win and woe.

Three long rings later, Greg answered. "Happy Thanksgiving, Leonard. And the answer is no, I didn't find anything yet."

"Oh, I'm not calling about that." Leonard checked for the cop in the rearview mirror. The last thing he needed was a city cell phone ticket to add to the list.

"Everything okay?" Greg asked, his voice climbing an octave.

"I'm getting a nasty speeding ticket. Just wanted to alert you. Consider it added to your list. The retainer yesterday doesn't include this ticket, obviously."

"Shit, Leo. Don't you have a bag of PBA cards? You've even given me a few."

Leonard peered at his glove compartment again, guilty. "I forgot."

Greg sighed heavily into the phone, enough for Leonard to pull his ear away. "Leonard, why did you really call me?"

"Did you find even the smallest of things?" Leonard bit his lip, spotting the officer leaving his car.

"Leonard, no."

Leonard hung up before Greg had a chance to release another heavy breath. The officer strolled back to the driver's window, holding a long yellow ticket and a smirk on his face.

"This'll be a Thanksgiving to remember." The officer waved the ticket in front of Leonard's face but did not hand it over yet. If only the officer knew what today really meant for Leonard. "Did you tell your daughter you're going to be late?" The cop further taunted.

"No."

"That's a shame."

It really was. "She's dead."

The cop's eyes filled with the first sign of humanity since their exchange as he studied Leonard. For an instant, Leonard believed he spotted a hint of humiliation filling the young man's face.

"I'm actually on the way to visit her at the cemetery. She passed away six years ago today."

"I'm very sorry to hear that." The cop stumbled over his words. He frowned and instantly crumpled the ticket in his hand.

"No, no, no." Leonard shot his hand out of the window, reaching for the nearly ruined paper. "I drove like an asshole. This is what I deserve. You're just doing your job."

The cop took a step away from the car. "It's a holiday. Let's forget this happened." It was as if a different spirit inhabited the bitter cop's body from a moment ago. He actually sounded like a decent guy.

"I insist. Give me the ticket." Leonard wiggled his fingers for the paper. He really wanted it and yearned for the punishment.

"It's really not a big deal." He tore the ticket from one corner, not making much progress in its destruction.

"Just give me the fucking ticket," said Leonard.

The cop pulled one sheet away and shoved another yellow ticket into Leonard's sweaty hands he didn't notice before. What was this second page? Leonard eyed the paper fast enough to realize it wasn't for speeding.

"What the hell is this?" Leonard asked.

"One of your taillights is out. Get it fixed."

"It's out?" Leonard was more shocked by the light than the speeding. He babied this car, and now a light wasn't working?

"Happy Thanksgiving." And the cop walked away. But the funny thing was, he really meant it.

Leonard punched the steering wheel with a singular knuckle and said, "Shit."

# October 2012 – The Restaurant

"Millie, you need to engage Jackie. You can't expect him to know what to do." Leonard rolled his eyes at Millie's clueless parenting.

Jackie squirmed like a worm in the black booth of the Chinese restaurant, known for its fish tanks lacing around the perimeter. Leonard chose this restaurant to celebrate Jackie's third birthday just in case the boy needed a distraction during a sit-down meal. Leonard wasn't wrong, but he didn't expect Millie's unwillingness to parent.

"He doesn't listen," said Millie through gritted teeth, yanking Jackie by his arm back into his seat.

Amy shot Leonard a fast eye at Millie's reaction.

"Just talk to him. Tell Jackie why it's important to stay seated," said Leonard.

Jackie slid underneath the table, laughing like an unhinged monkey.

Millie buried her face into her hands. "This is just too much."

"This is what being a parent is about."

"I can take Jackie for a little walk?" said Amy, who had barely touched her food.

"Millie, talk to Jackie. Kids are smarter than we realize."

"Not this kid." Millie rolled up her sleeves, ducking under the table to find him.

Leonard winced at her bitter words. What mother admits to such a statement about her own child, especially when it was anything but genuine? Jackie was clever and well-spoken; he was a Rosen.

"I just think it's nice we're together for Jackie's birthday," said Amy.

Leonard shot Amy a glare. "You do know this isn't his actual birthday, right? Remember Jesse had Jackie on the actual day and wouldn't let anyone see Jackie on his real birthday?" Leonard served the harsh reminder to Millie as she fished Jackie from the floor.

"He needs to learn." Millie planted the boy down a tad too hard in the seat, her face blotchy.

"You need to teach him." Leonard pointed at Millie's chest.

"When? The once a week or less when Jesse lets me see him? Since the accident, Jesse's given me the run around like it's his job."

"You still have custody of Jackie. You're supposed to have him during the week. You have rights, Millie. Use them." Leonard frowned, and in his gut, as twisted as it sounded, something whispered in his ear that Millie shouldn't have Jackie. He wasn't safe with Millie since the incident at the hospital.

"If Jesse gives you a hard time, maybe your father can call him to make the plan?"

"Watch me go, Grandpa... I'm a mouse!" said Jackie as he disappeared under the table for the seventh time that night.

"No, no, no. Jackie, I want you to come up and sit like a big boy right now." Leonard pressed a finger onto the table until all color drained from the flesh. "We are in a restaurant for your birthday, and big boys sit in a big chair at the table."

Jackie giggled louder and crawled onto Leonard's feet, untying his shoelaces. Leonard stuck his head under the table, almost bumping noses with Jackie.

"Hey, buddy. You're missing your birthday up here. We're going to order cake soon."

Jackie stared at him with bright eyes, emitting a light Leonard remembered Millie possessing once.

"Ice cream sundae?"

Jackie scooted backward, shaking his head. Leonard popped up as all the blood in his body rushed to his brain. He masked his utter failure in persuading Jackie with a weak grin.

Leonard cleared his throat, pulling his pants far too high for his style. "Jackie, wanna take a walk and see the fish? I think I saw a shark earlier."

The boy darted up from the table, jumping into an unprepared Leonard's arms.

Leonard carried Jackie to a medium-sized fish tank housing a scuba diver with bright orange fish encircling his treasure chest. The water in the tank emitted a fish food odor, with swaying plant decor mixed with turquoise pebbles on the virtual ocean's floor.

"Wow, Jackie, look at that big fish." Leonard pointed to a yellow and white monster of a fella. He had no idea about the fish species, but it grabbed Jackie's attention.

"Are we gonna eat him?" said Jackie.

Leonard twisted his face. "No, Jackie. These fish live here. We get to watch them live."

"And eat."

"Yes, and eat. Maybe sleep."

"And poop." Jackie's face broke into a smile. He knew he was being funny.

"Sure, that too." Leonard shifted Jackie to his other arm. The boy carried a decent weight to him. "Hey, Jackie? How about we walk for a little? Big boys walk."

"I like when you hold me, Grandpa." Jackie leaned his head onto Leonard's shoulder, hugging his neck tighter.

All the protests in Leonard's body melted when the weight of Jackie's body seeped into Leonard's arms. He patted the back of his grandson's head and proceeded to the monster of the aquarium tanks that handed the restaurant its reputation.

A lone shark swam around. There were no other fish with the shark for apparent reasons. Iridescent rocks and glow-in-the-dark pebbles highlighted the shark's environment. Two scuba diving figurines gathered pearls from a chest to keep the shark company.

"Whoa, Grandpa, look at him." Jackie stared wide-eyed in amazement at the creature. Leonard viewed the shark as the king of the aquarium. No one bothered him, and he couldn't bother anyone. "Will he eat you?"

"Me? Why only me?"

"Will he eat Mommy?"

"Aw, Jackie. You don't want anything happening to your mommy." Leonard swallowed his words. The eerie statement left him unsettled because he knew her problem was not getting better. Except, he couldn't worry about it tonight. Tonight was about Jackie.

"Maybe the shark will eat Daddy."

"Anything is possible." Leonard hoisted Jackie up again as the child slipped through his arms. "You're getting big, you know that?"

"I don't want anyone to eat you."

"Change of heart?"

"You buy me toys." Jackie flashed an innocent smile.

Leonard laughed, shaking his head, agreeing.

"Put me down. I'm a big boy."

"Put me down, *please*. Say please."

"Put me down, puh-lease."

Leonard planted Jackie's sneakered feet on the wood-tiled floor. They held hands, admiring the restaurant's underwater decor as they showed no signs of returning to the table soon.

"Grandpa? What do you do?"

"For what? You mean work?"

"Yeah. During the day. After you wake up in the morning."

"I buy and sell houses and buildings. I didn't always do that. But that's what I mainly do now."

A starfish caught Jackie's attention. He ran up to the glass, pressing his face against it, trying to kiss the creature. Leonard walked up to Jackie, planting a gentle hand on the kid's petite shoulder.

"Do you know what you want to do?"

"A starfish!" Jackie pointed to the mammal.

"You can be a starfish."

"Can I be a rock?"

"Sure, why not?"

Jackie walked away from the tank, moving on to the next exhibit. He grasped Leonard's hand, showing no signs of letting go this time.

"What else?" said Jackie.

"You tell me. It's your life."

"A cowboy. A racecar driver. A man."

Leonard threw his head back and laughed. "Sorry, keep going. I'm loving this."

"A teacher. A horse..." Jackie stopped to think what other absurd things he could unknowingly be. He looked up at Leonard, waiting to be noticed.

"Yes, Jackie?"

"Maybe I can go to work with you."

Leonard patted his heart. "I would love that. I think that's the best answer so far."

Jackie jumped up and down, not knowing how else to express his great answer to the career game. Leonard slowed in front of another tank filled with an array of tropical fish and knelt before Jackie, fixing his small collar from its wrinkling.

"I want us to try something. Whenever you or I say something great, we're going to make a round fist like this and tap our fists together." Leonard taught the entire motion to Jackie, who screeched the first time they did the fist bump.

"That was fun! Grandpa, again." This time, Jackie readied their fists to bump into each other. "I like doing these fist taps."

"There you guys are," said Amy, appearing from the shadows. "We were getting worried."

"Really? The both of you?"

"Well, Millie's been on her phone, but you've been gone longer than usual."

"Hey, Jackie, since it's your birthday, how about we take a picture?" Leonard snapped his fingers at Amy to grab her attention. "Get your phone out for a picture."

Amy obliged like a well-trained puppy, taking out her phone and waiting for the moment to take a picture. Leonard scooped Jackie into his arms as they posed in front of the ocean blue aquarium tank.

Amy held up her hand, signaling the boys to smile.

"Say cheese," said Amy, getting several pictures of the same smile and pose.

"Great job, my boy," said Leonard.

Jackie held up his fist, waiting for Leonard to reciprocate. Leonard chuckled and made a fist for Jackie to see. They pounded fists, with Jackie's hand being the aggressor.

"Let's go back to Mom," said Jackie.

Leonard nodded, understanding their moment ended and walked his grandson back to his mother.

# *September 2012 – The Dentist*

"Hi, this is Leonard Rosen, here to pick up Millie," he said into his iPhone. He needed to buy a new case desperately and planned to do it today, but everything got sidetracked by Millie's emergency dental appointment. Millie's car that Leonard paid for had broken down that morning, or so she claimed, and she couldn't drive herself to the dentist appointment that Leonard booked for her. She claimed her teeth had felt loose for the previous month—a sensation Leonard couldn't fathom or even make sense of. But lately, everything Millie said sounded odd, like a rambling lost person. Leonard had assumed today would be a great day. It was a hot August afternoon. He wanted to go to the Apple store after lunch for a new case and then sip a cold diet soda on the new float he had just purchased from Amazon. He was a free man under the guise of not being legally tied to anyone since the ink on his divorce papers had just dried from his fifth marriage to that bitch. He didn't even want to mention her name. She just turned so awful. But none of that mattered now because he was liberated. August would be Leonard's month, he declared. It was supposed to be that great day until he got the call from Millie in the morning that crashed all those plans. The start date turned into tomorrow, and all Leonard lived for was tomorrow at this rate. He had been sitting in his car for ten minutes since Millie called, saying she was done. So, what was the holdup?

He was about to write a semi-nasty 'I'm in the car' text when Leonard saw Millie dragging her feet toward him. She stared at the ground the whole time, not lifting her eyes to meet his. An instant scowl formed on Leonard's face. He tried to fight his blatant disgust with Millie these days, but just so much had happened. There were too many wounds, and she didn't seem to care either way. She climbed into his car before slamming the door much too loud for Leonard's taste.

"Hey! Watch it. What's wrong with you?" Leonard asked, eyeing Millie like a stranger.

"My mouth hurts." She rubbed her jaw, whisking her lips with her fingertips.

"I bet. You don't take care of your teeth."

"Dad, not right now." Millie rubbed her temple, her eyes unable to focus on him or anything.

"Don't give me that 'not right now' shit. You don't take care of yourself. I know you don't brush your teeth every day."

"What are you talking about?" She finally turned to face Leonard, squinting.

"I've seen your toothbrush in the morning, and sometimes it doesn't look wet. And your breath stinks half the time." The truth hit Leonard hard in the nose a few weeks ago when Millie passed by him one morning, and he caught a whiff of her stale, fishy breath. He had to stop himself from gagging. Leonard waited until she left that morning, decided to go to her bathroom, and examined her toothbrush. It was bone dry. On the days' Millie didn't have Jackie, which increased tenfold over the last six months, sometimes she opted to stay at Leonard's comfortable house with all its spoils. She said she didn't want to be alone. It wasn't every time she didn't have Jackie, but it was enough that Leonard kept a set of toiletries for Millie.

"You sound crazy right now."

"You pushed me to this." Leonard swallowed, burying his anger in the pit of his stomach. He didn't intend to attack Millie, but it just happened lately like a geyser exploding because that's what he morphed into around her. Picking at everything she did and didn't do, everything she was and was not. It was a cycle he found himself trapped in. "Do you feel better? What did he do?"

"I'm not sure."

"What do you mean?"

"I can't remember."

"These are answers Jackie gives when he comes home from daycare. Come on, Millie. What did he do?"

"He took some molds of my teeth. That shit tasted so bad, I almost gagged." Millie half laughed, swallowing more of the sour saliva.

"Molds for what?" Leonard's pulse skipped a beat. Molds were expensive.

"I need to go back next week." Millie shrugged.

"Next week? Millie, you better get your car working. I'm not doing this weekly. And I thought today was a checkup and cleaning. What's going on?"

"Dad, I don't know. I didn't ask why the dentist needed to do anything." Millie buried her eyes in her hand, shielding herself from the sun.

"You don't seem to know anything these days." Leonard shook his head. "Can I have the card back?" Leonard extended his empty hand, waiting.

"I'll need it again next week." Millie dropped the American Express card into Leonard's hand, never touching his skin.

"I understand, but now is a long time until next week. Do you have enough money?"

"I could always use more. I want to buy Jackie new sneakers."

"Sure, show me which ones, and I'll order them." Leonard met her bluff. She had played him too many times, asking for money to purchase something for Jackie, but it never happened. She accepted the money, but for what Leonard only learned when it was too late. He smartened up, even if it meant displeasing Millie.

"Forget it." Millie rolled her eyes. She brought her knees up to her chest, placing her feet on Leonard's perforated leather seats.

"Feet down." Leonard swatted at her feet. He revved the engine, loving the growl come to life. He was about to shift into first gear when his phone went off. It was the dentist's office. "Hello, this is Leonard." He listened to the receptionist speed talk as he stared at Millie from the corner of his eye. She studied the ends of her burnt hair. Nothing about her appeared healthy. "Sure, no problem. I'll be right in." He hung up. "Dr. Blank wants to speak to me. Do you know why? You paid in full, right?"

"I gave them the card and signed the receipt. I don't remember how much the bill was, so don't ask."

"Wait here. I'll be right back." He just shook his head and left Millie to herself.

Leonard sat in a brisk cool office with modern blue décor. He studied the doctor's family photos on the desk. Everyone in the snapshots had the perfect smile. Go figure. Although, Leonard thought the wife's teeth looked too white in contrast to her overly tanned skin. Next to her were three tall sons, probably in their early twenties. Dr. Blank positioned himself in the center of his family, behind their backs, so he wouldn't break the chain they created. They must have vacationed on an island, maybe Aruba. Leonard thought about the one vacation when he took Millie and Steven to an exotic island. Overall, it was a great trip, aside from the one night Steven drank too much and threw up everywhere. But he recalled how much everyone had bonded, how much he and Millie had spoken. Everyone got along, and it was a great time that, unfortunately, never really repeated itself.

A throat clearing jolted Leonard back into the present. Dr. Blank made his way behind his desk with heavy footsteps. His belly hung over his expensive brown belt as he plopped down, studying Leonard before speaking.

"I know I'm due for an exam. I've been a bad patient." Leonard wagged his finger in the air, trying to cut the odd tension created by each man in the room.

"Ah, yes. How long has it been?" Dr. Blank sank into his black leather chair. Another expensive accent. Leonard knew the price for everything, an innate skill.

"Two years. But in my defense, I bought this awesome electric toothbrush with an oversized head. They don't even make it here. I flew it in from Europe. My mouth has never felt better. I'll send you the brand."

Dr. Blank held up a declining hand. "Just come in for a cleaning, Leonard." Dr. Blank cleared his throat, scrunching his brow.

Leonard's stomach tightened.

"I wanted to talk to you about Millie." He leaned forward, clasping his hands on the desk. "She has a severe problem."

"Yeah, she mentioned something about you taking molds. I couldn't really get a straight answer out of her." Leonard fought a wave of nervous flutters in his chest. He'd shifted in his seat at least a dozen times by then, unable to figure out if he wanted to cross his leg at a ninety-degree angle or keep both feet planted on the royal blue plush carpeting.

"Nearly all her teeth are rotted. Maybe ten percent of them I can salvage."

"Excuse me?"

"She'll need implants and extensive oral surgery to complete all necessary work."

Leonard battled dizziness threatening to topple him forward. His eyes darted wildly. What was this man across from him saying? Where did this come from?

"We'll probably do veneers. Maybe a special bleach to prevent staining. Although nothing is foolproof. That'll probably cost between twenty to twenty-five thousand dollars."

"Whoa, whoa. Everyone needs to calm the fuck down." Leonard threw his hands up in the air, hoping to create a force field from this sudden information dump from the dentist. But it was Leonard who needed to calm down. Dr. Blank seemed perfectly relaxed. Leonard ran a stiff hand through his hair, inhaling any oxygen he found. "Let's start from the top, okay?"

Dr. Blank nodded in agreement.

"What is going on with Millie?"

"I've been practicing dentistry for thirty-five years."

Congratulations, Leonard thought.

"The only people I've seen with Millie's tooth decay and overall damage are individuals with a serious drug problem."

Leonard lost the ability to swallow. A severe drug problem? What the hell did this all mean, and where would he begin?

"Leonard? Would you like a glass of water?"

He hated water.

Dr. Blank frowned. "Has Millie ever shown signs of addiction? I mean, we can fix her teeth, but this should be addressed. Maybe even a program?"

"Um..." Leonard forgot how to speak. He never experienced complete body weakness until now. Millie, a drug addict? How could she be an addict if she cared for Jackie full-time? Leonard noted how she didn't watch Jackie most of the time, but he thought that had something to do with what had landed Jackie in the hospital that night. When did she have the time to slip into a debilitating way of life?

"You probably want to think about all of this and what to do next—"

"We'll fix her teeth. Of course, we'll fix her teeth. She's in pain. I don't want her to be uncomfortable. She needs to feel comfortable. I don't want her in any pain." And Leonard meant it.

"Okay, we'll rebuild her mouth. I have already made an appointment for her next week. She'll probably need someone to drive her to these appointments. Some of the work will leave her sore and maybe groggy."

"Understood." Leonard forced the words out. He comprehended nothing other than he had a real problem on his hands. Millie.

"I'm sorry you had to find out this way."

"You're certain it's drugs? She eats terribly. Only wants sugar. Maybe it's poor diet choices and not what you think it is." Leonard was desperate for any sign of hope from Dr. Blank but knew he had hit a wall.

"Her choices are all directed to the source. Drugs. Again, I'm sorry. I... I don't know what else to say." Even the air deflated from Dr. Blank's confidence. "I hope I'm wrong."

Leonard shook himself from the thick fog drowning him. "We'll start with her teeth and go from there."

Dr. Blank nodded, and the men shook hands.

Leonard stormed to his car. He was unsure what to say to Millie, but he knew a confrontation was imminent. Leonard had readied for battle and asked what the fuck was wrong with her when he stopped short in his steps. He reached his car to find Millie passed out, head was thrown back in the passenger seat, snoring. He decided to let her sleep instead and drove them home.

# February 2011 – The Hospital

Of course, Jackie would love a racecar, one of those model die-cast ones. He chose a red and yellow one, both Jeep Wrangler models. The last time Leonard saw Jackie, all the little boy did was pretend to crash cars. These would be a hit. He figured there'd be no harm in stopping at a toy store a minute from the hospital. Millie texted him, saying they just took Jackie for some imaging of his general body, whatever that meant.

About an hour ago, Leonard received a stumbling, slurred, hysterical phone call from Millie. Apparently, Jackie fell at home. Jesse wasn't there when it happened. For once, Jesse had been working, and his alibi of being at the shop held strong. So, it all fell on Millie. She was home with Jackie alone. Leonard didn't want to point fingers or enter the hospital with an accusatory eye, but how could he not? He didn't want to ask Millie questions, but he wanted answers. She didn't tell Leonard how Jackie fell. Only that he tripped. Those were the only details she revealed, and they didn't illuminate much of anything substantive.

About six months before, Millie and Jesse had broken up for good. From what Leonard heard, Jesse had already found a new girlfriend to fuck up. Better some random chick rather than his beautiful daughter to corrupt. But recently, and Leonard didn't want to lie, Millie didn't seem that great. Aside from breaking up with Jesse, something with her seemed... distant. Yes, that was a way to describe her current moods. When Leonard asked Steven if he spoke to his sister, all his son did was shrug. The shrug was Steven's answer to all questions regarding Millie. Leonard was unsure when his children's relationship soured or transformed into a terrain of estrangement.

Leonard blamed Jesse for many of Millie's social problems with her relationships. It was as if Millie lived to please and keep Jesse in line. Two tasks Millie failed miserably, and she held herself responsible. She blamed herself for Jesse breaking up with her for everything. Except for that day's occurrence. So far, Leonard didn't suspect the same remorse from Millie over Jackie's injury.

He found Millie sitting alone on a blue bench staring straight ahead at an empty space. She seemed tired from twenty feet away. Something changed, Leonard repeated to himself. Something seemed off. He walked to Millie, tightening his grip on the toy cars he had just bought.

"Hi, Millie," said Leonard.

"Hi, Dad." Millie did not make eye contact with him.

Leonard sat beside her and rubbed a hand on the middle of her back. "Are you okay? How are you doing?"

"I'm fine. Just can't believe this happened." Millie signaled to the double doors, indicating Jackie must be back there.

"When can we go see Jackie? How is he doing?"

"They're just finishing up some body scans. The doctors want to ensure there's no damage or anything like that."

"The doctor wouldn't let you stay with Jackie while he had the x-rays?" Leonard eyed his daughter.

"They needed to sedate Jackie. He was pretty upset. After he was out, I didn't want to risk anything. The doctor said I can just wait here."

"I got these for Jackie on my way here." Leonard held up the bag of cars.

"You stopped at a toy store?" Millie eyed the bag, unimpressed.

A shot of white anger pulsed down Leonard's spine. "Yeah. I figured I had two minutes because you said they were just taking him in for imaging. Don't you remember telling me that?" Leonard refused to be blamed for a centimeter of what happened to Jackie today. Or to be made a villain in this equation. Yes, he made a quick stop at a store to buy his grandson something to cheer him up when he got out of the hospital today. Big deal.

"Thanks, Dad. He'll love it," said Millie, having no idea what was in the bag, and Leonard didn't offer to show her either.

"Look at me," said Leonard.

She didn't move or lift her eyes.

"Millie, look at me." Leonard deflated at her oblivion. He didn't know what she stared at ahead, and something nudged at him that she didn't know either. He lifted her chin to force her eyes to meet his. Her pupils were barely there, like pinpoints, if he had to describe them to anyone. He dropped her chin, feeling her jaw grow slack under his touch. All he wanted to do was wash his hands from her cold, clammy skin. He didn't view Millie as his daughter right now. He regarded her as an awful mother to a victim child who happened to be his grandson.

"You should be ashamed of yourself," he scowled. Leonard walked a few steps from a silent and slack Millie before changing his mind and heading back to her. "You should be fucking ashamed." Leonard lost control of his voice, pointing a finger less than an inch from her deadened eyes. "And you're supposed to take Jackie home in your current state tonight? Over my fucking dead body."

"I said I was sorry."

"You haven't said shit." Leonard backed away from Millie, not believing what he was about to do, who he was about to call. But there was no choice, at least not tonight.

He reached the elevator bank just when the doors opened, and out busted Jesse, who already was jogging to find Jackie. Leonard grabbed Jesse's grease-stained clothes.

"Who the fuck?" Jesse whipped around but was not quite relieved to see Leonard. They didn't have the best relationship. "Where's Jackie? Is he okay?"

"I just got here. But from what I hear, he's going to be okay."

"Where is she?" Jesse asked, meaning Millie, as he cast an ominous glance down the wide cream corridor ahead.

"She's in the waiting area. I know emotions are high right now, but let's just try to take a deep breath."

Jesse threw a furtive glance Leonard's way, a silent warning to not overstep a boundary that was already crossed by Millie's negligence.

"Hell, I remember when Steven was nine. He fell and busted open his chin on a chair. We rushed him to the hospital, and anyone who tried to tell me to calm down, I wanted to crack their jaw."

Jesse sucked a sharp breath through his nostrils, not relating to Leonard's anecdote. The favor Leonard needed to ask Jesse, even though he hated himself for doing it, was about to spill out of his mouth.

"Listen, Jesse. I was actually going to call you. I didn't know you were on your way over…" Leonard swallowed, preparing himself.

"Of course, I was coming. The moment I heard, I dropped everything at the shop and ran. Goddammit, Leonard." Jesse flailed his arms, running his hands and long fingernails through his oily hair.

"You're right, Jesse. You're one hundred percent right. I didn't mean anything when I said it. I don't think anyone is thinking straight right now with Jackie in there. He should be home instead of here."

"You've got that fucking right." Jesse crossed his arms at the declaration. "What do you want, Leonard?"

"Millie's pretty thrown off from what happened."

"Thrown off." Jesse scoffed. "That's one way to put how she is." They both knew what Millie was without needing to say it. Neither man wanted to admit to it either. Millie was the mom of Jackie and also Leonard's daughter. They both shared a stake in this; all that mattered was Jackie's safety for tonight.

"Can Jackie go home with you tonight? I know it's last minute, but I think we can both agree it's the right move for tonight. I would offer, but I think it would confuse him even more, and my house isn't child safe, really."

Jesse rubbed his tired eyes like this was the last thing he was prepared for. Leonard reached into his coat pocket, finding his wallet.

"I know you're not prepared. I wouldn't be either. Here, let me help." Leonard whipped out a wad of twenties and counted out one hundred in three seconds. He pushed the money into Jesse's black, grease-stained palms.

"A hundred?" Jesse asked, unimpressed. "I didn't have time to go food shopping."

Leonard shook his head as if to say, of course and gave Jesse another five twenties.

Jesse peered from his green-covered palm back to Leonard.

"There's a good chance Jackie will stay more than a night."

Leonard rolled his eyes, so Jesse couldn't see the growing disgust. Of course, Jesse would use this as a bargaining chip to his advantage. Make a buck off his son. Leonard built his wealth on perceiving people's next moves and forecasting a real estate market and its trends to gain from. But whenever it came to Jesse, Leonard failed miserably. He never gauged just how much Jesse would push, and no matter the amount offered, Jesse would ask for more.

Leonard kept counting the twenties in his wallet, only to transfer all of them into Jesse's hand. Seven hundred and sixty dollars. Leonard's wallet now lay empty in his hand.

"That's all I have, Jesse."

Jesse shook his head, satisfied. "That should be enough." He stuffed the wad of cash into his back pocket. "Everything will work out, I'm sure. Jackie will be fine."

Funny how money shifted the mood, Leonard observed.

"I'm going to grab a coffee and wait to hear from Millie. I won't be far," Leonard said.

"Do what you gotta do. We'll keep you updated."

"Thanks, Jesse." Leonard massaged his lighter wallet with only singles left to his name for the night.

"Anytime. And Leonard? It was nice seeing you." Jesse nodded, patting his back jean pocket.

# *November 25th, 2021*

The Rosen plot held fifteen spots, with eleven already occupied. At first, when the family heard the most senior of the Rosen clan had purchased fifteen spaces, everyone laughed. Like fifteen Rosen family members wanted to rest next to one another for eternity when the moment arrived. Everyone said there was no way the plots would fill up. But with untimely and odd choices when their various deaths came, each respective Rosen chose to be buried with their relatives, whether by chance or on purpose. The youngest of the Rosens to rest underground was Millie. Leonard found her stone too quickly. He didn't remember the walk from his car to the gravesite.

The instant he landed in front of the plot, he kicked himself for forgetting sunflowers, Millie's favorite plant. She, like Leonard, adored yellow and the sun. Putting both together, she decided a sunflower must be her favorite flower. It made sense to Millie, but they laughed over her reasoning to everyone else. He stared at her tombstone, questioning if he chose the correct wording, even though the rabbi he had consulted at the time said there was no wrong verbiage for remembrance, but Leonard didn't buy it. Thirty-two years old, way too short of a life to brag about timewise. Less than half of Leonard's age. He couldn't imagine living only half of his life, all the things he would have missed, and all the things he wouldn't have done. Millie would never know better than the half sweet and half sour years she spent on Earth. Not all her years were terrible, but the last ones made the final impression. On his way over, he had grabbed three rocks and placed them on top of her stone. One for him, one for Steven, and one for Jackie. He recited aloud who the stones represented as he placed them down.

Dozens of people sprinkled themselves throughout the enormous layers of the land. Leonard assumed the cemetery would be empty by this time. Of course, he was wrong. He was wrong about a lot of things lately. Underestimated people and overestimated the good they could do. He wished Steven had come with him to show respect to his sister. Maybe Leonard would confront Steven over his coldness, or he would just let him be. He watched other mourners talk to their lost loved ones. He thought it looked strange talking to oneself out loud but guessed these people didn't care. It was a holiday, and everyone wanted to be with their loved ones on special days. So, if talking to a skeleton buried six feet under helped normalize the day for some, then Leonard could understand why they did it. He wished he had that bravery to talk to Millie aloud, but something in him couldn't live up to the challenge. Instead, he just looked at the grass covering her disintegrated body. Her bones had probably already vanished to dust. He wondered if he dug her up right now, what would he find? It was an image he swiftly pushed out of his wandering mind.

Someone's labored sniff snapped Leonard awake. He whipped his head and caught an image of a stunning brunette passing behind him. She wrapped her arms around her slender waist and pushed her feet to move forward. She couldn't have been older than fifty. Leonard took pride in people thinking he was much younger than his age. A woman's age never intimidated Leonard into not making a move, and all Leonard wanted to do was move closer to this sobbing woman. He wanted to know her story. Who was she here for today?

Leonard reached into his pocket and grabbed the handkerchief to guide him to an opening.

"You look like you need this?" Leonard extended the white silken tissue in her direction.

The woman stopped to consider his offer, long enough for them to study each other. She was beautiful. It was the first thought to enter Leonard's mind and the last to leave. Green eyes. A green-eyed woman. He could melt into her gaze. The tears decorated the color surrounding her pupils as if mother nature had sculpted this female creature by hand. Would she even give Leonard the time? It was the first time he doubted if he was good enough for someone. And usually, in Leonard's mind, he was always better.

"It's clean, I swear." Leonard inched the immaculate tissue closer to the mysterious woman, flashing a smile that screamed at her to trust him. It had usually worked in his past conquests.

She smiled, probably for the first time today, Leonard guessed. She seemed very alone as a mourner on Thanksgiving, noting her bare ring finger. He couldn't let her go without finding out some information about her. If things didn't go anywhere today because of their morbid circumstances for being here, then there was always tomorrow. This was his perfect woman, he suddenly realized. On paper, at least. Could she be the one he waited for during this dry spell? He needed to find out.

"Please, I insist you take this." He pushed the tissue almost into her hand. She didn't stop him and dabbed her gorgeous, brilliant eyes silently. Once finished, she nodded her appreciation.

"I visit my daughter every holiday. I like to think by doing that, she's not alone on these important days of the year," said the woman in the most perfectly steady, soft-spoken voice Leonard had the privilege of hearing. Her tone fit her beauty, and both traits were equal in strength.

"That's very noble of you. I'm sure she knows you're here." Leonard never sounded this sympathetic, but it was the only thing to embody to keep their conversation afloat.

"Who are you here for?" She nodded to Millie's grave.

Leonard had almost forgotten where he stood until her reminder hit him. He was supposed to reflect today. His mind didn't want to deal with all those troubles once this woman entered his shrinking picture to honor and focus on Millie only and to think about how to get Jackie. Not that he wouldn't revisit them later, but he wanted to do something else right now. He wanted to win this woman over.

"My daughter, Millie. She's been gone for six years now. Today is actually the anniversary of her death. I miss her every day." Leonard felt a strange weight lift off his chest, admitting to these details. He had never actually said them out loud to another woman, but this stranger did something to him. She made him want to speak honestly.

She moved closer, standing shoulder to shoulder with Leonard, staring at Millie's stone. Her eyes glazed over with a fresh sheen of tears as she read, 'Daughter, Sister, Granddaughter, Mother...' on the grave. "She was a mother?"

"Had one son. My grandson. His name is Jackie. A really handsome and bright kid. He's twelve."

The woman frowned. What was her name? Leonard needed to know her name but didn't feel ready to ask. "Are you close with him? With Jackie, I mean."

Leonard knew who she meant. "Yes. Very close. We see each other once a week." And then he stopped speaking because that wouldn't be the reality in a few months if he didn't think of a solution to keep Jackie here.

"That's a beautiful thing. I always envisioned what kind of grandmother I'd be to my daughter's children, but life happened." She motioned toward her child's mysterious grave. Leonard tried to pinpoint where the woman pointed, but he didn't collect his answer.

"I'm sorry." He reached a hand and placed it on her shoulder. She didn't flinch or display any sort of reaction. Instead, she kept staring at Millie's grave.

"What are the stones for?" She gestured to the small rocks on top of the smooth tombstone's finish.

"I usually place one for each important person I want to be represented here. Just so Millie knows she's remembered by her closest loved ones." Leonard thought about Steven's rock and wanted to remove it. He wasn't worthy of a spot on her stone today when he so adamantly refused to visit his only sister. "I was going to bring flowers today, but I forgot." Leonard tapped his skull, messing up his salt and pepper hair.

She smiled, squinting into the sunlight as she gazed at Leonard's face. She fixed a strand of displaced hair and tucked it behind his ear. He followed her thin fingers out of the corner of his eye. This was the closest he'd been to a woman in months, yet he knew little about her. His pulse danced across his chest. She reached down into the grass and picked up a small rock, nearing the size of a large pebble, and held it up to Leonard's nose.

"May I?" she asked Leonard.

"Of course." He motioned her to go ahead, utterly fascinated by this warm, feminine creature.

She placed the pebble on the stone, touching Leonard's rock. "Even though I never met Millie, I feel like there's a strange connection as if we already knew each other. Have you ever felt that way about someone?"

"My name is Leonard Rosen." He couldn't rip his eyes away from her perfect complexion. Her cheeks grew rosy against the chilly air.

She turned her eyes back in Millie's direction. "I'm sorry we had to meet this way, Leonard, but I'm oddly content to be standing here with you and Millie. Thank you for letting me share your space today." She inhaled a cool stream of oxygen through her nostrils, never quite allowing the air to escape. "Happy Thanksgiving, Millie. My name is Jill." Jill finally turned to meet Leonard's mesmerized face.

He knew Thanksgiving wouldn't be so bad because Leonard planned on getting to know the perfect woman named Jill today. He raised his arm, welcoming Jill into his personal space, and she glided right into his nook. They walked down the cobblestone pathway, away from Millie. He turned his head to peek at her shrinking tombstone when he felt a gentle hand press against his sturdy chest.

"Are you ready to go?" asked Jill. Her eyes ignited something in Leonard that made him want to live this day. They fed a new motivation into Leonard's soul that, until now, seemed deadened under rocks of restraint.

"Where would you like to go?"

"Anywhere you want to go sounds good to me." Jill's smile was all Leonard needed to keep moving.

# December 8th, 2008 – The Announcement

Leonard planned to start a low-carb diet today after waking this morning, stepping on the scale, and freezing in place when he saw the number read one hundred and ninety-six pounds. He never got this high for a man with his average stature and it wasn't like it was a happy weight, either. He devoured a garden salad with grilled chicken sprinkled with balsamic dressing for lunch, and for dinner, he aimed to eat some sort of protein. Of course, nothing went to plan in Leonard's life. Judy called him about an hour before his day ended, telling him Millie and Jesse wanted to eat at the new Italian restaurant that just opened a few months ago. He pushed back at first, but Judy always had a way of incessant nagging that made even the most confident of men roll over and lose a part of his soul to her pushiness. He would find a way to eat healthy at this family-style restaurant, even if it meant bringing his own goddamn food from home. Leonard chuckled to himself at Judy's reaction if he dared bring outside food into a dining establishment. It made him laugh and roll his eyes simultaneously. He needed a change, for sure.

He sat at the table with Judy, fighting a constant leg shake, not wanting to be there. Judy eased into the restaurant's ambiance, enjoying a vodka tonic.

"Are you sure you don't want to try a sip?" Judy offered Leonard a taste of her cocktail.

Leonard scowled, turning his head away.

"You're so boring," she said.

"You know I hate anything with alcohol. The taste, Judy."

"It's all tonic water."

"You're missing the point." Leonard rubbed his temple, losing patience and hope.

"You're in a great mood tonight." Judy finished her drink, searching for the waiter for a refill, snapping her fingers in the air.

"I know Millie is going to say she's engaged to Jesse. He's a bum. And she's barely working."

"Maybe they just wanted to go on a double date with us."

"And they chose the most expensive restaurant in town that I'll have to pay for." Leonard pushed the bread basket to the table's edge, fighting the starchy temptation as his stomach growled.

"Try to be a little positive, Leonard."

"It's called being realistic. You're either wrong or realistic in my world." The latter is how Leonard built his success.

"And how has that worked out for you, that thinking?" Judy squinted.

"It's how I run my business. So far, so good." Leonard downed half of his Diet Coke, crunching on some trapped ice.

"And personally?" Judy asked, raising a singular penciled eyebrow.

"Well, you are the fifth wife." Leonard laughed for the first time today.

"Ugh, go to hell," Judy said, crossing her arms.

"Right back at ya, baby." Yes, Leonard thought. He really needed to start that diet.

Millie and Jesse suddenly appeared, holding hands in front of Leonard. He didn't buy their image of love tonight. He'd seen it many times from them. Leonard did sneak a look at Millie's fingers and noting there was not a ring in sight.

"Hi, Dad."

Everyone hugged and said their hellos before sitting at the table. Jesse even shaved tonight, which Leonard found shocking.

"I've wanted to try this place out for the longest time," Judy said to Millie. "But your father is so stubborn."

Leonard rolled his eyes. If only Judy could see who she had married. Why did all the women become so surprised with Leonard towards the end? Judy didn't know the end was near, but Leonard made up his mind. He just needed to figure out the timing.

"Well, that's Dad for you." Millie nudged Leonard's foot.

"Watch it. New shoes." Leonard snarled to Millie.

"Your father isn't in the best mood tonight." Judy shot a dagger eye at Leonard. "He's dieting."

"You look good, Leo," said Jesse, emerging from his muted state.

"Leonard. Always call me Leonard." He caught Millie and Jesse exchanging nervous glances. Good, Leonard thought. They should feel uneasy. What was this news, anyway?

"So, what's the big announcement?" asked Leonard, clapping his hands together. His stomach tightened.

Millie opened her black patent leather purse Leonard was almost sure he paid for and fished out a black-and-white picture. Leonard wasn't dumb. He knew instantly what that was. His first reaction to his hunch? One big fuck of a miracle that he didn't regurgitate across the white linen table cloth.

Millie and Jesse squeezed each other's hands as she held up a clearly visible sonogram picture of a fetus. Leonard bit his bottom lip so hard that he tasted blood. He'd definitely lose weight from tonight's meal. Leonard couldn't stomach a single ice chip from their announcement.

"We just came from the doctor. We're officially thirteen weeks today." Millie's cheeks blushed, and Jesse planted a kiss on her head.

Judy threw a shocked, happy hand over her mouth and clutched Leonard's frozen arm on the table.

"You're pregnant?" Leonard forced the words out.

"Yeah, Dad. I just said thirteen weeks."

"I heard what you said." Leonard eyed Millie, simply shocked. He couldn't turn his head to peer at anyone else's reaction.

"Aren't you happy? You're going to be a grandpa," said Millie.

Leonard threw his napkin on the table, huffing what oxygen remained in his body.

"Leonard, relax," said Judy. He instantly pulled his arm out of her wiry grasp.

"You're really going to keep the baby?" Leonard asked Millie as he pretended Jesse had vanished from the table. He saw his daughter's cheeks redden, a sign he caught her in something she knew he disagreed with.

"Dad, of course, we'll keep the baby." Millie's eyes darted to Jesse's for confirmation. Jesse sat there, not moving a muscle. "How could you even suggest something like that?"

"You barely work. You just cut back a day from your job because you claimed three days were too stressful." Leonard already held two fingers in the air for everyone to see. "Jesse just started a new job." Now he pointed at Jesse's pale face.

"This one will stick. I know how to fix bikes," Jesse said to Leonard.

Leonard didn't know what to say. The tingle in his chest returned. A wave of numbness washed over his left cheek. The panic always started on one side of his face before spreading like a blazing wildfire. He needed to stop it from happening, and it couldn't happen here, not in front of Jesse. Leonard despised the guy and refused to display weakness.

"I really thought you'd be so happy," said Millie.

"C'mon, Leonard. A baby is a blessing," said Judy, who birthed no children of her own. Leonard just glared at his fifth wife. She never got it. She never understood him. Why couldn't she just take his side right now? "How about we order some appetizers and let things settle."

"You really want to keep this baby?" Leonard asked Millie, ignoring Judy's ludicrous suggestion about ordering food. He couldn't bring himself to swallow air if he tried.

"I'm not going to get rid of the baby," said Millie.

"I think it's something the two of you need to seriously consider," said Leonard, clicking his jaw and trying to avoid looking at Jesse.

"We don't believe in that here," said Jesse.

"You don't believe in that," Leonard repeated, adopting a mocking tone. "Well, I'll tell you what I believe about this whole thing." Leonard pushed an inch back in his chair, jarring the table and leaving the waters rattling. "The two of you really screwed up this time. Forget about those domestic disturbances where the cops showed up at your apartment. Now you're bringing a baby into the picture? Have you lost your fucking minds?"

Judy shushed Leonard over his language. He shot his fire eyes at Judy's face. They were enough to shut her up for the moment. Tears coated Millie's face as she cried silently. Leonard did not know when she lost it, but he didn't care.

"I don't know what to say. I really thought you'd be happy." Millie wiped away a rogue tear that raced down her cheek. "Are you happy?" Millie asked Judy.

"Her opinion doesn't matter," Leonard said, holding a hand in front of Judy's face. Her nostrils flared at his rejection, leaving Leonard only to shrug.

"We're going to have the baby," said Millie, staring at the white linen tablecloth.

"How will you do this? Logistically, how? You guys don't have much money and aren't making a lot of money. You fight." Leonard filled an entire hand with reasons to end this terrible plan. "Seriously. How will you make this work? Raising a baby."

Jesse draped a casual arm around Millie's slumped shoulders, pulling her close. "We'll manage."

# November 25<sup>th</sup>, 2021

They shared a bowl of matzah ball noodle soup for now. Jill sipped her cranberry juice with a slice of lime balancing on the glass rim while Leonard nursed a Diet Coke. They chose a booth for the impromptu lunch that overlooked the empty street. Leonard guessed people didn't feel like cooking this year as he observed the packed diner. Either way, he welcomed the busier atmosphere. Yes, he wanted to get to know Jill and intended to, but he didn't yearn for quiet, not today.

"What does the lime do for the juice?" Leonard asked, pointing to the sliced fruit.

"It's refreshing. It's a nice break from the straight cranberry flavor." Jill took the wedge of lime and squeezed it into the beverage. She guzzled a hefty serving of the juice and smacked her lips together, sealing it with a wink. "Would you like to try?"

"No, no. I'm good." Leonard held up a declining hand. But he really wanted to say to Jill how good she looked sitting across from him in this plush booth.

"Can I take a taste of your Diet Coke? I haven't had it in years."

"Sure, go right ahead." Leonard signaled her to drink.

Jill reached for the extra straw on the table and inserted it into his drink. He hid his disappointment at the idea she wouldn't choose his straw to drink from but soon pushed the silly thought from his mind. They ended up at this diner simply because it was convenient and less than ten minutes away from the cemetery. After twenty minutes of sitting in the restaurant, the only new detail they uncovered about each other was their love for soup. Otherwise, they kept the conversation light, with quick insertions of witty banter. It was only a matter of time before one dug deeper into the other's life. Leonard decided to go first.

"What was your daughter's name?" Leonard asked. She stopped drinking her juice, pushing the glass to the side. "I'm sorry. If you don't want to talk about it, I understand."

"Melissa." Jill gazed out the window.

"Do you have any other kids?"

"I have another daughter. She lives in Florida with her husband. They just had a baby girl."

A genuine smile spread across Leonard's face. A loss to be padded with new life. One could never replace the other, but these were motivators to live for. At least, that's how Leonard viewed Jackie.

"My granddaughter's name is Isabella. I'm still getting used to saying *my granddaughter*." Jill chuckled. "It's funny. I thought I would never want to be called Grandma. It just sounded so old to me. But now I can't wait to hear that little girl call me that." Jill cradled her square jaw in her hand, waiting for Leonard to speak.

"I totally get it. When Jackie was born, I wasn't ready. I mean, Millie wasn't even married to the father. It wasn't the most well-planned thing. But I love him so much. He's my boy, you know? And he's all I have left of Millie here on this Earth." Leonard cast his eyes into his lap, fearing he would give himself away. He needed to look tough. That's what he did with women. He was supposed to save them. Never the other way around. He wanted to be taken care of by a woman but not saved. He was the knight.

"At least you have Jackie." She reached across and took Leonard's hand. He didn't flinch or move away. He invited her warm touch. "I remember Melissa saying she couldn't wait to have kids one day. And I would always say, don't rush. You're so young. There's so much time." Jill half laughed out of the irony, not the facts. "She would have been a good mom, too." A single tear slid down her cheek.

"What happened?" Leonard's soft voice traveled across the table. Jill lifted her gaze to his face, deciding if she should answer. He didn't want to push her or lose this moment. He squeezed her hand to encourage a response. The light pressure pushed her forward.

"I'm not sure what came first. Alcohol or drugs, drugs or alcohol. Either way, they got to her before she beat them. She would have been twenty-six."

Leonard winced at the even younger age than Millie when she passed. Both were young and should be here today, sitting with their parents, maybe even in this booth, where they could have all gotten to know each other.

"The day I got the call plays in my head at least once a day. It doesn't consume me anymore, but it produces a fleeting thought, I guess you can call it. It used to be much worse." Jill released a shuddering breath.

"I can relate." Leonard studied Jill's face. He offered her a clean napkin to dry her eyes. "If your daughter is in Florida, why are you here today? Thanksgiving's a family holiday."

"I told you every holiday I visit Melissa, so she's not alone."

"That's right. I'm sorry. I get distracted whenever anything about grandkids is mentioned."

And then Leonard told Jill about everything. His dilemma with Jackie and seeking custody, from the Thailand curveball to not being permitted to see him today for dessert. His whole day appeared to crumble until he met Jill at Millie's grave by chance. They discussed fate and faith. Leonard stood staunch by 'life is too short, so why settle,' hence his reasoning behind his many failed marriages and broken engagements. Jill never seemed phased by many details that would trigger a woman to flee.

"So, are you going to go for custody of Jackie?" asked Jill, toying with Leonard's fingers until they intertwined with her own.

"My attorney said going through the system would be difficult and not in my favor. Unless I dig up nasty stuff on Jackie's home life."

"The system?" asked Jill, not understanding. Her face oozed a naive and virtuous glow Leonard could bathe in for years.

"The courts. It's complicated." Leonard shook his head, realizing for the first time that it might be best to let Jackie go to Thailand. He was sixty-five years old. How many raging uphill battles did he have the energy for? And maybe Jackie wanted to be with his father and step-siblings. Leonard knew there was no replacement for a father and a mother. But Leonard also knew he could provide a life ten times better than Jackie experienced now. And Margot? Forget her, that bitch.

"Could you live with yourself if you didn't try?" Jill's green eyes penetrated Leonard. "You're in a very tough spot. If he does go, you could always visit."

"I could. But his father is tricky. If Jackie goes, he's gone." Leonard needed to fight, but how? He hadn't a clue.

"I know you'll figure this out. You're a smart man."

"Thanks," said Leonard, rolling his eyes, retracting an inch away from Jill for the first time today.

"I'm serious. You don't come across genuinely smart people too often. When you do, you just know they are. Haven't you felt that way before, Leonard?"

He loved how his name sounded coming off her tongue.

"Sure. But I've been burned by many people I thought were smart." Like Millie. And Jill knew who Leonard meant too. Maybe Jill's daughter duped her own mother too many times, but Jill kept believing for whatever reason. "Do you ever blame yourself for Melissa and what happened to her?" He didn't expect this to become a therapy session for himself with a complete stranger, but Jill made him want to talk so far. To speak about everything he hadn't wanted to address with the high-priced therapist he had seen for two years after Millie's death. Something about Jill welcomed him and his inner thoughts to be vocalized. He felt free.

Jill exhaled, not hinting whether she'd answer Leonard's probing question. "At first, I did."

She considered her answer before continuing.

"Yeah. Every day, for probably the first year, I blamed myself." Her eyes never appeared wider than right now.

Leonard winced at her admission, as he never blamed himself by book standards. Regret bloated his veins, a nuance he experienced difficulty explaining to the ordinary person.

"How about you?" Jill asked.

"I wish I did things differently earlier in Millie's life. I blame her mother. Those were the bad genes." Leonard always pointed the finger at Millie's mom. She was the bad one, and he should have fought her for the kids but didn't. The only result of his inaction was a regret that ran to the ocean's most extraordinary depth. He got Millie too late and Steven just in time, a way he rationalized the good and bad kid.

"I know what you mean. That's how I view my ex-husband." A shiver wracked Jill's body at the mention of him, a man Leonard instantly disliked. "But I don't blame him. I blame him for certain things, but not for her death. I'm sure he has his regrets, too. We'll suffer together at the end of it all, right?"

"You have a big heart." Leonard smiled.

"I guess that's a good and bad thing." Jill blushed, hiding behind her cranberry cocktail.

"I like it." Leonard squeezed her hand. He thought he had completed his confession about Millie, but more details tugged at his heart to be freed. "I'm glad I didn't listen to everyone with how I dealt with her when she was spiraling."

"It's difficult." Jill shook her head, swimming in her own muddy reminiscence. "I'd keep Melissa in the basement. Help her withdraw. Keep track of her. And just when I thought she was on her way, all it took was one bad day to set her back. I tried everything, and I think Melissa knew that. It's how I came to terms with not blaming myself anymore for her death."

"Everyone said to cut Millie off. But I couldn't do it. What was I supposed to do? Throw her onto the street and let her die in some alley?"

"You followed your heart; there's nothing wrong with doing that." Jill waited for a beat before popping a morsel of a matzah ball into her symmetrical mouth. Her teeth were straight and white, almost too perfect but he couldn't complain. She was a complete angel, and Leonard wasn't ready to let this perfect human go.

"What are your plans for the rest of the day?" Her answer didn't matter to Leonard because he had already decided on their itinerary.

"You're looking at it." Jill gestured to the sparsely covered table.

"Good. Because I hear this place has pretty good turkey and pies. It is Thanksgiving, right? We have to have a little turkey." Leonard lifted his brow twice and shot Jill a menu across the table.

"I like your thinking, Mr. Rosen. Is it okay if I call you that?" She browsed the menu, never shifting her eyes away from the food-jammed pages.

"You can call me anything you like." And he let her because she was just that special. And the plans he had for the two of them today, she would never guess. She was his perfect woman, and he had every intention of spoiling her.

# November 2007 – Domestic Disturbance

It was an absolute miracle from the gods that Leonard did not get pulled over by a cop. He sped to Millie's apartment, not dipping below fifty miles per hour on a drive that consisted mainly of residential streets. He had received a frantic, sob-ridden call from Millie, imploring Leonard to come over as soon as possible. He asked what had happened but couldn't get a straight answer. Only when Leonard detected Jesse's loud, slurred words in the background did he drop the phone and jump into his car.

Fifteen minutes later, he arrived to find two cop cars with their flashing lights already parked outside of Millie's apartment. Fucking great, Leonard thought. Millie already had issues with the landlord, which certainly would not help.

Judy called him right before he exited the car. "Hey, baby... I know. I'm so sorry. I'll come home right after this. I promise... Love you too." Leonard ended the call with two kisses and jogged over to the rookie cop, who couldn't be older than twenty-two.

"Are you the father?" the cop said.

"Of Millie Rosen. I'm Leonard." He offered his hand to the cop, who shook it with an iron grip.

"My partner is inside talking to the boyfriend. Seems like he's been drinking, and things got out of hand."

Leonard ground his molars, unable to speak. He warned Millie about Jesse. This wasn't their first fight, but it never escalated to cop calling.

"No one is hurt. Your daughter seems pretty shaken up. We don't suspect she's under the influence of anything. The guy in there seems pretty wild right now." The cop adjusted his belt, shoving his gun into better view.

"Wild? What do you mean wild?" asked Leonard.

"He's drunk. We suspect some drug use," said the cop.

Leonard's throat dropped into his stomach, his eyes darting everywhere, trying to make sense of why Jesse was in Millie's apartment, the rent Leonard paid for. "Can I go in?"

"Wait here for a few more minutes. We'll bring her out when everything is settled."

"Okay, but she's safe in there now?" Leonard pointed to the brick building.

"My partner's in there."

It didn't answer Leonard's question, but he decided not to push it and ended the exchange with a slight head nod.

Another cop emerged from the building, leading Millie by her hand. Leonard's breath caught in his throat at the sight of his daughter. Black makeup smeared both cheeks unevenly, and her eyes resembled those of raccoons. The moment Millie locked eyes with Leonard, he opened his papa bear arms wide and embraced his girl. He buried his nose into her poorly colored hair and let his baby girl cry. The tears soaked through his green long-sleeved polo shirt. He gently pushed Millie away, keeping her a safe distance close to his chest. He cradled her chin in his hand to examine her face.

"Did he hurt you? Did Jesse touch you, Millie? Are you doing drugs with him?"

She shook her head as another wave of sobs wracked her body, and, out of pure, fatherly instinct, he pulled her back in, riding out her cries as he peppered her with shushes.

"He just got so mad. I don't even know why." Millie forced out the words through hiccups and stutters. "I think he was drinking with some friends when he got off of work."

"He shouldn't have been in your apartment in the first place. You guys are broken up, and he's stalking you while being drunk and high."

"Dad, please." Millie waved her hand in the air to stop Leonard's rant.

"You can't have someone around you doing drugs. Do you understand me? I'll kill him if I have to." He meant every word as he stared Millie dead into her eyes.

"I invited him over, okay? This is my fault." Millie buried her shamed face into her shaking hands.

"Why did you invite him over, Millie?" Leonard said through gritted teeth.

"It's sort of complicated."

"Is it really?" Leonard took a step back to catch his breath and carefully chose his next words. "Don't lie to me. I will find out the truth. I always do."

Millie sucked in a sharp breath, wiping a final tear away. "We're kind of getting back together."

Leonard threw his arms up and kicked at the black gravel, creating a budding mushroom cloud inches off the ground.

"Please don't get mad." Millie clasped her hands in front of her face, begging.

"You promised me, Millie. You promised me you'd never see him again after how he treated you in the past. Clearly, not much has changed. He'll just grow tired of you again when he thinks there's someone better. And he's on drugs!" Leonard pointed to the red and blue flashing lights and the apartment building, his heart pounding in his eardrums.

"He's going to get better. He already is. Tonight was just a slip-up. Everyone has a bad day."

"Keep telling yourself that, but by that time, it'll be too late. All it takes is one bad day for everything to end, Millie. Why would you put yourself in that position?" Leonard took a step closer. "Also, part of my agreement to get you this apartment was not to see Jesse."

"Sometimes things change." Millie shrugged.

"Don't give me that bullshit." Leonard glared at his daughter. The moonlight caught her face and illuminated every feature clearly for him to view. Everyone always said Millie was her father's spitting image, and tonight, Leonard finally saw it, but under the worst circumstances. "You lied to me. Again."

"I swear, Jesse is so much better. I wouldn't have gotten back with him otherwise." Millie reached for Leonard, who pulled away. The gravel crunched underneath her unbalanced feet as fresh tears flooded her eyes.

"You made Judy sound like a bad person, too. You said you needed this apartment for some distance because the two of you didn't get along. But now that I think of it, she's been nothing but nice to you." Leonard scanned his eyes at the off-kilter Millie. He started to see her for the thing she had sprouted into. "I think you're the problem."

"Dad, I'm really sorry." Her eyes grew raw from her constant bare-handed swipes.

Leonard pursed his lips and offered her a clean napkin. He grabbed a few extra before he left the house, figuring she'd need them.

"Are you mad at me?" Millie said, replacing her hands with the white handkerchief.

Leonard rolled his eyes, so done with this. He released a sullen breath, glancing at the idle cops. "Do you want to come stay with us tonight? I'm worried about leaving you here." He pointed to the apartment door.

"Are you going to yell at me when we get to your house?" A shiver rippled through Millie. The air did carry a brisk undertone this evening.

But Leonard couldn't believe it. A twenty-five-year-old woman, scared to be in trouble with her dad. Why did she make these bad choices if that were the actual case? He'd find a way tomorrow to convince Millie to drop Jesse. He removed his sports blazer and draped it around Millie's prickled arms.

"Come on. Let's go home." He pulled Millie close into his warm cocoon and drove the speed limit the entire way to his house.

Leonard arrived home to find a few lights on and a cold dinner on his placemat. She cried most of the ride home, and he didn't think her face could grow puffier, but science proved otherwise. He led Millie into the kitchen and told her to sit down before planting a kiss on the top of her blonde bleached hair, her brown roots needing a retouching soon.

"Here, put these under your eyes." Leonard handed Millie two frozen pea packs. She obeyed silently. "Do you want anything to drink? Eat? Did you eat dinner yet?" Leonard's sudden need to nurture Millie overwhelmed his body as he fought off inner trembles.

"I'm not hungry," said Millie, eyes glued to the live edge wood custom table.

"How about some ice cream, at least?" Leonard dangled a tub of cookies and cream in the air, tempting Millie. He finally grabbed a smile from her and fist pumped the dessert in the air. "Ha-ha! How about a drink?" A rush of optimism shot through his veins as he reeled his baby girl back into his safe web.

"Do you have any regular Coke?"

"Only Diet Coke in this house."

"I only like regular Coke."

Leonard twisted his face, grimacing. "Ew, really?"

Millie shot him a dose of side-eye.

"How about some fruit punch instead?"

"Sure, sounds good." Millie balanced her chin on her forearm and sprawled onto the table.

He placed three hefty scoops of ice cream into a bowl, topped with whipped cream, and the glass of red fruit punch onto Millie's placemat before watching her devour the food and mouthing a silent "thank you" to Leonard. After taking a sip of the punch, she placed the cold glass onto the smooth wood's finish.

Leonard darted over with a coaster. "Gotta be careful with this table. It's a custom piece."

She flitted her eyebrows, the only acknowledgment of hearing his protest.

"Leonard, darling, is that you?" A face-masked Judy entered the kitchen, fully robed in light pink silk, her hair wrapped in a terry white towel turban. She kissed Leonard on the lips, cutting the embrace short when she spied Millie a few feet away.

"Millie. I had no idea you were there." Judy pulled her robe closed even tighter. She sat perpendicular to Millie's chair, taking the girl's hand in her smooth, lotion-based palm. "Are you okay?"

"Judy, just let her eat."

"It's okay, Dad." She clearly was not okay, as a new round of tears dripped down her face.

"Oh, honey." Judy wrapped her thin, robed arm around Millie's trembling shoulders and rocked her.

Leonard couldn't believe it when Millie leaned into Judy as if she were the mother. It only confirmed the doubts that lay at the bottom of his stomach. Millie had duped him into thinking Judy was the reason she needed the apartment. Millie planned to see Jesse behind his back and on his dollar. Now wasn't the time to grow angry with Millie, but how could he not?

"I'm going to go upstairs," Leonard said, walking out of the kitchen, but no one paid attention.

"You can stay here as long as you like," Judy said into Millie's ear.

Leonard rolled his eyes and went to bed.

# October 2006 – A Night at the Knicks

"Here's to new friends and business ventures," Leonard said, raising his glass of regular soda with the tiniest splash of vanilla vodka to a group of men who drank straight, neat liquor.

Leonard had eyed this property in Brooklyn for months and assigned Greg to do his magic research to find out everything about the property owner. He came through again, so much that Leonard signed on the dotted line today at a seamless closing, one of the best throughout his career as a developer.

He offered a million dollars cash and picked up all the closing costs and fees the sellers incurred. He also sweetened the deal by throwing in two years of season seats for Knicks games. Clever Greg uncovered this minor, which turned into a vital detail about the seller: He was a diehard Knicks fan and couldn't say no to the game. Two months later, Leonard possessed his golden property.

"Leonard, you are one hell of a guy," said James, one of the sellers with a beer belly in full bloom, and he had just started drinking for the night.

"Gentleman, tonight is on me. Do not hold back. And consider this a taste of what life will be like at the Knicks games." Leonard signed for the suite for the evening, and he stipulated these season tickets would entail private suites on reserve. No one understood this property purchased today except for Leonard because it would be worth upwards of twenty million dollars in fifteen to twenty years with the real estate market trend. He saw Brooklyn and what it was becoming and had to be part of it. Now he was, in the best way possible.

"Oh, so, you're going to pay whenever we're here?" James said, shoving drenched guacamole chips down his throat.

"In your fucking dreams, unless you invite me to every game." Leonard winked, but here was the killer: He despised basketball but appreciated its aura for humoring clients.

"I just might. So, clear your schedule." James clapped Leonard on the back, jolting him forward. "C'mon. Drink up." James pointed to Leonard's untouched vodka Coke.

Leonard nodded and timed it where he and James threw their drinks back, James squeezed his eyes shut, recovering from the tequila sting, and Leonard dumped his bitter soda into a potted plant.

A tap on Leonard's shoulder grabbed his attention to the suite's hostess, a tall, waif blonde that Leonard probably would pursue if he didn't find himself currently smitten with Judy and engaged. He was happy, and satisfaction always proved key to his loyalty to anyone.

"Mr. Rosen?"

"Please, call me Leonard." Leonard shook the young woman's cold hand.

"There seems to be a problem with your card." She revealed his shiny Platinum American Express card hidden in her other hand.

"Problem? What kind of problem?" Leonard's pulse skipped a beat.

"It's been locked because of suspicious activity. Do you have another card we can keep the tab running on?" The words rolled off the blonde's tongue so casually.

"Wait. Back it up." Leonard held up a hand. "What kind of suspicious activity? And what do you mean, locked? This has never happened before." Leonard turned quickly to James and company, ensuring no one caught onto this financial fiasco.

"I'm not sure. This is the error the computer gave to us." The blonde shrugged.

"I'm going to call up Amex now. Keep the tab running. You know I'm good for the money."

"I'll have to ask my manager first." The blonde shifted in her step, not handling the challenge well.

"Sweetheart, no one has to know about this. It's just a little blip. I have company I'm entertaining." Leonard signaled to the inebriated bunch just a few feet away. "You think I wanna be embarrassed in front of them?"

The blonde shook her head.

"Give me five minutes." Leonard held up five beefy fingers and skipped out into the hallway.

Six minutes later, Ernie from American Express fraud went through the recent purchase history with Leonard.

"Could you just read them a little faster? Only point out the charges that would trigger fraud." Leonard ground his teeth in all directions from every other word uttered by Ernie. "No... none of these charges sound suspicious. Can't we skip forward?" Leonard listened to a few more mundane charges.

"Oh, wow, Mr. Rosen. This one here is a biggie," said Ernie in crisp excited delight.

"What biggie? What's the fucking charge?" Leonard caught his breath, clutching his chest. "I'm sorry. What is the biggie charge?"

"There seems to be a charge at a Ford dealership located on Long Island, NY for a sum of twenty-four thousand five hundred dollars, swiped today at five in the afternoon."

"What? Someone bought a car using my fucking credit card? How could you guys allow this to happen?" Leonard's vision shifted enough to send him reeling back onto the concrete-painted wall. This was the only card he took with him tonight, and his office was twenty minutes across town, where he kept his extra cards locked away in a small safe under his desk.

"It wasn't your card, sir. It was a card linked to your account. An authorized user's card, it appears."

"Who?" Except Leonard already could guess.

"A Millie Rosen."

Leonard released a hiss of air out of his nostrils unevenly.

"That's my daughter." Leonard's fucking daughter.

"Her card has been locked, too."

"Why would she buy a Ford? She doesn't even like the brand." Leonard confided in Ernie, trying to figure it out with this stranger from across the Midwest.

"I don't know, Mr. Rosen. Perhaps it was an enormous gift?"

"A gift? A Ford?" It all made sense in one massive rush. A sliver of nausea crawled through Leonard's stomach when he figured out who wanted the Ford and who Millie purchased it for. He didn't know who he'd kill first. He'd figure that out later because right then, he needed to find a way to pay for the fucking bill.

Leonard rushed to his office in record time. He planned to call up Millie, screaming missiles, but he figured he'd do it after the game, saving his voice for his guests. He had more properties they owned in mind, and he wanted to talk about them tonight. Figuring he had a few minutes to spare from his office, Leonard speed walked rather than hailed an armpit-smelling cab. At least it was one of the nicest nights in the city, with the air and humidity dancing together in perfect harmony.

His phone buzzed, breaking his moment of peace when he saw Millie called and answered on the first ring.

"Where are you?" said Leonard, his eyes bulging as he listened to her whining. "I'll be right over. Stay there."

Leonard hailed a cab on his first try, instructing the mute driver to a restaurant less than ten minutes away in Manhattan.

Leonard didn't dare enter the Italian restaurant Millie dined in with her friends. It was also too expensive for her to afford on her limited hourly salary, hence her call to Leonard. She probably wanted to use the American Express card linked to his locked account, but it was declined.

Millie emerged wearing a corset top and far too much red lipstick for Leonard's approval. The more he looked at Millie, the more he detested everything about her. She looked cheap with her top polished hair bun and oversized gold hoops. Who did she believe this impressed?

"Hey, Dad. Perfect timing, right?" Millie had no idea she stepped into her own lethal trap.

"I know what you did today, Millie." Leonard glared at his daughter.

"What do you mean?"

"Why did you call me just now?" Leonard planted his hands on his hips.

"The Amex wasn't working, so I thought you needed to know." Millie gulped her sluggish words down.

"Bullshit. You planned on using it to pay for this expensive meal. I'm paying for another expensive dinner. And you don't even invite me. Ever." Leonard didn't know where that last final line came from. He never wanted to be a part of her crew.

"You don't like any of my friends." Millie pointed to the restaurant over her shoulder.

"Tell me why the Amex isn't working?" Leonard's blood thumped through his blue veins, awaiting an answer he didn't want to be true.

Millie rolled her eyes. "Look, if you know why the card isn't working, why don't you just say it?" Millie released a half snort. "I hate when you play detective."

"You bought him a fucking car this afternoon, didn't you?"

Millie stood there, frozen. Her eyes darted everywhere but Leonard's scrunched sweaty face.

Leonard took one step closer to his guilty daughter. "You bought him a fucking Ford pickup? Jesse put you up to this?"

Millie shook her head but didn't mean no.

"Did you buy Jesse a car today? Yes, or no?" Leonard lost control of his voice.

"You're going to embarrass me." Millie shot her father a guilt-ridden yet warning glance.

He never wanted to hit any of his children until now. The thought released a wave of shame, but how much could a person be pushed? The worst part for Leonard was that Millie did not care. What power Jesse exuded over Millie, Leonard never understood. The guy was a total loser, in Leonard's opinion.

The tips of his fingers tingled as he wiggled them. He breathed, expanding his diaphragm to its limit before deflating. His eyes shot to her black patent leather satchel.

"Give me that." Leonard yanked on the purse, almost snapping the strap off Millie's veined neck.

"Dad! What the hell." Millie scowled, twisting her bronzer-stained face as she massaged the irritated skin.

Leonard clawed at the inside of her bag until he found her wallet, grabbed her Amex card on his dime, and shoved it into his pocket, chucking the bag back into her hands. Millie stared at her disappearing credit card, losing a shade of color on her face, if that was even possible, with the amount of makeup caked onto her complexion.

"Seriously, what the hell are you doing?"

"I'm taking the card back, and tomorrow, you and I are going to that fucking Ford dealership and returning the fucking truck you bought Jesse, and then after that, you're not to see that asshole again." Leonard pointed a rigid finger, almost touching the tip of Millie's shiny nose.

"Fine, we'll return the car, but you can't tell me who I can and can't see." Millie's eyes trailed over Leonard in disgust.

"Oh, I can't? Then, if you want to be so independent, you're off my payroll."

Millie sucked in a sharp breath. "Let's talk about this."

Leonard laughed a mad man's chuckle. "That's what I thought. I'll see you tomorrow."

He started to walk away, grinding what was left of his teeth and refused to turn back to Millie. He'd never spoken this harshly to her before.

"How will I pay for my dinner? That was my only card." Millie's voice echoed off the buildings.

"Call Jesse. Maybe he'll finally buy you a meal for once."

# September 2005 – First Impressions

"Greg, I finally feel like I'm getting closer to the seller," said Leonard to a dubious eyebrow raised Greg.

"What is it about this property, Leo?" said Greg, flicking a piece of lint off his shiny sharkskin three-piece suit. "Also, this guy isn't selling." Greg peered around at Leonard's modern office. Ceiling-to-wall windows lined the room's perimeter. "Nice office, by the way. Did you decorate?"

Leonard nodded, huffing on his fingernails and wiping them on his lapel. "You know how I get." He looked around, admiring his work. "I have a certain vision and go for it."

"You're telling me. By the way, are you married yet?"

"Engaged. It'll probably be a fast wedding. Why wait? It's not like it's our first marriage." Leonard cast his eyes away from Greg.

"Who's the lucky gal?" Greg popped his eyebrows up and down.

"Judy. She'll be number five?" Leonard stared at the ceiling, squinting his eyes.

Greg waved a hand in the air. "I lost count after number three with you. Will there be a prenup?"

Leonard smiled. "There's always room for a prenup."

"Remember. If you plan on building anything with the lady and take out a loan under your names, I'd recommend a postnup."

Leonard rubbed his chin, considering the piece of information. "Let me marry her first before I start thinking about divorce."

"Wow, Leo. I never saw this side of you before. You're so romantic suddenly. I think I might have a heart attack right here in this fucking expensive chair." Greg clutched his chest, producing a gurgling choke.

"Anyway, back to this property." Leonard fanned the air, reeling Greg back into the zone. "I already know what I'd offer these guys. A million in cash and go from there."

"What's the from there part?" Greg leaned in with his shark fin on high alert.

"That's where you come in. Look these guys up and find things to entice them other than money."

"Like what?" Greg half laughed.

Leonard sat behind his leucite desk, pulling out a checkbook and scribbling a check, sliding it across the spotless surface to Greg's side.

"That's for you to find out." Leonard winked.

Greg folded the check without looking at it, stuffing it into his snug front pocket. "If only I counted how many retainer checks you slid my way, I'd be a very rich man."

"I have made you a rich man."

"I said *very* rich." Greg held a finger up at the correction.

The intercom buzzed, cutting the room's ambiance in half.

"Yes?" said Leonard into the machine.

"Millie is here. She said you were expecting her?" said the secretary's robotic voice.

Leonard scrunched his brow, wondering if he simply forgot. "Sure. Send her right in." He shook his head, almost positive this was a surprise visit.

"I should go," said Greg, pointing to the door.

Millie and a fellow similar in age to his daughter, standing six feet tall who easily won the height contest, entered the room. The mysterious man wore black trousers, needing a visit to the dry cleaners, a crisp white shirt, and a blue tie in a half Windsor knot.

Leonard cocked his head, trying to get a better read off the guy, but the detail that struck him most was the folded Wall Street Journal paper underneath his sweaty armpit.

"Dad," said Millie, shooting a side eye at Greg. "Hey, Greg. What are you doing here?"

"Greg and I were about to grab a power lunch…"

Greg cocked a surprised eyebrow before nodding to the impromptu plan.

"Hi, Millie. How ya doing, sweetheart? Good to see you," said Greg.

"Wait, come here." Leonard walked over to Millie and engulfed her in a bear hug. He never tore his eyes off the new guy, studying him like a petri dish specimen. "Would you like to introduce us to your friend?"

"Dad, this is Jesse."

Jesse stepped forward, jutting out an oversized pasty hand. "Very nice to meet you, Mr. Rosen."

Leonard took Jesse's hand as a courtesy to his daughter. Immediately, Leonard smelled something off with the guy. This man hadn't bought the ensemble. And who wore a tie without an accompanying suit jacket?

"We were in the neighborhood, and I wanted to introduce you guys." Millie motioned back and forth between her father and Jesse.

"From what Millie has told me about you, it sounds like you and me have a lot in common," said Jesse.

Leonard winced at the poor grammar.

"Oh, yeah? Like what?" asked Leonard.

Jesse did a double take at the question and cleared his throat a notch too loud for indoor quarters. "Well, we both think Millie is a great girl and really smart too. She must get it from you."

Leonard shrugged. "Guess so." He looked in Greg's direction, whose eyes remained plastered to his Italian leather shoes. "Would you guys like to join us for lunch?"

"That's okay." Millie placed a hand on Jesse's bony chest. "We already have a date planned for an early dinner." She glanced up at Jesse's dull eyes for an absent approval.

"In that case, consider it on me." Leonard whipped out his wallet, removing two hundred in twenties from his Gucci wallet, and handing the money to Jesse.

"Thanks, Mr. Rosen." As Jesse took the cash, his eyes darted in Greg's direction, watching the lawyer readjust the time on his Rolex watch.

"Oh, my apologies," said Leonard, pointing to Greg. "Jesse, meet Greg. My divorce attorney."

Jesse didn't move.

"This guy is a shark." Leonard came around and put a solid hand on Greg's shoulder. "He can sniff bullshit like it was the first thing the doctor put under his nose when he was born."

Jesse stared at Greg and then at Leonard, taking a hard gulp, right before he and Millie exited Leonard's office.

"What do you think of Jesse?" asked Leonard.

The two men ascended a skyscraper heading to one of the city's ritziest restaurants, known for their raw bar.

"He's a little weasel and full of bullshit."

"The Wall Street Journal planted under his arm gave it away, huh?"

"And who wears a tie with no suit jacket? Is the guy a waiter or something?" Greg rolled his eyes. "He was trying to impress you. Were you impressed?"

"I'm impressed he landed a girl like Millie." Leonard frowned. His daughter deserved better, so why did she feel the need to settle?

"He's handsome," said Greg.

"Looks fade. Trust me, I know."

"That you do, Leo."

"If this Jesse guy screws Millie over, I'll kill him. Maybe I can tell her to stop seeing him now?"

Greg threw his head back, releasing a bellowing laugh. "Yeah, right. You know how it goes: You tell them not to do something, and it only motivates them to do it more, especially with daughters."

"You only have sons."

"Thank god for that, no offense."

Leonard clicked his jaw, fighting off the comment.

"The only thing I tell my sons not to do is get any girl pregnant who they don't want to marry."

"And I'm assuming this pep talk worked?"

"So far," said Greg, pursing his lips. "Once an unwanted pregnancy happens, then everything goes to shit."

"I don't even want to think about it." Leonard stepped off the escalator, not waiting for Greg.

"You got that right, Leo. You're stuck with the other side for life when pregnancy happens. You'll always be connected."

Leonard just peered at Greg, not wanting to dive deeper into this conversation, and instead, he led his attorney into their power lunch.

# *November 25th, 2021*

"Do you ever think about your daughter's last day?" asked Leonard. He walked, arms linked with Jill, down a sparse path in Central Park. He didn't know how they even ended up in the city. They got into his car after the diner and decided to drive, not knowing the plan. Leonard hadn't done something like that since he was a teenager.

Jill tightened her grip around Leonard's arm, snuggling closer to his soft wool coat.

"I just hope she didn't feel alone that day."

Leonard stared into her emerald green eyes, waiting for more.

"At least we had a nice conversation the night before." Jill released a breathy laugh. "This might sound silly, but I never expected the next day to happen... even though I knew it was possible at any moment."

"I used to tell my son that I would just sit around and wait for the call saying she's dead." A cold breeze whipped his face.

"It's a terrible way to live for a parent." Jill pulled Leonard's arm closer. "You sound like you think about that day often."

"Sometimes I do. And when I do, it consumes me. Who knows how I'll feel if I lose Jackie to Thailand." Leonard kicked a stray pebble back onto the winter's coming grass. "But I can tell you one thing. I didn't expect today to happen." Leonard paused in his step, facing Jill, where their cold breath clashed between their faces.

"I didn't either. Usually, I have a hard time with family holidays, but today it's been the easiest one." Jill couldn't conceal her smile as it spread across her perfect oval face.

A loose strand of black curly hair fell against her forehead. Leonard followed the hair's path, and when it settled, he pushed it behind her head, leaning in and meeting his lips to her warm, waiting mouth.

First, their top lips pressed together, only for their bottom lips to melt into one another. He wrapped his loose arm around her waist, pulling her against his broad chest while her cold hand cradled his cheek. A sharp wind broke the embrace. Jill opened her eyes first, and when Leonard regained focus, those eyes he dreamed of stared right back, burning into him.

"I think if you keep focused, Leonard, you'll see anything can happen." She caressed his cheek like petting the softest material in the world.

"Focus, eh?" Leonard kissed the hollow of her cream neck, landing another on her forehead.

Another bitter wind shot through the park, causing Jill to recoil.

"It's getting cold out here," said Leonard.

"It's just the wind making it feel worse than it really is." Jill buried her hands into her coat pockets.

"We should go somewhere."

"Oh, yeah? Like where?"

"Somewhere inside. That's warm." Leonard leaned forward, pressing his head against Jill's forehead. "There are a bunch of hotels around here with restaurants, bars…."

"You don't drink."

"You remembered," said Leonard, planting a hand over his heart. "So, what do you say? How about we check out one of those hotels? No pressure."

Jill planted a quick peck onto Leonard's lips, running her fingertips along his square jaw. "Sounds good."

"I know."

# May 2003 – Gap Year

"It'll just be one year, and then I'll reassess," said Millie.

Leonard and Susan were the audiences for the impromptu speech, and to think, just five minutes ago, they were deciding where to eat dinner when Millie barged in unannounced. She was supposed to be in Connecticut finishing her sophomore spring semester when that plan clearly changed for Millie, with no one else knowing yet.

Despite Millie's surprise visit, the only person in the room who didn't love the idea of her presence right now was Susan.

"What will you reassess? You need to be more specific, Millie," said Leonard. He noted Susan's paled complexion, hoping she wasn't coming down with anything.

"I'm going to figure that out while I'm home."

"Home?" asked Susan, tugging on her pearl necklace.

Millie's eyes shot to Leonard. "Yeah, home. I thought it was implied that I'd be staying here."

"Won't the change of pace from a wild college life to a boring one here be too much of a change? I'd go crazy in your shoes," said Susan, swallowing hard.

"Susan, let's not," said Leonard, holding a silencing hand. "Of course, you can stay here while you figure things out, Millie. But I'd like to know the plan. You can't just sit home and do nothing."

"Or party here and sleep off your hangover at home," said Susan.

Leonard glared at her, saying he was the actual parent, not Susan. Something was up with her lately, and if things didn't change, he didn't see this marriage lasting much past the one-year mark, and it killed him because everyone warned him about Susan and her shallow ways. Of course, Leonard's built-in blinders were on high alert, and he didn't see that part of Susan, the part everyone advised him about.

Millie's eyes darkened, searching for a rebuttal to Susan's accusation. "Dad..." Her voice quivered.

"It's okay, Millie." Leonard got up from his seat and hugged Millie. She released a quick sob the moment his arms touched her shoulders.

Susan just stared at the scene.

"I'm sorry," said Millie. She cried into Leonard's chest, leaving quarter-sized tear stains behind.

"We're going to figure this out. Go upstairs and wash your face." Leonard kissed the top of Millie's hair, patting her back. "Think about what you want for dinner. We can all go out."

Susan's eyes widened at the suggestion. Leonard shook his head in her direction, throwing off a silent warning.

"I think I'll just stay home," said Millie.

Leonard offered a light grin, handing Millie a tissue from a bejeweled tissue box. Susan must have picked that out during her quest to redecorate and leave her mark in Leonard's home.

"Well, if you want us to bring you home anything, text your father," said Susan.

Only once the sound of Millie's shower commenced did Leonard find his breath, plopping down next to Susan, who immediately bounced up.

"I didn't expect that," said Leonard.

"Do you want a drink?" asked Susan, already pouring herself a cold glass of white wine.

"Sure. You know what I like."

"I'm not sure I do anymore, Leonard." Susan poured a glass of diet chocolate soda with too much ice.

"What's that supposed to mean?" Leonard sipped the watered-downed beverage but decided to swallow his complaint.

"I don't know. Steven is fine. He's not a bother."

"A bother?" Leonard twisted his face.

"He's quiet. Doesn't get in the way." Susan chased her words down with a hefty gulp of wine.

Leonard glared at her, trying to make sense of this rant.

"Millie is trouble. And now she's going to be home with us for a year?" Susan clutched her breastbone. "The whole idea makes me want to leave."

"We'll get to what you just said in a second. But fuck, Susan. Do you hate my kids or something?"

"Ugh. I hate when you swear."

Leonard stormed over to Susan, startling her to where she almost dropped her crystal cup.

"This is my goddamn house. I'll have whoever I want living here. You understand? And you clearly have a problem with my kids."

Leonard took an unsteady step backward, trying to catch his waning breath, begging himself not to allow the panic to win.

"It's not what I expected, Leonard. That's all. I'm surprised."

"Look, I didn't expect it either. But it's Millie. This is how she operates. She decides on something and then springs it on me." He shrugged, staring at the stone floor. "I'm not going to force her to go back to school. If I do that, she'll just drive to school, sit in the parking lot, and wait until class is over to come back home. It's a waste of her time and my money."

Susan's eyes bulged. "You mean you would send her back to a local school?"

Leonard threw his arms up, turning his back to Susan. He chucked his bland soda into the sink, almost breaking the cup.

"Millie is trouble, Leonard. I see it all the time. She'll ruin us if she's around."

"I can't believe you treat people for a living with how you're talking right now. Where is all of this coming from?" Leonard flailed his arms to the ceiling.

"This wasn't our plan," said Susan, stone-faced.

"I have kids. I'm not sure what your plan entailed." Leonard tapped his forehead.

"You had one child in college and another about to go away to school. That was the plan."

Leonard rolled his eyes at the creature Susan, his wife. This conversation had lasted too long. Suddenly, his stomach growled as a bitter reminder of their original evening plan.

"Do you even want to go to dinner still?" asked Leonard.

Susan crossed her arms over her flat chest. "I've lost my appetite."

She wasn't alone in this sentiment, Leonard thought. He pushed off the counter with shaky hands and began to walk towards the kitchen's exit.

"I'll be back in a little."

"Where are you going?" asked Susan.

"I'm going out to pick up food for Millie."

A crash was followed by shards of glass littering the kitchen floor by the breakfast nook. Leonard lurched forward and stared at the ruined wine glass. He gaped at Susan. His blood boiled. He wanted her out of his house.

"Have you lost your fucking mind?" Leonard squinted at Susan, grabbing onto the counter for balance.

"What about me, Leonard? How about you ask if I want some food."

"You just said you lost your appetite."

"I am last in your mind. It's evident." Susan stepped forward, crunching a piece of glass below her black stiletto heel. "Side with your wife, for once."

Leonard was about to say something, but he would only add fire to the rage simmering between them. She wasn't worth it. To think they hadn't made it a year before facing their first major challenge as a married couple. But to Leonard, Millie's gap year declaration wasn't a hardship. It was just something to figure out and adapt to. What was Susan's fucking problem?

"It's me or her, Leonard."

His pulse skipped a beat, but not from heartbreak. More from the shock of this woman who morphed into a grotesque stranger in his kitchen, looming over the marble island.

"Clean up the glass, Susan."

"Answer me."

"I said clean up the fucking glass." The vein in his forehead throbbed a well-defined zig-zag shape, something he became known for when his blood was about to burst every capillary in his body.

"It's me or Millie. We can't both be in this house and be happy."

Leonard snorted. Suddenly, out of the corner of his eye, there she stood, just beyond the kitchen's entrance. Millie's hair dripped onto the floor as she wrapped herself in one of Susan's expensive French blue silk bathrobes. He wasn't sure how long Millie was there or what she heard from the exchange, but she stared at Leonard with the same eyes from when she was six, looking at her dad for every answer in the book.

"Leonard. This isn't a hard question. Now answer me. It's me, or Millie," said Susan through lipstick-stained teeth.

Leonard half laughed. "Her."

# November 25th, 2021

Leonard stood naked in a pitch-black bathroom with his cell phone to his ear. He dialed Greg's number, hoping his attorney would answer. He left Jill asleep in bed.

She wouldn't be waking up anytime soon after the fuck session they'd just had. Even just shy of sixty-five, Leonard fooled the youngest of them, and he'd had them young, the biggest age gap being twenty-five years, but just for pure fun. In a relationship, he wanted a woman close enough to his age, so they could reminisce about similar events encountered instead of educating someone about history.

"Pick up, pick up, pick up."

On the third ring, Greg answered the phone.

"Leonard."

"Aw, no, Leo?"

"Why are you talking so low? Are you in trouble?" Greg actually sounded concerned.

"Did you find anything?" Leonard bit his thumbnail, waiting for his scolding.

"Leonard. It's a holiday. I promised my wife no work today, okay? I'm about to carve a whole fucking turkey that I have no idea how to cut. That is the only thing I'm focusing on this afternoon."

"Why do you keep calling me Leonard?" For once, he missed being called Leo because he knew he had Greg on his side when referred to by the pet name.

"Why are you talking so low? I can barely hear you. Where are you?"

"The truth?" Leonard half laughed. "I locked myself in the bathroom of a hotel room at The Waldorf Astoria."

"Aw, that's cute. Staycation?"

"Until tomorrow morning. I met a woman today at the cemetery. She's perfect."

"Of course, you did, and you think she's perfect. That's how it always starts."

"Her name is Jill."

Leonard strained to hear if she awoke but was met with dead silence.

"What do you mean this is how it always starts?"

"Forget I said anything. I need to go."

"No, wait. Tell me. I want to hear it." Leonard leaned against the wall, listening to his quickened heartbeat, and for whatever reason, his nerves increased, standing on high alert.

"It's nothing bad. It's just who you are." Greg cleared his throat, the confidence draining from his words.

Leonard couldn't recall hearing Greg so uneasy, as if he was a rookie in law or making things work that appeared impossible.

"Tell me who I am, Greg. You've intrigued me."

"Leonard, c'mon. It's Thanksgiving—"

"I fucking know what day it is. Now tell me who the fuck I am." Spit ejected from Leonard's mouth.

The air hissed out of Greg's nose into the phone's receiver. "You talk a big game. Say you're going to focus on your family, like your grandson, and getting custody of him. And then you meet the perfect woman. You build her up, and everyone else gets pushed to the side. I don't know anything about Jill, but she is the fastest woman to hypnotize you. It's just who you are and what you do. There's nothing wrong with it. But don't you see? Being with Jill now—is the fight to get Jackie to live with you, have him become number one in your life suddenly worth it?"

Silence fell between the men. Leonard didn't think the pitch-blackness of the bathroom could get any darker, but it did. His breath hiccupped up his throat, catching on his tongue. He understood Greg's way with words could sting the other side, but he was supposed to be on Leonard's. Wasn't that always the unspoken plan?

"Leo? Are you there?"

"Oh, now you're back to calling me Leo after you ripped me a new asshole."

"You wanted to hear the truth."

"So, you think I'm an asshole, huh?" Leonard ran frigid water and splashed his face in the dark.

"You're not an asshole to me. I think you're just a guy who wants to please everyone in the messiest of situations."

Leonard swallowed, suddenly realizing his face didn't need the water, but his sandpaper tongue did. In a biblical sense, he quickly threw his mouth under the running faucet and guzzled at least a gallon of water down his throat. It didn't help much.

"If you find anything, please call me."

"I'll try my best. You know I always do with you."

Leonard was a centimeter away from hanging up when a sharp breath before Greg interrupted.

"Hey, Leo? You didn't use my name for the room today, right? I just realized my wife might be hosting a titty brunch there in a few weeks for the holidays."

Leonard smiled so brightly that his white teeth lit up this bathroom. "I have no idea what you're talking about, Mr. Cohen." He ended the call when he heard Jill stir.

"Leonard?" said Jill from the bed, her voice muffled. "Leonard, where are you?" Her tone, thick with sleep and some hoarseness, meant she needed him.

Leonard pulled the white sheets away to reveal her lean, soft body. He crawled between her legs, positioning himself for something.

"Wait, not yet." Jill pushed Leonard's hair back to reveal his whole face. "Who were you on the phone with?"

"No one." Leonard kissed her lips, lingering to taste her a moment longer.

She tapped the tip of his nose. "You lie."

"My attorney." He kissed her chin, traveling to her neck and down to her chiseled collarbone. "Don't ask."

"I wasn't going to, but I can only imagine." And then Jill climbed on top of Leonard, her body ready for more.

# *July 2000 – Bermuda*

"She's only seventeen, Janet. What do you mean, don't worry?" Leonard paced the room on hold with hotel security. They hadn't even been in Bermuda for forty-eight hours, and already Leonard swore he'd never retake another family trip.

"She's not dead if that's what you're thinking," said Steven, playing on the latest Gameboy model.

"No one is dead. Let's not use that word," said Janet, rubbing Leonard's lower back.

"I'm sorry about this. I'm so embarrassed," said Leonard to Janet. He wrapped his free arm around her shoulder, pulling her close.

Steven rolled his eyes underneath the lowered baseball cap, not shielding them enough for Leonard to not notice the disgust.

"Don't you roll your eyes." Leonard snapped his fingers at Steve, to no avail.

"How about all of us go back to my house and resume the calls?" said Janet.

Leonard didn't know what he should do. He couldn't even form words to answer anyone. All he could do right then was stay on hold for the moron security guard to tell him Millie was still lost. If they never found Millie, Leonard would die. He should have listened to Janet from the start and stayed at her house in Bermuda.

"And here everyone thought I was going to be the bad kid," said Steven, eyes still glued to his video game.

Leonard stormed across the room, ripping the Gameboy out of Steven's hands and flinging it in the air. It hit a glass of water, shattering into a million clear pieces on the tile floor.

Steven jumped out of his seat, half a second from lunging after Leonard when Janet threw herself between the Rosen men. Everyone in the room emitted a fire to explode the entire hotel to the ground.

"Fuck you!" roared Steven, his hat slipping off his head.

"Stop it, just stop!" said Janet, placing a hand against Steven.

"Stop acting like your sister is dead," said Leonard, huffing. "How about I send you home? Would that make you happy?"

"Fucking vacation, my ass." Steven walked towards his bedroom door in the spacious hotel suite. "The only reason you took us anywhere is that you couldn't find anyone to watch us, so you could visit your girlfriend." Steven slammed his door, shaking the walls of the room.

Leonard dropped the phone back onto its cradle, going after Steven when a steady hand pulled him to a stop.

"Let him go. No one has slept all night. This is probably how he's dealing with worrying about his sister," said Janet.

"Sometimes, I forget how good of a therapist you are."

"I guess that's why I get to charge what I ask for." Janet shrugged, cracking an exhausted smile.

She didn't deserve this, and what was worse, Janet was too level-headed to want to deal with all of Leonard's shit and baggage he brought to Bermuda in the mere two days of being here. He probably wouldn't see her after this trip. It was the only fair thing he could reciprocate to Janet. To let her go.

"Do you want to call back security?" asked Janet.

Leonard threw on a royal blue windbreaker. "Nah. I'm going to walk around the area and find Millie."

Janet didn't show any signs of challenging his decision. "I'll stay here with Steven."

Leonard traversed the partially lit streets of God knows where in Bermuda. He had no idea where he walked. Every few steps, he'd call out Millie's name and met with the terrible silence he always expected. Was this how it ended? To lose a child? He didn't want to cry, no. He wanted to collapse. He never knew this level of exhaustion until now. Even when both his kids were newborns and the few nights he stayed up with that ex bitch of their mother, he never experienced the full-blown body fatigue aching through his bones tonight. His grandfather always echoed the motto of it only getting harder when the kids grew older, and that night Leonard believed his grandfather's words to their fullest.

He stopped in front of a jewelry store. Most of the precious stones must have been removed from the window display for the night when they closed. Funny, he thought. The next day, meaning the current day, Leonard had planned to take Janet into town to buy her a bracelet, or a watch, just a little something special to show his appreciation for her. Not anymore. They were done. Their fun ended too quickly before being inundated with Leonard's complicated reality. And now, his daughter was missing on a tiny island that swallowed the notion of Millie returning.

A buzzing emerged. At first, Leonard thought a group of bees whizzed by his ear. It was hard to tell where the noise originated since being in this foreign town at night had him disoriented, to begin with. The buzzing grew louder, quickly transforming into a growl. He recognized the growl from a closing distance.

It was an engine coming towards him. And then he saw the lights. Leonard bolted against the building, pasting his body to the stucco siding. The car flashed by him with a group of people, and in the mere seconds of its passing, he pinpointed a whiny voice.

"That's my dad!" The voice shot from the car straight through Leonard's eardrums, igniting the air back into his lungs. Millie's voice. And then it all hit him. Millie was alive in a car, heading back to their hotel with strangers, leaving Leonard running after them in the night streets of Bermuda.

Leonard burst through the revolving glass doors of the resort, panting. He had never run so fast in his life. His vision shifted to where he almost lost footing on the shiny tile floor. A fake green potted plant broke his stumble.

Laughs heard in the distance pulled Leonard's attention to the sharp left, and there stood Millie, carefree, very much alive, giggling with a group of three boys and an equally trashy girl. The dry screech against the hotel's floor grabbed Millie's attention away from the group of misfits.

"Dad?" Millie eyed Leonard from head to toe.

"What the hell are you doing? Where were you?" Leonard sniffed his daughter, catching a whiff of something putrid. "Are you still smoking? And what is that, gin? You've kept us all up tonight."

"Calm down." Millie shot her eyes back over to the group of youths. "I was just having some fun tonight."

"We thought you were dead."

"You always jump to the worst conclusions," said Millie, rolling her eyes. "I'm alive, see?" Millie twirled, showing way too much skin between her barely visible shorts and a t-shirt revealing her midriff.

"Let's go. Now." Leonard ground his teeth, forcing himself not to pull Millie through the hotel lobby.

Millie just crossed her arms, not moving an inch.

"Millie, don't test me. Come with me. Now." Leonard jerked his hand towards his body.

"Is Janet there?"

"Yes, Janet is in the room with Steven. Is that a problem?" Leonard swallowed his own words. Of course, it was a problem. He learned it quickly tonight.

"Ugh, this is embarrassing. I'm going to crash on a couch down here."

"Like hell you are. Come with me or else."

"I thought Janet had a house here. Why is she staying in our room?" Millie crossed her arms tighter over her chest.

"She was worried about where you were tonight. We all were."

"Janet doesn't even know me. How could she worry about me?"

She had a point. But this was the trip's goal, for everyone to get to know each other and Janet. The air deflated from Leonard's body, understanding what he needed to do.

"Come, Millie." He extended his hand for his daughter to accept. "I promise we'll go back to our room, and I'll walk you straight to your bed. No one will speak to anyone about tonight."

Millie stared at Leonard's steady, outstretched hand. He didn't know if she would accept his genuine offer.

Millie inhaled a sharp breath before lifting her eyes to meet Leonard's. "I hate Bermuda."

"We'll talk about it in the morning."

"I want to go home." Millie took two steps towards Leonard and took his bare hand.

Leonard looked from his hand to Millie's tear-streaked face. "Me too."

# November 25ᵗʰ, 2021

"She put me through a lot." Leonard gazed at a bowl of the reddest strawberries his eyes had ever seen. He sliced small pieces with a knife, feeding them to Jill and himself, switching off every other bite. "Sometimes, I wonder how I didn't completely lose it on her."

Jill's eyes remained half closed but entirely attentive to Leonard's voice. She opened her lids wide enough for him to revel in her hypnotic eyes. He kissed only her bottom lip, catching a taste of sweet berries off her swollen flesh.

"You practiced great restraint from how it sounded. I don't know if I could've let Melissa get away with what you did with Millie."

Leonard creased his brow, cocking his head like a curious puppy. "Like what, specifically?"

"All the lies. The broken promises. Buying the boyfriend a car on your credit card."

Leonard dropped his chin a notch. "You're telling me Melissa didn't lie to you? They were addicts, Jill."

Jill ran the tips of her unmanicured fingernails up Leonard's skin, producing a trail of goosebumps. "Of course, of course. I'm just saying Millie lived a larger life. And with that came larger lies."

"Isn't it all relative at the end of the day?" Leonard never noticed her unpolished nails until now. Why did he think they were red?

"I guess that's one way of looking at it. I mean... Melissa lived her final years in my basement. Maybe I don't know what I'm talking about, even." Jill cast her eyes away, rejecting Leonard's offer of a sliced strawberry.

"Hey..." Leonard turned Jill's chin gingerly towards his face with his hand. "Are you still with me? Did I say something wrong?"

Jill encircled his wrist with her hand. "No. Of course not. You've been nothing but wonderful today." She blinked the tears away.

Leonard believed she had become an expert at stopping the imminent waterworks before they commenced.

"Do you want to leave?"

"Leave? No. No, I don't want to leave." Jill reclined backward onto the marshmallow pillows until the covers fell away, revealing a soft nude breast. "Do you want to go?"

"Eventually."

Jill raised a weary eyebrow in half protest.

"We only have the room until eleven tomorrow morning."

Leonard winked, climbing towards Jill, eyeing her with thirst. She welcomed Leonard's advances, wrapping her arms and legs around his body as he buried his nose into her neck, taking in her sugary scent.

Jill giggled. "You are something else, Rosen."

"Rosen? No one has called me by my last name since... God, I don't even know." He explored her mouth with a touch of his tongue and pulled back. "I like it, though."

"Good." Jill engulfed Leonard's mouth with hers, not letting him breathe the hotel's air until her lips broke away for selfish reasons. She needed to breathe too.

Leonard gazed at her hand, cupping his cheek, catching a glimpse of her untailored nails. Some tips were uneven and maybe one bit down to their stub. "Hey. This might sound weird, but I could have sworn..."

"What is it, Rosen?"

"Weren't your nails red earlier today?"

"My nails? Oh, Rosen. I hate getting my nails done. I never do."

Leonard blinked down the facts before fucking her for the third time that day while noting the first crack in the facade, his perfect woman showing an imperfection.

# December 1999 – Aruba

"There you go, buddy. Just sleep it off," said Leonard, rolling a very inebriated Steven onto the king-sized bed. A whiff of hard alcohol hit Leonard's nostrils, stinging them to the moon. "How much did you drink tonight?"

"Prolly as much as I threw up," said Steven, slurring his words into the pillow.

"Ew, gross." Leonard shook off the stench if that was even possible. "First thing in the morning, you shower. If you even remember this conversation."

"Hold on. Hold on. I need to tell you something." Steven reached for his father with zero focus or precision. "This is the best trip ever."

Leonard laughed. "Of course, it is. You're drunk, and I'm not threatening to take everything you know away." Leonard laughed while rustling Steven's hair, watching his son pass out for the final time that night. Once Steven's snores filled the room, Leonard dragged his feet out into the hall.

"Dad, out here," said Millie from the balcony.

Leonard planned to join Millie, but first, he wanted to make a phone call.

"Dad? I see you."

Leonard fished his phone out of his pocket. "I just need to make a call."

"To who? It's late." Millie stretched on the lounge chair, clothed in tie-dye pajamas, letting the thick ocean breeze wash over her tanned face.

Leonard pointed to his phone screen and was about to say who but stopped, unsure why. But he sensed a moment over the two of them, more potent than the Aruba ocean's gusts falling off the crashing waves. It was a moment he decided not to interrupt.

"Do you have a new girlfriend already?" Millie raised an eyebrow to Leonard, who paused over his lounge chair. "Oh, my God. Do you?" Millie's voice took a sudden shift into panic mode.

"What? No. God, no. I just got divorced. I'm taking a break now." Leonard swallowed. She wasn't a girlfriend he wanted to call, just a friend, a close, intimate friend who he allowed to refer to him as her boyfriend.

"I'll believe it when I see it."

"Why are we even thinking about that? We're here on vacation. Just the three of us."

Millie burst into laughter, shaking her head and rolling her eyes. She reached for a tropical punch with an orange sliver on the glass and sipped a hefty serving of the beverage.

"Is that alcohol?"

"Yes. You wanna try it? It's sweet."

Leonard considered it, but the thing was, he just detested the taste of anything bitter, sour, or however, alcohol that clashed with his tastebuds.

"C'mon. It tastes like fruit, but better." Millie outstretched her arm, teasing Leonard.

"I'll pass." Leonard held up a hand, curling his lip. He already smelled the liquor.

"Okie, dokie." Millie shrugged and finished the drink to its final drop.

"Woah, take it easy. Do you want to join your brother in the bedroom? It reeks in there." An unsettling queasiness settled in the bottom of Leonard's stomach, and it wasn't about the odor, either. The possibility of Millie being found vulnerable in Steven's position rattled Leonard to his core. Millie would always be his little girl.

"It's mostly juice. Plus, I'm not drunk."

"Do you drink?"

Millie waved the question away.

"I'm serious, Millie. Do you drink?"

Leonard breathed, trying to capture the beach air to coat his burning lungs and push away the panic filling his chest just as quickly as it appeared.

"I don't drink, Dad. Maybe just a little here and there."

"Because you shouldn't drink, you and Steven. You're both underage."

"You have nothing to worry about."

Leonard shook his head, grinning. "One day, you'll see. There's always something to worry about when you're a parent."

"That doesn't scare me. I'd love to have a child one day." Millie gazed at the white stars, entirely at peace.

"You have plenty of time to have kids. Enjoy your life now."

"How old was Mom when she had me?"

Leonard sucked in a sharp breath as the subject of the mother, Claire, was seldom broached, mainly because Leonard detested and threw the Rosen death stare into the blank space ahead whenever she was mentioned. Why did Millie have to pierce a serene moment like this to mention Claire? Leonard couldn't hide his disappointment, his glare emerging across his face so naturally that he didn't even realize it was happening.

"Forget I asked."

"I was twenty-seven when you were born."

Millie did the math in her head, looking at the white sparking stars for the answers. "Okay, I have time."

Leonard pointed his steady finger at Millie's face. "Yes, you do."

She laughed a laugh Leonard would never tire of hearing. "This is nice. I like single Dad."

"Is that my new name?"

"When you're single, yes." She offered her hand to Leonard. He took it without hesitation. "This is nice."

"I know. Aruba during this time is great."

"I mean, just us hanging out." Millie squeezed Leonard's hand, studying it.

Leonard couldn't pinpoint when it was just him and Millie together, having real father-daughter bonding. He just hoped his latest ex-wife, Becky, moved all of her crap out of his house during this vacation. That was really the point of this impromptu Aruba trip, to return home and have it be his home again.

"I know why you booked this trip, Dad. You didn't fool anyone."

Leonard snapped his head up, peering at a heavy-lidded Millie. He sat back onto his lounger, reclining for the first time this evening.

"I have no idea what you're talking about." He unscrewed a cold bottle of water, letting the brisk liquid wash down his throat, and then remembered how much he despised the bland taste of it. Even the color didn't entice any fiber of his body. "Don't look at this trip like that. We're together, right? Isn't that something?"

"I'm just saying you don't fool me."

"I never said I was trying to."

"You really thought Becky would adapt to suburban life, didn't you?"

Leonard shrugged. "Well, she moved there, didn't she? She should have been more upfront if she didn't want to."

"Didn't she try to convince you to move into the city?"

"Yes, and I explained to her it wasn't an option. You guys are still in school, and I hate the idea of not being able to leave the city, ever."

"You have a way of convincing women to relocate for you."

"Yeah, but it seems like things don't go as planned once they move in. Look at my history." Leonard stopped himself from pouring out anything from within to Millie and was in a bit of shock he even admitted to his relationship failings with her.

"Maybe don't have them move in every time?" said Millie.

"What kind of marriage would that be to live separately?"

"Why do you always have to get married?"

Leonard was about to say something, maybe even something that would spoil this moment between him and Millie, when his phone buzzed in his pocket, saving both from God-knows-what type of verbal exchange. He took out the device to reveal Shelly calling, the friend he planned to call before this conversation took the lead. Leonard frowned at the phone and then at a closed-eyed Millie, thinking what the right thing to do now would be. What was the proper choice? When Millie's voice cut through his dilemma, he was about to return the phone.

"Take the call, Dad."

"Nah, I'll call her back." Leonard winced the moment he let the word slip.

Millie smiled, showing her hunch was correct the entire time. "I won't be upset, just answer.

"You promise? This isn't a trick or anything."

"I promise," said Millie.

# *November 1998 – A Wedding to Remember*

"What do you mean she's here?" said Leonard to his brother. He searched wildly over his brother's broad shoulders for the trespasser, his first ex-wife, the mother to his only two children. "Who let her in?"

"It doesn't matter. No one knew who she was. But she's out in the lobby now and refuses to leave until you come talk to her," said Robert. He placed two solid and steady hands on Leonard's shoulders to still the new groom and keep him from fainting.

"At my fucking wedding, Robert? Is she serious? I have nothing to say to that pig."

Leonard forced the rising bile down his throat, thinking how thankful he was for opting out of breakfast this morning. Otherwise, it certainly would have been on the floor by now. For this monster to show up on a happy day, his fucking happy day. She knew what she was doing. She always did.

Two minutes later, Leonard stood outside the elevator banks in an empty room, face to face with his first ex-wife, Claire. Her skin sported a permanent clammy sheen, and her weight ballooned well over the obese mark. Her appearance suggested a struggle Leonard didn't care to hear about, but he knew she'd force serve him a taste of all the supposed agony he caused.

"What do you want?" said Leonard, not hiding the oozing disgust spilling from his pores.

"I didn't come here to fight," said Claire.

"What do you want?" He hated how her eyes scanned his body. He hated how she saw him on what was supposed to be a joyous, memorable day. Today would be unforgettable, all right.

"I forgot how well you wear a tuxedo."

Leonard clicked his jaw, grinding his teeth to their stubs.

"Anyway, I don't want to keep you. I wanted to ask a favor."

"You... want to ask a favor of me?" Leonard's eyes popped. "You should be lucky I haven't filed restraining orders against you. Against your own kids."

Claire recoiled, squinting her eyes while retracting like a turtle.

"Oh, did you forget already? How you abandoned your kids, you let them live in squalor. They only had three fucking hours to empty their lives from that shit hole. How could you do that to them? At least you could have told me. I would've been able to save more things. How could you do that to them, Claire?" Leonard spotted the spit flying from his mouth. He wiped his bottom lip, forming a saliva stain on his midnight blue tuxedo.

"Well, if you wanted them sooner, why didn't you just ask me to hand them over?"

"It's my biggest mistake. Don't think I don't hate myself for not doing things differently. But you're their mother. I thought this was what you wanted. And the courts always side with the mother. Crazy or not." Leonard gestured over Claire's body.

She glared at him.

"So, you think I'm crazy?" said Claire.

"Why are you here? What do you want from me?"

Claire blinked her crocodile tears away, peering into the high hats. "I want to see them."

"No."

"I am their mother. I want to see them."

"How did you find me?" Leonard's pulse thumped in his chest, threatening to pop his silver buttons.

Claire half laughed. "Well, honey. When you marry a hotshot from Manhattan who wants a wedding announcement splashed all over the papers, it's easy to find you."

Leonard threw his head back, bumping it against the wall, knowing Claire was right, and he warned Becky against a tacky wedding announcement. Still, he didn't consider Claire tracking him down because with his original protests to Becky over a wedding story, he simply didn't want the attention. But Becky was Becky and needed to keep appearances for their glitzy, wallet-melting wedding, only to be crashed by a crazy ex.

"I want to see them. I'm their mother and have the right to see them."

"You walked out on them. They haven't heard from you in a year. What makes you think you have any rights?"

"Don't tell me you're going to be that kind of father. Where he doesn't allow the mother to see her own children." She laughed, and a snort escaped in the horrible mix.

That's precisely what she was. A fucking pig.

"Is Millie a bridesmaid? Or maybe, maid of honor? Is Steven your best man?" Claire crossed her arms, pushing her fat together, adding to the layers of rolls on her doughy torso.

"Goddammit!" Leonard punched the wall, producing more damage to his bare knuckles.

"I hope this isn't how you act in front of the kids." Again, Claire snorted.

Leonard spun around, almost toppling over from the zero traction nature of his new black shiny shoes. He raised his fist in the air, not intending to punch anyone, but he found his hand unable to lower.

Claire glared at his fist. "Do it. I dare you."

"Mom?" said Millie.

Leonard dropped his hand to his side, pinning it against his hip.

"Millie, honey," said Claire. The words rolled off her tongue like slime, and, now, Leonard wished he did have her thrown out of the venue. At this moment, he failed to protect his children, the children she abandoned.

Millie hugged her body, her bare arms catching a breeze shooting through the empty lobby while taking a step away.

"How have you been? Are you safe?" asked Claire.

Leonard twisted his head in Claire's direction, scowling at the creature he once believed to be perfect.

Millie shook her head no, her eyes forming a glassy texture. She tightened her grip around her body and whispered, "Why..."

Millie ran away up the staircase.

"Millie, wait!" said Leonard, bolting after her, never turning back to see Claire's face again.

# *November 25ᵗʰ, 2021*

"That was the last time I saw her," said Leonard. He laid against Jill's chest, tangled between her limbs and the crinkled bed sheets.

Jill ran her smooth-skinned hands through his hair, slick with some sweat from their latest session.

"What do you mean last time? She wasn't at Millie's funeral?" asked Jill.

Leonard shook his head. "She was a no-show and knew all the funeral details too. Claimed she couldn't make the proper travel arrangements, even though she lived only an hour away."

"That's very sad." Jill moved her hands down to his neck, rubbing the knots away.

"She was an awful, awful person. Just horrible."

"She passed away?"

Leonard almost laughed at how politely Jill prefaced a horrible person's death. "Yeah. She died a year ago." Leonard stretched his neck and leaned back in Jill's cocoon, groaning. "Keep doing that. It feels so good."

Jill chuckled, obliging. She raked her fingernails across his chest, sending chills down his spine.

"Every year I knew her, Claire always threatened that she was on her deathbed. Every. Single. Year. No one took her seriously. Just an absolute nutcase."

"It's scary how certain individuals can fool us, innocent people, you know?" Jill's breath tickled his earlobe. "Do you ever wonder why you married her?"

"She was astute. Duped everyone who came into contact with her. It happened to me. And then I got to know her, but it was too late."

"My ex sounds like he could be her brother," said Jill, pausing her massage.

"I actually liked Claire's brother. He was normal."

Jill resumed the massage, returning to his shoulders. "How did Steven take his mother's death?"

"Steven buries everything. At first, I thought it was bad, but I'm not sure anymore. He's here at least, right?" Leonard grabbed one of Jill's hands to stare at her raw nails. He still couldn't believe her nails weren't red earlier. It's as if he was totally blinded by something he wanted to see until now.

"What? Still about the nails?" Jill extracted her hand from Leonard's. "Do you have a thing about nails or something?"

Leonard sat up with a sudden need to make a call. He threw on his boxer briefs for the first time in hours and ducked into the bathroom.

The phone rang four times before Greg answered.

"For fuck's sake, Leo. What now?" Greg huffed into the phone, chewing on something.

"I'm glad I'm back to Leo. Anyway, you know I'm with this new chick right now?"

"Yeah, yeah, glad to hear you're still going strong."

"Very funny. Here's the thing." Leonard cleared his throat. "Her nails..."

"Again, with the fucking nails," said Greg. "What's wrong with her nails? Are they too long? Too short? What the fuck is your obsession with the goddamn nails?"

Leonard watched his reflection in the oversized bathroom as his breath fogged up the glass inches from his nose. "I could have sworn they were red earlier, and after one of the times we had sex, I noticed they weren't." He scratched at his premature five o'clock shadow. "What do you think that means?"

"Are you serious right now? This is why you called?"

"I could have sworn they were red, Greg."

"Okay, so they're not. Big deal. Maybe you're getting Jill confused with another woman."

"That's impossible. I haven't been single for this long, God knows when, and I haven't slept with anyone for the last three months until today." Leonard drummed his filed nails on the marble vanity, waiting for an answer. "I just can't seem to get over it. Whenever I see her nails, it's almost as if I thought she was someone or something else."

"I'm not sure what to say, Leo. But this is what you do. You build someone up in your head and start breaking them down, noticing their flaws. This new chick, Jill, sounds like it's happening in record time."

Leonard bit the inside of his cheek and didn't appreciate Greg's analysis, but he wasn't entirely wrong, either. At least with Leonard's track record, it was what he did with all the women in his life, but Jill appeared so different from everyone in the past.

"And I know you always tell me that the new woman differs from the old one. But it's never different. It always ends the same."

"Why are you being so fucking harsh?" asked Leonard.

"Because you've made it a point to call me every hour on Thanksgiving, and now my turkey gumbo is officially cold."

"So, should I forget about the nails? Is that what you're telling me?"

Greg slurped what Leonard guessed was his cold soup, pulling the phone away from his ear.

"All I'm saying is learn to tolerate people. Perfection? Not possible. Tolerable? Sure."

"But why do I need to settle, Greg? Why should anyone need to settle?"

"Nobody is perfect."

Leonard squeezed the bridge of his nose, rejecting all the words, all of Greg's wisdom.

"And Leonard?"

"Yes, darling?"

"If you call me one more time today, I'm pretty sure my perfect wife will kill me."

Greg hung up.

# June 24<sup>th</sup>, 1998

There weren't enough boxes for this move. There was no way Becky could fit all of her shit into the forty-six extra-large and tall wardrobe boxes, no less from her sprawling penthouse apartment into Leonard's humble mansion. Rich people's problems, as his brother would whine about. But seriously, they needed more boxes, and to top off this far from the perfect, crumbling afternoon, Leonard kept missing Millie's calls, and he knew precisely the origin of her panic.

"Robert, please, I'm begging you. I'm in a real bind here," said Leonard into his phone, the beads of sweat pouring down his tanned, clean-shaven face.

"She's hysterical, Leonard. How am I supposed to drive her for three hours," asked Robert.

"If you won't do it, just tell me so I can start making other calls." Leonard kept making sure Becky wasn't within earshot for any of this ill banter. He was being pinned between his fiancée and his daughter right now, during the worst timing for both women in his life.

"I'll do it. I just don't know how I will. There's the nuance."

"Thank you, Robert. Just tell me how much you want. I'll write you a check when I see you next. Or wire. I can wire you the money." Leonard's pulse slowed for the first time this afternoon until the sound of packing tape slapped onto another box reverberated throughout the emptying apartment.

"You can't buy me, Leonard." Robert cleared his rattling throat into the phone.

"I've paid you before when I've been in a bind." Leonard scrunched his brow. A fresh headache seeped into his skull.

"I'll let you know when Millie's all checked into camp." Robert hung up, not even offering a real goodbye, as Leonard surmised he didn't deserve one. The whole optics of the situation made him look like a complete asshole father and quite the cliche to choose the fiancée over his child, but today was different. Too many plans and too much money would have fallen through the gaping cracks in this less-than-ideal situation of moving a princess from the city to a mundane suburb on Long Island.

Becky's unexpected wiry hand landed on his shoulder, giving it a neutral double squeeze. "You okay there? Was that Millie, again?" Her hair was wrapped in some silk turban, a style Leonard had never witnessed until now. He wanted to see her hair, not parts of her hidden.

"No, Robert. He's going to drive Millie up to camp in the morning." Leonard's jelly limbs led him to one of the few leucite chairs remaining in Becky's space.

"How could she say you don't care? You're sending her to one of the ritziest summer camps in the country. Doesn't she get it?"

Becky sat at the base of Leonard's chair, trailing her hand behind Leonard's cramping calves, squeezing his aching muscles.

"I get it, and I don't get it. She's sometimes so complicated."

"It sounds like a case of Daddy issues to me." Becky shrugged her shoulders.

Leonard was about to tell her to watch her fucking mouth but then remembered how her mouth looked earlier this morning, her only goal pleasing him in her fluffy white bedding that was now being packed up for the big move. He ran his hand through his black hair, wondering how many new grays today's episode would sprout. To imagine last year, he sported zero grays, and now, they kept popping up.

Becky stood from the ground, wrapping her arms around Leonard's lean body. "It'll all work out, baby," said Becky into his hair.

"It doesn't get easier with kids. The older they get, the harder it feels sometimes." Leonard pulled Becky's body into his, yearning to melt into her skin.

Becky pushed away from Leonard, throwing her arms up into the air, clanking away in her heels. "Can't help you on that. Maybe it's why I never had kids?"

She disappeared into the living room, leaving Leonard stewing in his swirling thoughts. When his mind reached a teetering simmer, his phone rang again. He groaned when he saw the caller ID.

"Hi, Millie." Leonard gulped.

"Dad, are you serious about Uncle Robby?" Millie sounded like she held on for dear life on the other end.

Despite Leonard picturing her tear-soaked face, he had already made his decision.

"It'll be fine. Uncle Robby promised to not play his country music."

"This is my final year at camp. You promised we'd drive up together." Millie's voice adopted the screech of a bird dying.

"I know, but with Becky's move happening tomorrow, I have to be here. I have to be. I'm sorry, but I'm doing my best here. Try to understand this time around."

"But you promised me." Millie's voice had the power to shatter glass at this new octave.

"Look, what do you want from me? I'm being pulled in a million directions here. Sometimes I have to do things that aren't part of your plan." Leonard winced, instantly regretting his last words.

"Oh, I see your priorities now."

"It came out sounding bad. In a few weeks, Becky and I will be up for visiting weekend, and then I'll drive you back. This is just a hiccup."

"I know you're about to marry Becky, but sometimes I just need you. Why does Becky need to be a part of every sentence? Sometimes it's nice when it's just us." Millie sobbed.

"You have me, I promise." Leonard clutched his chest.

Millie released one last cry and hung up the phone. Leonard dropped his cell onto the teak wood floors, producing a deadening thud.

Becky reappeared, towering over Leonard's hunched frame. "Was that her again?"

Leonard peered up at the giant of a woman holding a wine spritzer in one hand and an unopened bottle of something else in the other.

"Here, try this. It's fruity." She placed a Mike's Hard Lemonade in front of Leonard, the sweaty drink kissing his shoe. He didn't understand or agree with the gesture. Didn't Becky remember his hatred for alcohol? And then Leonard couldn't stop wondering what the Mike's Hard Lemonade signified coming from Becky. Maybe she forgot what he liked and hated. Perhaps she wasn't that perfect after all.

# *February 1<sup>st</sup>, 1998*

Leonard just got the call four hours ago about the house, not his house, but about Claire's house and how the town slapped an eviction order onto the property. Millie and Steven had three hours to get all of their precious items out before the town's sheriff permanently locked them out. For all these months, Leonard gave Claire money to pay for the rent, the utilities, and the general upkeep of the house per their divorce decree. It wasn't a big deal, but what did she do with all of that money? And now she had disappeared from their kids' lives.

A knock snapped Leonard out of his maddening trance. Thinking about Claire and all the damage she caused could trap Leonard for days. The knocks grew louder. He had a state-of-the-art doorbell, and whoever stood at his door chose to knock like a psychopath. He forgot to look through the peephole as the incessant pounding drove him crazy to the point of carelessness.

He yanked the door open, revealing a sullen Millie and Steven, holding gigantic cardboard boxes about to burst onto the slate ground.

Leonard's eyes popped, and all the rage coursing through his body seconds ago morphed into a chocolate belt lining his heart, warming his chest.

"Welcome home, children," said Leonard, opening his arms and welcoming them in.

Millie and Steven rolled their eyes in unison while sweat prickled their faces. Leonard grabbed the boxes from his children's hands, tossing them to the ground.

"I called the movers about an hour ago. They should be here soon to unload everything," said Leonard, motioning both kids into his house... No, their house for good. "Did you get everything you needed?" Leonard slapped Steven twice on the shoulder before pulling him in for a half hug.

Steven shrugged. "I gathered as many pictures, photos, albums as I could. I probably missed a few. There was just so much shit to go through."

"I already called Greg. He's going to call the town to see if we can get back in there. He's going to explain the circumstances."

"Good old Greg, right? What would you do without him?" said Millie, crossing her arms.

Leonard frowned. She was right. He pulled Millie into a hug, though it never felt natural hugging his kids. He couldn't explain why. No one hugged Leonard growing up. It wasn't a Rosen trait.

"Are you okay? Did you find what you needed?" Leonard softened his voice for Millie. He understood what she needed.

"Don't worry. She packed all her hair products," said Steven.

Millie gave Steven the finger. "Well, it's expensive. I can't go and buy everything new." Millie signaled to her clear taped box on the floor.

"Don't you worry about that. If you need anything, you just ask. That's how we roll here, okay?" Leonard looked from his kids to the boxes just outside the entryway. "Aright, everyone shower up, get changed, and then come back down."

"I'm not in the mood to go out to eat."

"Yeah, we stopped at McDonald's on the way back. Millie scarfed down a giant shake," said Steven, smiling at outing his sister.

Millie glared at Steven from the staircase.

"We're going shopping," said Leonard.

"Oh, my God, really?" Light filled Millie's blue eyes for the first time today.

Steven crossed his arms, lowering his baseball cap over his eyes. "I'm not watching Millie try on clothes all day."

"We're not just getting new clothes. We're buying everything new. C'mon, It'll be fun. This is a new beginning. A new life," said Leonard. "Get ready." He pointed to Steven. "We're going to the city."

Ninety minutes later, Leonard guided his kids down the most expansive aisles in some ultra-modern electronic store. Leonard's goal was to buy Millie and Steven everything new and the shiniest products. There was no budget for today's trip. He didn't divulge this detail to his children, especially Millie. She would have gotten carried away when given the blessing.

Leonard caught Steven eyeing a fifty-inch flat screen television mounted to one of the display walls. "I think the sixty-inch would look better on your wall."

Steven snapped his head in Leonard's direction, forgetting how to blink. Leonard laughed, wrapping his arm around his son's shoulder.

"I told you everything new, right?"

"These are expensive."

"Don't you worry about that, okay? Never worry about that. You're living with me now. Things are going to be different."

"Mom always made it sound like money was tight, you know?"

Leonard didn't know, and he detested Claire more than ever. He swallowed the bubbling bile rising in his throat at the mere thought of her.

"Things are different now, okay?" Leonard stared at Steven until he nodded, his understanding of this new life being offered to him in plentiful, expensive electronics. This was only a taste of what a new life would be for them.

"Could I get surround sound too?" asked Steven, perking up while shaking off Leonard's arm.

"Get a salesperson. I'm going to find your sister."

Leonard wandered away from Steven to find Millie. His heart quickened when he didn't spot her after two minutes of searching for her. He finally found her sitting in the most expensive massage chair, dreaming the minutes away. He nudged her leg, trying not to startle her.

"Wake up, sleeping beauty."

Millie pinched her left eye open, continuing to relish the massage chair. "If I owned this chair, I think I could die peacefully."

Leonard peeked at the price tag. Fucking shit, he thought, but today was a new beginning for all of them. He wanted them to remember this day, how their dad was the most fantastic guy on earth.

"Let's get it," said Leonard. "But just don't say the dying part."

"Seriously? Where would I even put it? This is huge." Millie snapped straight up, examining the chair's girth.

"Your room is large enough. And just picture the chair in front of the big window. You can overlook the yard while getting a massage." Leonard kind of wished he had bought the chair for himself.

"Oh my god. This is crazy. This day is crazy." Millie melted back into the leather seat, covering her eyes. When she removed her hands, there were tears. Tears she couldn't control as they rolled down her cheeks. "This is a lot."

Leonard knew she didn't mean the price either.

"Things are going to be so different now, aren't they?" asked Millie, peering up at her father, waiting for all the answers she never had.

Leonard kneeled next to Millie, staring at her as he would when she was a four-year-old girl. "Things will be different. But different is sometimes better. You know what I mean?"

"Do you think we'll hear from Mom soon?"

Leonard then realized he could never replace their mother, even if he bought them the tallest buildings in the world. These were just things, and their mother was an emotional force in their lives, whether good or bad, so maybe he couldn't replace her, but hopefully, he could distract his children enough to where they wouldn't feel the sting of her absence when those moments hit.

"I wasn't close with my mother growing up either. By the time I left for college, we barely spoke." Leonard's mouth went dry, and a white-hot rage shot through him whenever he thought about his mother. He fucking hated her.

"But I don't hate Mom. You must think I'm crazy, but I don't." Millie peered down at her chipped nails.

"How about after this, you go get a manicure? I think there's a nice salon that Becky goes to not too far from here."

Millie's face paled at the mention of Becky's name. Leonard saw it but decided to ignore Millie's disappointment.

Millie looked over Leonard's shoulder, and her face lost another shade of color. "Oh, wow, it's Becky."

Leonard whipped his head around, smiling the instant he spotted his fiancée. He stood up and wrapped his arms around Becky. Her hair appeared salon fresh and smelled like a bouquet of roses. He could take in her scent all day. She was immaculate, and he loved when she wore black high-heeled boots. There was something about the edginess combined with the sexiness of a heel. Today, her shoes were ultra-black and ultra-high.

"It looks like you've found yourself a very nice chair." Becky's eyes scanned a supine Millie in the expensive piece. Millie shifted in her seat while glancing at Leonard, who moved from the left-to-right foot.

"It's Dad's gift to me for moving in with him... finally."

"I guess good things come to those who wait, huh?" said Becky, shooting her eyes at Leonard's. She played with the back of Leonard's neck, prickling his skin with her teasing fingertips.

Leonard cleared his throat, stepping away from Becky. He needed some distance. "Won't this look awesome in Millie's room? She thought she didn't have enough space," said Leonard, wagging his finger at Millie.

"Of course, you have the space." Becky took a step closer to Millie. "Your father's house is huge. To think, we'll all be living there soon enough."

"Oh, you're going to spend the summer with us?" said Millie.

Leonard buried his eyes into his sweaty palm. He didn't want anyone to find out this way, but the timing never played on his side in this life.

"No, silly," said Becky. She wrapped an arm around Leonard's shoulder, pulling him into her web. "I'm moving in. Didn't your father tell you?"

Both women shot their eyes at Leonard, pinning him with their stares.

Leonard nearly choked on his saliva as the pressure emitted from each woman sunk deep into his chest. "It's true. Becky's going to move in by early June." He took Becky's hand, hoping she didn't notice his sweat-coated skin.

"I know we won't have much time together with you shipping off to camp, but when you get back, we'll catch up," said Becky.

Now, more than ever, Leonard wanted Becky to shut up.

"I thought you loved the city. Didn't you grow up here?" said Millie.

"Well, after your father made it abundantly clear he'd never move to the city... even though his office is here... I decided to make the jump. Jump into the burbs." Becky shot Leonard a semi-sour smile. "Plus, we're engaged. What were we going to do? Live separate lives?"

"Sometimes that's what makes certain relationships last," said Millie, squinting at Leonard.

"Millie," said Leonard, glaring at his daughter.

"It's fine, Leonard." Becky pressed her smooth hand against his thudding chest. "This is a big change for everyone today. Right, Millie?" Becky pinned the girl with her dazzling black eyes.

"It'll be a lot of fun," said Millie, not lifting her eyes from the ground. "I'm gonna sit here a little longer. Make sure this chair is really worth it."

Leonard forgot how to swallow at this point.

"You do that. Your father and I are going to hunt around for little Stevie." Becky pulled Leonard's arm with such force he almost toppled over those boots he thought he loved a minute ago.

"Watch it, Becky."

"Does she hate me?" The air hissed through Becky's nostrils.

"Don't be ridiculous, Becky. She's had a rough day. Jesus." Leonard scanned his eyes over Becky as he fought the disgust. He never got angry with Becky and wasn't used to this simmering anger he suddenly held for his fresh fiancée.

"I know when I'm disliked, Leonard." Becky crossed her arms, pressing together her perky breasts.

"Are you really going to do this? Today of all days?"

Becky said nothing and stuck her pointy nose even higher into the air.

Leonard placed a hand on her elbows, turning her body to face his without a choice. "You know I hate it when you're upset. Tell me, how can I fix this?"

Becky shrugged. "Maybe it's a mistake me leaving the city. You know, all I want is for you to move here."

Leonard shook his head, squeezing her elbows tighter. "It's not an option. I have to stay in the school district for them. I won't pull them out."

"I've never left the city before. This is hard for me, too."

"I know it is, baby. But I'm telling you, you'll love it on Long Island. Plus, we're a forty-minute ride to the city." Leonard ran his hands up and down her slender arms, hoping for a miracle. "I'm begging you, just for today, let anything the kids say slide. You don't know what they just went through. Imagine being deserted by your mother out of the blue?"

"Was it really that bad?"

"Baby, they lived in squalor."

Becky blinked extra hard, grimacing and clutching her chest. "Oh, my god. Where is that?"

# November 25<sup>th</sup>, 2021

Jill laughed and laughed and laughed. She couldn't get over Becky; quite frankly, neither could Leonard. How did he fall for a woman so stupid at one point?

"Oh, my God," said Jill, fighting to find her breath. "How did she? How could she think squalor was an actual place?"

Leonard shrugged. "And she always bragged about the fancy schools she attended growing up in the city. I guess she didn't pay attention."

"Wow, Rosen, just wow. And how long were you married for?"

"A year, I think? Yeah, a full year. Susan only lasted nine months, but that wasn't my fault. Susan was a complete and total bitch. I started talking to Susan while Becky moved out of my house and back into her city life." Leonard twisted his face, thinking about Becky and all of her goddamn wardrobe boxes.

"You don't get tired? Meeting new women, going through the motions? Getting married? I did it once, and the divorce sucked my life out."

"Did you date?" Leonard roped his hand around her leg, staking his claim.

"Of course. But settling down with someone? I'm not sure. I never found the need to have someone with me to feel complete."

Leonard examined Jill from head to toe. She still looked great, unclothed, but something about this conversation unsettled his nerves. As if she exposed his flaws, except for Leonard, everyone else claimed they saw. He knew his faults were glaring to others, but he didn't care. He refused to settle in life or fit into a mold others deemed appropriate.

"I guess I always wanted a perfect life. Come home to a wife who cared for the house and kids. Had dinner ready for me on the table and asked me how my day was. That kind of thing."

"Did any of them come close to giving you that?"

"I guess my first wife. She was the longest marriage, after all." Leonard flashed a smile. "Ten years from start to finish, legally."

"Wow. What an accomplishment." Becky patted Leonard on the back. "How do you pick them?"

"I've never had a problem meeting women who led to serious relationships. I just know how to date, I guess?"

Jill half snorted. "And how do you see me?"

Leonard dragged his eyes over her naked flesh. "I really like what you don't have on right now." He lifted his brows twice.

"I'm serious."

"I am too." Leonard leaned in, kissing Jill's waiting lips.

"How about some dessert?"

"Whatever you want." Leonard pulled Jill on top of him, only to be met with her resistance.

"No, I mean actual dessert. All of this activity has left me famished." Jill pushed off Leonard, fetching a terry cloth bathrobe from the closet, sauntering back into the space, holding the room service menu, flipping through its pages.

Leonard glanced at the clock, seeing it was almost four o'clock and knowing he should have been at Jackie's house for dessert and not in a hotel room. Instead, here he was with Jill, a relative stranger, who served as a decent distraction, but by no means a replacement for where he wanted to be. He studied her bare legs, thinking they were longer and could have sworn they were. It was the same assumption he made, believing her nails were red. What was going on with him? Was Leonard losing it or finally seeing what everyone else did about what he built in his head?

"Earth to Rosen?"

Leonard lifted his head from the floor, meeting Jill's dull green eyes. Why did he think they were brighter a few hours ago? He remembered them as booming emeralds when contrasted with her porcelain skin.

"Why do you call me Rosen?"

"Sometimes, I forget what your first name is." Jill smiled.

"Seriously? Usually, it's the other way around." Leonard swallowed, pushing down the ball forming in his throat.

"Oh, a fruit platter with whipped cream sounds refreshing." Jill pointed to some spot on the menu Leonard didn't care about to ask for further details.

"We just had strawberries." Leonard studied Jill. "What's my name?"

"I know your name. I said it earlier."

"I suddenly don't believe you." Leonard wrapped an arm around Jill's waist, pulling her closer, yet keeping a distance to not touch their bodies together.

"Have some faith, Rosen."

But there was no faith to be had in this minute of crippling doubt. Leonard didn't know what to think. He believed he knew Jill and everything he needed to know about moving on from this hotel room into tomorrow. But now, he wasn't sure about anything. Then, the sudden realization of forgetting about Jackie and losing him for a few months came crashing back onto his shoulders like a tidal wave breaking at its peak.

A vibration broke the silence in the room. Jill reached for Leonard's phone and tossed it onto the bed, where it landed beside his thigh. It was Steven.

"It's my son." Leonard lifted the phone, ready to answer.

"Answer it, and I'll order us some dessert."

"Only if you say my name."

Jill laughed. "I'll say your first name when you say my last name."

Leonard had never learned it. That was a fact. He watched her disappear into the bathroom before answering his phone. "What's up, son?"

"Dad. Where did you go?" said Steven.

"I've been gone the whole day, and only now you notice?"

"Nah, I noticed. I just decided to give you space."

Steven did have a point.

"But you know how I get. Sometimes I'm slow to react."

Understatement of the century, Leonard thought.

"Are you okay?" said Steven.

"Of course, I'm okay. I'm breathing, aren't I?"

"Where did you go? Are you coming back to Uncle Robert's?"

Leonard looked up to see Jill emerge from the bathroom, her footsteps silent on the carpet.

"Nah. I'm going to hang out for the rest of the day."

Leonard watched Jill toss the room service menu onto the glass table, crossing her arms casually, waiting for Leonard to return to her.

"You're not going to see Jackie later?" asked Steven.

Leonard froze in his seat. Steven never mentioned, let alone uttered, Jackie's name. His denial of his nephew's existence remained known to anyone familiar with the convoluted situation, and to have Steven ask about Jackie in any capacity equated to some step forward. Leonard witnessed progress and loved it.

"Why? Do you want to come? I could call Jesse and ask if there's a chance to see Jackie today."

"Ha! Yeah, right. Like that asshole would ever do anything to make you happy." Steven sighed. "I don't know. I guess knowing that Jackie will be leaving for Thailand... fucking Thailand." The word fell off Steven's tongue like a clumsy, tumbling boulder. "It made me think that maybe I need to try more with him while I still have the chance."

Leonard's eyes fell to the ground, unable to lift them a centimeter. "It's never too late to start, Steven."

"I feel ashamed for how I've blocked him out. Do you think he'll forgive me?" Steven's voice trembled.

"Without a doubt. Jackie's a good kid. Once you get to know him, you'll see he doesn't have a mean bone in his body."

"I guess he takes after Millie." Steven's voice filled with a light that had been missing since Millie's passing.

Leonard's throat tightened, and he could not catch his breath. He noticed Jill staring at him, twirling her hair around her index finger as the pools of concern darkened her eyes even further.

"Anyway. When does he leave for Thailand?"

"Three months. But knowing Jesse, it could be sooner. I don't put anything past that guy."

"You'll figure everything out."

"I really hope so, Steven."

"You will. Look, I'm gonna go. I'll bring you home some pie if you want."

"I'll let you know."

Leonard hung up, staring at the black screen of his phone. He needed to figure this out. He needed to find a way to keep Jackie here, and suddenly he felt like a fool for believing Jesse had planned this gigantic move for three months. It would happen sooner, and if he sat here much longer, he couldn't figure out anything.

"The food should be arriving any minute," said Jill, her voice cutting the thick tension in the air. She dragged her feet over to Leonard's slumped frame at the edge of the bed. She sat in his lap, draping her arms around his neck, running her cool fingers through his silver hair.

He never stopped watching her, catching her wrist mid-stroke. "What do you do for a living?"

Jill rolled her eyes, lifting her arms from Leonard's body.

"I'm serious. I want to know more about you. What do you do? Do you have a job? Run charities? Trust fund baby?"

"You're acting silly now."

"How? Becky was a trust fund baby, dumb as wood. We know this. But you're nothing like Becky. So, I don't think you're a trust fund baby."

Jill shook her head, failing to conceal a spreading smile.

"Tell me who you are. What you are? What do you do when you're not with me in this room?" Leonard was one step away from throwing himself on his knees, begging Jill to give him more details of her life. The more he thought about Jill, the more he realized just how little they knew about each other. Well, not Jill. He opened himself up to Jill. Leonard knew next to nothing about her life other than sharing a common tragedy over the loss of their daughters.

"I'm a psychologist."

Well, Leonard thought. It explained the ease Jill possessed with people opening up to her.

Two knocks from the door filled the hotel room. Jill popped up to answer and, ten seconds later, waltzed back into the room, showcasing a dazzling assorted fruit bowl of freshly whipped cream and a bottle of champagne. Her robe fell apart at her chest, leading down to her torso, but he wanted Jill to cover up for whatever reason.

He watched Jill pour two flutes of champagne from the green Moet bottle. Moet? Alcohol? Who was paying for this? He was, of course. But he didn't want any of it, the champagne he didn't want mainly. Everything else was tolerable.

"Champagne? I thought I told you I detest the taste of alcohol," said Leonard.

Jill cocked her head like a lost canine stumbling upon an intriguing stranger. "I could have sworn you liked a spirit."

Leonard snorted, his tongue spewing the type of saliva when nausea kicks in. "You must be thinking of the wrong guy."

Jill drank half the glass, smacking her lips at the last drop. "I guess I heard wrong."

"I thought you didn't drink. Isn't that what you said back at the diner?"

The light spilling from the parted drapes caught a section of crow's feet at the crease of Jill's left eye.

"I declined to have a drink at lunch. I never said I didn't drink." Jill followed up with another sip of champagne, her glass almost empty. She took a bite from the bowl's largest and most succulent green grape. She offered the other half, the paler side, to Leonard.

"You're doing that thing therapists do. They play with words." Leonard pointed a finger towards Jill's face.

She waved her hand away, shooing the comment into oblivion.

"Is that what you think of therapists, Rosen?" She crossed her arms. "Or is that what you think of me?"

"Oh, don't be silly." Leonard walked over to Jill, closing the space between them. He bit into a plump blackberry, taken aback by the sweet juices exiting the fruit onto his tongue. "Holy shit. This is some good fruit."

Jill rolled her eyes, sitting down, away from Leonard, peering out the immaculately clean window.

"Can I refill your champagne?" Leonard took a whiff from his glass, hating the bitter aroma of the alcohol.

"Why do you dislike therapists?"

"Are you taking it personally?"

"I take my job seriously, and it's my career, but no, I don't take it personally, your dislikes."

Leonard kept smelling the champagne, growing increasingly thirsty and disgusted, but all he really wanted was Diet Coke.

"Oh, just take a small taste already. It won't kill you," said Jill.

No one told Leonard what to do, especially not fucking Jill. He tossed a half-eaten slice of pineapple back into the pile and plopped back onto the bed. The distance between them stretched across the room, coating it in a novel, uncertain energy. It was electric, but not the kind you wanted to touch.

"I've been to a therapist twice in my life. Different therapists and both experiences didn't agree with me."

"Sometimes, it takes time to find the right one. I tried out numerous therapists after Melissa died. And after my divorce."

"You couldn't just talk to yourself in a mirror?" Leonard's smile waned, already regretting his lame half-joke.

"That was insensitive."

"I know. I'm sorry." Leonard really was sorry.

"Can a doctor operate on himself?" Jill crossed her legs, looking like a therapist listening to a bumbling patient.

"You're right, and I'm wrong, okay?"

"I'm not trying to prove anything." Jill drummed her pale fingers on her bare leg. "I'm sorry therapy didn't work out for you. But for some, it's a wonderful tool."

"I don't doubt it, but it's not for me."

Jill remained silent, peering at the chilly cityscape below. Everything from the hotel room appeared miniature, like tiny moving particles against a gigantic uncertain world below.

"What would you think of me if I were your patient?"

"Let's not even go there." Jill raised an eyebrow.

Leonard wanted the challenge. "Seriously. What would you think of me? From what you know so far? What do you think? Am I doomed?"

"Doomed? What could you possibly think you're doomed over? You've lived your life doing as you pleased."

"Let's say I went to find out if I made mistakes in the past that led me to my present. Do you think I had a chance? With the therapy and all that."

"Probably not," Jill said with no trace of life threading through her voice.

"Really." Now it was Leonard's turn to cross his arms. He pulled the heather gray covers up to his waist as the cold air danced across his goose-bumped skin. "And you're so certain about this, why?"

Jill locked eyes with Leonard, not shifting once. "Because men like you don't change."

# *May 1997 – Guy's Night*

"Steven, get your butt down here," said Leonard, clearing the table for their impromptu steakhouse takeout night. He detested a cold steak, and this food was divine, cooked and delivered from the best restaurant on Long Island, and the creamed spinach could stop the nastiest of world wars. Leonard hated most vegetables, so for him to rave about any food the color green, it had to be special and decadent.

Steven dragged his feet onto the terracotta kitchen floor, sporting a baseball cap pulled down enough to cover his eyes.

"No hats at the table." Leonard pointed to the baseball cap.

Steven rolled his eyes but obliged as he plopped onto a chair, licking his lips and eyeing the feast on the table.

"Where's Millie tonight?"

"She's at her friend Lauren's house." Steven didn't hesitate to cut into the perfectly cooked medium rare filet mignon.

"How's she doing? Whenever I ask Millie how school is, she gives me one-word answers."

"Fine, I guess."

"Do you know what group she hangs out with?"

"No? You know that we're in two different schools, right? She's in high school, and I'm in the middle until next year."

Leonard shut his mouth and realized he looked like a real jerk at the table. He didn't know what schools each of his kids attended. He filled his fork with slices of steak, shoving it into his mouth with brute force.

"You guys have been coming over a lot more lately. Is everything okay at home?"

Steven's eyes shifted, slowing his chewing to a snail's pace.

Leonard reached across the table, moving Steven's water to the side to get a better view of his son's face.

"You know, whatever you tell me won't go further than this table. Is everything okay with your mother?"

"Yeah. It's just that... I don't know. Your house is more fun. It's just better here."

"Oh, you need to be more specific than that. And fun? I doubt that."

"No, I don't. It's pretty obvious, I would think." Steven locked eyes with Leonard, the lump of food stuffed into the corner of his mouth.

"Well, anytime you want to stay here, you're more than welcome to."

Steven nodded and resumed devouring the steak and beloved creamed spinach. Leonard regretted not getting a double order as he watched Steven scarf down the side dish. The only piece missing from this meal was Millie. If she were there, then dinner would have been perfect. Leonard cherished having one-on-one time with Steven, but something about having all your children together at one table with you proved to be a privilege.

"What if I wanted to come to live with you?"

Leonard's heart skipped a beat. "Why? You don't want to live with your mother anymore?"

"I don't know. I just like coming here, I guess."

"Anytime you want to come here, you have a key. The door is always open." Leonard cut into the juiciest piece of steak, revealing a black and blue temperature. He twisted his face, plopping the too rare piece of meat onto Steven's plate.

"Can I come over for dinner tomorrow?"

Leonard peered up at the tray ceilings, considering the answer. "Can't. I have a date tomorrow night."

"Oh. Someone new?"

Leonard shrugged. "No, with Becky. We've been seeing each other for a few months now."

Steven nodded, freezing for a moment the instant the rare meat hit his tongue. He forced a squinted grin as he chewed through the steak.

"Let's just keep things as they are now. We've got a good thing going. I don't want to rock the boat, you know?" said Leonard.

"All good." Except Steven never made eye contact with Leonard.

"Hey. How about after this, we go over to the sporting goods store on Route 110 and pick out new gear for baseball this season?"

"I already have everything I need." Steven's eyes grew wide at the possibility of fresh stuff.

"Nah, c'mon." Leonard waved off the comment. "Finish up. We're getting you everything new, and consider it done."

"Seriously? Everything new?"

"Brand new. Stop talking and finish your food. I think they close at nine." Leonard checked his watch, even though he knew they closed then.

Steven shoveled the food into his mouth, not even coming up for air. Leonard laughed as he watched his son's zeal steer his utensil.

"Should we ask Millie if she wants to join? She'll probably need new volleyball gear soon."

"You didn't know she quit?"

"Quit?" Leonard dropped his fork, crashing it to the floor. "When? What do you mean she quit?"

"All I know is she stopped going. When I asked her about it once, she said it wasn't for her anymore."

"This is bullshit. I thought she was going to go for a scholarship."

Steven frowned, putting back on his baseball cap, pushing back from the table, signaling that he had finished eating.

Leonard wiped his mouth with a lone napkin, tossing it onto his plate, thinking how an expensive meal suddenly tasted so cheap and rotten on the tongue. "I'm sorry, I'm not mad at you. I'm just caught off guard, and you know I don't like being surprised. I'm going to talk to her. What time is she going to be at your mother's?"

Steven shifted his eyes away, closing his mouth into a straight line.

"Let me guess. You don't know what time she comes home. Are there any rules there?"

"Let's just forget it."

"Do you have a curfew?"

"Dad, it's just different, the rules with Mom versus here."

Leonard was about to drill into the importance of discipline, rules, structure and anything else regarding the basic foundations of parenting. Still, he had already noticed Steven shrinking in his chair. Leonard decided to drop it and treat Steven to a shopping spree at a store instead. Plus, as long as you followed his rules, he was the cool parent. Who wouldn't want to follow Leonard's rules? Everyone liked nice, new shiny things, right?

# February 1997 – The Meet

Millie was a natural on the volleyball court, with a serve that sliced just over the net, defeating any opponent waiting for the ball to pass over onto their side. The rival stood zero chance against her lightning bolt serve. Millie became known as the shark on the volleyball team in the school. Leonard loved it. He bought her the best volleyballs to practice with at home, whether at his house or her mother's. He wanted Millie to shine on and off the court, wanted Millie to own the best equipment, and wanted Millie to wear the best sneakers that promised higher jumps. He wanted her to be the best, period.

Leonard shuffled back and forth on the middle bleacher, a few rows up from the court. He never thought he would become a parent who shouted from the sidelines, but he was from the first game.

"Millie! Millie!" Leonard shouted from the stands, deciding to wear all denim today.

Millie spun around, her ponytail whipping her face, and her cheeks flushed rosy red.

"Remember what we practiced earlier. Try that next play." Leonard threw a rigid thumbs up, waiting for Millie to return the gesture. He recently built a volleyball court in his backyard and practiced with her until ten at night, right before heavy matches. He loved it and only assumed she did, too.

Millie lined up at the baseline, winding up to deliver the serve that shook the gymnasium. Leonard mimicked the moves they practiced together. She threw the ball up in the air. Leonard tossed his imaginary ball in the air. Millie tipped back, and Leonard twisted his back into the motion.

BAM! The other team never stood a chance. Another ace under Millie's perfect record. Leonard jumped high up, almost losing his footing once he landed back onto the narrower than expected bleachers. He followed up her victory with two claps and a whistle.

Millie shot back a look at Leonard, and when she saw him jumping up and down, she smiled her approval, skipping to the center to join her teammates in their huddle.

Leonard glanced to his right, catching a woman trying not to laugh... at him. He looked behind his shoulder, making sure he wasn't mistaken as the object of this stranger's amusement.

"Hi..." said Leonard, turning his body in her direction. "Did I do something?"

"I like your enthusiasm," said the woman, gesturing to the volleyball game starting.

Leonard turned back to the court, realizing he missed one of Millie's starts, and it was an occurrence that never happened, but he decided to drink in this woman's presence. She was almost as tall as Leonard, so above average for a woman, with stick-straight black hair, fair skin, and big wide eyes that already swallowed him whole. Her subtle style balanced out her urban appeal. She definitely did not live on Long Island.

"My daughter is on the team. The home team. She's the best server they've got." Leonard pointed to Millie, who obviously just scored another ace.

"I'm watching my niece. I'm not sure which team she's on. But she's not on the same side your daughter is playing on," said the woman, wincing at her cluelessness. "Her mom couldn't make it, so I'm here to support the game, I guess? I'm the cool aunt."

Leonard just smiled, unsure of what to say. He cast his eyes back onto the court, seeing Millie's serve was up, only to realize he must have missed a play between the brief banter.

"I'm not from here. I'm a city gal," said the woman.

"I know."

"How do you know?" She crossed her arms, straining the fabric of her midnight blue blazer with gold buttons across her sharp shoulder blades.

"I can tell these things." Leonard's eyes scanned the woman from head to toe, eliciting a brief shiver from her.

"So, you're clairvoyant, is that what you're telling me?" The woman scooted half a step closer to Leonard.

"I'm a lot of things. Where in the city do you live?" Before he allowed her to answer, Leonard held up a finger. "Let me guess. You're an uptown girl."

She couldn't fight the smile from his perception. "Yes. Yes, I am."

Leonard tapped his chin, mock thinking. "Upper East side?"

Her jaw dropped half an inch. "How did you know?"

"I work in the city. I see your type out to lunch every day."

"So, I guess you frequent the places my kind eats in?" She raised her eyebrow.

Leonard nodded his head to concede.

"Dad! Come here." Millie motioned Leonard to join her on the floor.

"Wait here. I'll be right back," said Leonard to the woman. He jogged to Millie in no time, skipping half the risers to his daughter. "You're doing great out there. Your serve is on fire today."

"I missed a shot before, you didn't see?" said Millie, her eyes darkening.

"Nah, you're being hard on yourself. You're doing great."

"You missed it when you were talking to that woman." Millie peered over Leonard's shoulder to the stranger on the risers. "Who is she?"

Leonard followed Millie's gaze before turning back to Millie. "I actually have no idea. We just started talking. I don't even know her name." Leonard searched her face, knowing he had lost a piece of Millie to the woman he had just met. It was always a battle between Millie and whatever woman was in Leonard's bed. It shouldn't be this way, but he expected it and grew used to the game of see-saw he had no choice but to play. "Hey, I'm here for you. Just focus on the game and nothing else. I'm cheering for you the whole time, okay?"

Leonard also wanted to say he envisioned a beefy scholarship to any college, but he didn't want to freak Millie out completely. He patted her twice on the back before she launched back onto the court and landed another ace. He clapped and whistled, watching her score another brilliant serve, watching how his girl was a natural volleyball player, and he pictured great things ahead. He couldn't pinpoint what for sure, but he knew they existed.

Leonard skipped his way back onto the bleachers. The woman stood in the same position, with her arms crossed with an amused smile plastered to her face.

"What?" Leonard asked, scanning his eyes over the stranger.

"You're cute acting like a father," she said.

"I am a father." Leonard stepped back, a tad offended.

"You look young to be a dad." She nodded towards Millie.

The compliment washed over Leonard like a warm velvet shower. He chuckled, smoothing his thick hair back. "I'm Leonard. What's your name?"

"It's nice to meet you, finally."

"Finally?" asked Leonard, tilting his head.

"I'm Becky."

# *November 25ᵗʰ, 2021*

Leonard just finished recounting to Jill how he met the social climber, Becky. It was also the first time since saying the story aloud when he realized that was one of the last times he had witnessed Millie at her best.

When Leonard often reminisced about his past, he would go out of order with the sequence of events, only to relive the night when the dinner ritual spawned. He viewed it as one of the rare organic moments in his life because, during those dinners, there were no distractions, no women to pull Leonard's attention away. It was just him and Jackie in the booth.

"I'm not sure how I feel about Becky," said Jill, amused by the anecdote. She lay supine across Leonard's bare torso, twirling her hair around an index finger. She chuckled, staring at Leonard, whose eyes were glued to the ceiling.

"What are you thinking?" Leonard propped himself up on an elbow.

Jill snorted. An actual snort escaped her nose. "This guy can clearly be bought off, Rosen."

"I know where you're heading with this, and I already told you the answer is no."

"But why not? You want to keep your grandson here. It's just money."

"I'll never be able to match his price. Six hundred a month and a few free meals, sure. And that's just to see him once a week, guaranteed. Look what happened to today? They refuse to let me into their house, and because I never extended myself for more than the weekly stipend... dessert canceled." Leonard shook his head. The more he spoke about the arrangement, the more pathetic he sounded. He was a cunning man, at least in his business dealings. But personally, he landed flat on his face the more he thought about his past relationships, dealings with his children, even in this hotel room with Jill. Everything appeared off and not how it should be. Nothing clicked.

"Everybody has a number," said Jill.

"You're making it sound so simple."

"Jesse doesn't sound that complicated. He's motivated by money."

"Everybody is to a degree. But what? I'm supposed to ask him to hand me his son for a price? A grotesque number?" Leonard twisted his face, thinking about what Jesse might challenge as the right price to agree to such an agreement.

"What's your number?" Jill raised an eyebrow.

"A million dollars."

"Wow, you had that number ready to roll."

"I'm ready to give it. But I know it won't be enough."

"You really think someone who doesn't have much money will turn down a million dollars?"

"Yes. He's not a fool. A million dollars these days, sounds so generic. And they're a young family. It only gets you so far."

Jill laughed, throwing her head back, annoying Leonard a bit. He fought off an angry leg shake.

"What kind of fancy life do you expect these people to lead?"

Leonard shook his head, not humoring the mocking tone thrown in his direction. He locked his lips with a twist of his fingers. Jill rolled her eyes.

"I'm just saying don't lose hope yet. You got your night with Jackie for all these years for the right price. And as I said before, everybody has a number."

"Would you ever give up your kids for the right price?"

"I would never give up my kids. And I would never be bought off to allow them to see a close relative once a week. But Jesse did that. He has a number."

She wasn't wrong. Leonard barely knew Jill, and she barely understood the full scope of the situation, but she was not incorrect in her observation. Jesse bartered a social arrangement with Leonard once. Maybe it could be mimicked again but in a much grander scale.

"You know, for once, I might just listen to a woman in my life and take their advice." Leonard ran a hand up and down Jill's silk smooth arm.

She watched his hand move. "Don't lose focus, Rosen."

"I'm just taking a break."

Jill squeezed his hand until his fingertips turned a shade pink. "You will figure this out."

"You really believe so?"

"Everybody has a number, Rosen. Everybody."

# *May 1994 - Blended*

"You're going to love Rachel," said Leonard, standing over a wild, carbohydrate-fueled spread of breakfast debauchery. It was his weekend finally, after what felt like an eternity because all he wanted to do was tell his kids about his second fiancée and to get their approval so he could move forward. Not that their disapproval would deter him from continuing the plan with Rachel, but it was nice for everyone to be harmonious and on the same page.

Millie and Steven barely touched their croissants filled with the smoothest and most decadent chocolate money could buy. At least that's what the pastry shop owner explained to Leonard as he purchased the overpriced delicacies.

"Kiddos eat up. I went all out on today's food." Leonard's eyes shifted from Millie to Steven and then back to Millie. "What? Is something wrong?"

His kids exchanged a look only they shared an understanding for and no one else. Leonard was a known outsider, and he detested the feeling.

"I'll give five dollars to whoever decides to talk first." Leonard wasn't kidding as he reached into his wallet and pulled out a crisp five-dollar bill. Both kids' eyes grew wide within mere seconds. Leonard smiled, knowing he had won this battle. They were going to talk. "C'mon. I'm waiting..."

"Mom said this was going to happen," said Millie.

"Hey! That's not fair. She didn't give me a chance to talk," said Steven, who crossed his arms as his ears turned a shade of beet red.

A dark shadow flashed over Leonard's face, causing Millie to recoil in her seat. Steven was still transfixed on the money, not paying attention to anything else.

"What do you mean? What did your mother say?" said Leonard to Millie.

Millie bit her lip, squirming in her seat. She wanted to speak, but Leonard saw her nerves seeping out of her skin. He reached across the table, taking her hand. "You can tell me anything. You're not in trouble, and I won't get upset."

"If I talk now, can I have some money?" said Steven.

"No, you had your chance." Leonard slid the money in front of Millie.

She took the bill and gave it to Steven without hesitation. As Leonard always described her to his clients, Millie was his girl with a golden heart. He referred to Millie as his prize and Steven as the troublemaker, yet he still loved them equally.

"Mom said you would find a new woman with a new family, and they would become your family while forgetting about us," said Millie.

Leonard's skin clammed up as he fought a maddening heartbeat. "She said that?" He could barely speak, holding a steady tone.

"Are you going to say anything?" said Millie, crossing her arms over her body, keeping in the warmth. "She'll get upset with us. We promised not to say anything."

"Yeah, she'll get so mad," said Steven.

Leonard smiled. "I won't say a thing. I promise." He cleared his throat, straightening his posture. "But, listen. I want you to meet

Rachel. She's actually going to join us for breakfast. She's really excited to meet both of you. And guess what?"

"What?" said Millie and Steven in unison.

"She has twins. Two identical boys. Isn't that cool?" Leonard couldn't contain his smile. "It'll be like the brother you never had." Leonard pointed to Steven. "And twin brothers you always wanted," said Leonard to Millie.

"I never said I wanted twin brothers," said Millie.

"Twins are cool. I have twins in my school," said Steven.

"And what's even better? They're eight years old. So, you'll be close in age. We don't have to deal with any babies," said Leonard.

"Aw, but I love babies," said Millie.

"Babies just poop and cry," said Steven.

"That's not entirely true, but you guys can jump in and play together. Won't that be so much fun?" said Leonard. No one sounded convinced.

"I love babies. I can't wait to have one," said Millie.

A flutter rippled across Leonard's chest. This conversation really gave Leonard's vital organs a beating so far. "Relax, you're only ten." And his little girl, Leonard, wanted to add but decided to stop talking.

"I still can't wait to have a baby. Do you think I'll be a good mommy?"

Leonard wanted to say, of course, just do the opposite of your mother, but he kept it simple. "You will be the best mommy. But wait a few years and find yourself a nice husband first. You promise?"

"Okay," said Millie, with the widest dreamy eyes staring back at him.

"I never want to have kids, gross," said Steven.

Leonard scrunched his brow and bit his tongue. Steven was only eight and was right in not wanting children. But Leonard suddenly wished to teach his kids to avoid resigning to the term 'never'.' It wasn't in his blood, and he wanted to ensure his own kids followed his thinking.

"Let's not make any heavy decisions today, deal?"

"Dad?" asked Millie, picking at a strawberry-filled croissant. "Are Rachel and her kids going to live here with you?"

Leonard swallowed a hefty amount of saliva before answering. "Yes. They're probably moving in within the next few months."

"They're going to live here every day? With you?" said Millie.

"I'm not sharing my room. I want my own room," said Steven, scarfing down a blueberry muffin.

"Well, yeah, every day. Don't worry. Both of you will keep your rooms. I'm already planning an expansion, so everyone won't feel cluttered." Leonard searched Millie's face for approval, but she wasn't breaking, and it broke him instead. "Millie, you know that you and Steven will always be my kids first. We're just expanding now as a family. Moving on to exciting things, you know?"

"How come we can't live with you every day?" said Millie.

"It's how your mother and I worked things out when our family changed." Leonard exhaled, running a sweaty palm through his gelled hair. It was something new he tried for a hair product. "Do you guys want to live here all the time?"

Steven rolled his eyes, so over this sappy conversation, while Millie shot a glance at Leonard, enough to reveal her answer.

"But Mom will be alone all the time," said Millie, not making eye contact with anyone.

Leonard pursed his lips. It's not like anyone thought about his loneliness on the days when his kids weren't with him. He also knew Claire didn't date.

Leonard was about to respond when a black Jeep turning into his driveway from the window caught his eye. Rachel and the twin boys had arrived. It was now or never to introduce everyone, and Leonard couldn't suppress his excitement. He created an urgent drumroll on his custom live edge wood slab table and leaned over the feast. "They have arrived. Here, follow me."

Leonard had to stop himself from running to the front door just so he knew his kids weren't far behind him. Before he turned the brass knob, he spun around, almost bumping into Millie. "Just promise me you guys will at least be polite. No one has to be best friends right away. But we're going to be a real big family soon. Okay?"

Millie and Steven nodded, not a hint of emotion tracked across their faces. Leonard returned with a forced smile, sucked in his breath, and opened the door.

"Welcome, welcome," said Leonard, motioning Rachel and her invisible children into the house. He looked over Rachel's shoulder, searching for her boys. "I thought you were bringing the boys?"

Rachel rolled her eyes, spinning around to the car. "Boys! I said get your asses out of the car!"

Leonard jumped back, a bit startled by the outburst and the language. He turned around to quickly check his own children, flashing a weak grin at them.

Rachel sighed. "They are being so difficult today. I swear, I can't wait until it's their father's weekend." She popped her gum, still staring at her Jeep, waiting for her two brats to emerge.

Leonard placed a hand on her shoulder. "We all have those days with kids."

"Those days?" Rachel scanned Leonard like he had two heads. "It's every day with these monsters. I swear, they're just like their father. They didn't get these genes from me."

Leonard half smiled. "I do recall you getting testy at a waiter the other week when the bread served wasn't warmed to your liking."

"Oh, come on. I asked for warm bread, and they brought it barely toasted to the table. The nerve." Rachel popped her gum twice between her cheesy white teeth. She peered behind Leonard's shoulder, her eyes landing on a frozen Millie and Steven. "Are these them?"

Leonard winced at the choppy grammar he suddenly noticed just now. Did she always sound this common? He spun around and gestured to his children. "This is Millie and Steven. In that age order, too."

Rachel scuffled over to them, her red heels punching the marble entryway floor. "Oh my god, look at the two of you. You are so cute." Rachel squinted through her puffy eyes, examining Millie and Steven. "We're going to have so much fun together, and you can call me whatever you want. Just not mother. That sounds old. And no one is old here, right Leonard?"

Leonard raised his eyebrows, agreeing with Rachel, and she smiled at him, revealing a red lipstick-stained tooth. He tried to signal her to lick her tooth by pointing at her mouth, but she didn't get it.

The twins opened the rear passenger door on the driver's side, each hopping out, revealing their blond, spiked hair. They looked like the oldest and most challenging eight-year-old boys Leonard had ever witnessed. They were carrying something, though; whatever it was, it had a hose hooked up to black backpacks. It was too late for Leonard to warn everyone in the house when he realized each twin came equipped with fully loaded, bazooka-sized water guns, already firing off jet streams of water from the Jeep's trunk.

Leonard threw himself in front of Millie and Steven, taking the brunt of the water being fired in their direction, as Rachel charged at her devil sons, kicking up gravel from the circular driveway.

"You little shits! Give me those guns," she screamed at the top of her lungs. "Just wait until your father has you."

Her threats didn't quell the twins' gusto as the boys laughed and ran while firing water in her direction, soaking their mother shamelessly.

Steven tugged on Leonard's soaked pant leg. "Dad, I'm not sharing a room with them."

"I know, I know. Don't worry. Nothing will change." Leonard shifted his gaze to Millie, who had just studied the wrecking ball scene unfolding in the driveway, and his heart ached for his little girl, but he didn't know what to do to make anything better.

Leonard knew he needed to call Greg first thing in the morning and redo his drafted prenuptial agreement and will. Leonard just sensed that things might not go as planned if the scene in his driveway indicated the future.

# May 1991 – Custody

Greg devoured the bloodiest, ketchup-filled burger, the likes of which New York had never seen. Leonard almost lost his appetite watching his divorce attorney scarf down this heart attack on a plate in record time.

Greg caught Leonard staring with the driest of mouths before extracting a napkin from the aluminum container, wiping burger juice from his chin. "Don't act like you're not jealous."

"Jealous of what?" said Leonard.

"That I look this good eating like this." Greg slapped his pot belly.

Leonard wiped his spotless mouth since he barely touched his food, fighting off waves of queasiness induced by stress from the divorce. Greg warned Leonard before battle that this would be a sticky proceeding, and he'd just never clarified that his prediction would be a gross understatement.

"Greg, what's next? I can't take this much longer."

Greg scrunched his eyebrows, pushing his plate to the side. "I'm surprised this is getting to you. I have two groups of clients, and you, I assumed, would fall into the category of easy divorces."

"What's that supposed to mean?"

"You started the divorce. You painted her as a horrible person. I thought you'd be thrilled to get rid of her." Greg jammed a pinky into his mouth, dislodging stuck food.

"I am relieved, but you don't know what she does to me. She's trying to torture me."

Greg laughed, causing his belly to jiggle.

"I'm serious. She's turning all my friends against me. Spreading these vicious lies. Meantime I'm stuck with all her credit card debt she rang up on my cards."

"If your so-called friends are this easily swayed by a pathological liar, then you didn't want them as friends to begin with."

Leonard drummed his fingers on the table, searching around for the unknown. "That raises the nagging question of what's next with the kids."

"I thought we agreed to joint custody. You get the kids every other weekend. Both parents must reside in the same school district. That's key. Don't forget."

Leonard started shaking his head no while Greg's face dropped.

"What am I missing here, Leo?"

It was the first time anyone had called him Leo, and Leonard didn't challenge it.

"I'm thinking I should go for sole custody."

Greg squeezed the bridge of his nose, producing a guttural groan. "This is a slippery road. And expensive."

"I mean, if Claire is spreading lies to adults about me, God only knows what she's telling our children. Also, she's fucking nuts."

"I'm not arguing with you. I know a liar when I see one. But..."

"I can't believe this." Leonard slammed his hand onto the table. "What rights do I have?"

"The courts like to grant custody to the mother and let the father have them on the weekends. Every other weekend."

"Why? She's a fucking loon."

"Well, we'll need to prove just how crazy she is, then. But it's not easy, and it ain't cheap."

Leonard crossed his arms. "Talk to me numbers-wise, first."

"Consider your legal bills just shot up by another ten grand. Remember, you're probably going to be held responsible for her legal bills since she had no access to her own money while you were together. So, your bill goes up, and so does hers."

Leonard tugged on his tightening shirt collar. "Just fucking great. You know I had a bad year with the housing market. I couldn't concentrate because of Claire. And then, on top of it, she maxes out the credit cards. Here, I'm scraping to make it through the end of the day. And now, to do what's right by my kids, I need to figure out if I have enough money to even pay for it."

"How is business for you?"

"Don't worry," said Leonard, waving a hand at Greg's question. "I'll always have enough money for your bill."

Greg pursed his lips, fighting off his original question.

"I've started to flip houses, and I think I'm onto something. Now tell me, what else is bad other than the money?"

"We'll need to first have Claire evaluated by a psychiatrist to determine her mental health. And then we'll need to find a child specialist to question your kids on the stand to hear them say where they want to live. All this happens while your ex and your kids live together, by the way."

Leonard wiped the sweat from the back of his neck, losing a vicious battle with his petulant leg shake.

"And none of these decisions are made overnight," Greg said. "So, while your kids say they want to live with you, let's assume there could be nights between that testimony and the court's decision to rule in your favor. All the while, home with the fucking loon, as you call her."

Leonard kept shaking his head, darting his eyes wildly about the spinning cafeteria room.

"Wait, it gets better." Greg held up a single index finger. "Let's say your ex is deemed unstable and unfit to care for your kids. Yes, you'll get custody, but do you know who else you'll need to take care of?"

Leonard's jaw dropped, already knowing the answer.

"Claire. She'll become your responsibility."

"What? But how? How is she my burden once we're divorced?" The numbness flashed across Leonard's right side of his face. He blinked the tingling sensation at the crease of his eye away.

"This is how the laws and courts work. No one said it was fair."

"It's more like fucking twisted if you ask me. What kind of responsibility would I have towards Claire if she failed her mental exam?"

"You'd be responsible for her financially, her medical costs, if she were ever institutionalized... that would be on you. Her overall well-being. This is what happens sometimes, and no one ever said it's fair. The law isn't fair, my friend."

Leonard pushed his chair a foot away from the table, attempting to inhale the fresh air, despite his lungs weighing in his chest like cinder blocks.

Before Leonard blinked, his feet carried him away from the table and into the men's room. He splashed cold water over his face before soaking his hair. Fighting to catch his breath, he breathed into a pile of crumpled white napkins in his hands. He was going to lose this battle, and he didn't even care about the cost of his wallet. He couldn't put his kids through the testimony against their mother, only to send them home with her while they awaited the judge's decision. There were no guarantees here. Leonard could lose his custody battle after having ugly truths come out, resulting in an unchanged outcome. No one would be safe, and it would be his doing.

He knew he would head back to the table once his heart calmed and tell Greg to forget the whole idea and any other notion that already changed the hashed-out plans Leonard agreed to with Claire. If his children were safe, then it was all Leonard could ask for. He just hoped his final decision in this bathroom was the correct one.

# *December 1990 – Gregory*

"I heard you're the best," said Leonard to an attorney named Greg Cohen. Mr. Cohen came highly recommended by one of Leonard's contacts within his inner real estate broker circle. His pulse remained rampant from when he stepped into the mahogany-rich waiting room and the equally wooden room riddled with higher education diplomas. Leonard counted at least ten nailed to the wall, circling him like sharks.

Greg held up two tanned hands, fingers decorated with various rings probably from colleges, jewelry draped on each pinky finger, and a sunlit gold wedding band, as if to show off that he conquered many of life's milestones. "Where did you hear about me again?"

"A real estate broker of mine. He said he used you for his prenup and said you'd be the guy if he ever got a divorce."

"Ah..." Greg gazed at the ceiling, shaking his head. "I love it when they plan ahead." He shifted his focus to Leonard, a sudden dark shadow crossing his face. "And what is it you do? Real estate, I assume?"

"I was a real estate broker...I am. I still am. I still have my license. But I'm looking to switch gears. I still want to be in real estate, but I'll be honest with you. I've hit a bit of a rough patch." Leonard's rough patch equated to a year of no sales, poor stock market investments, overspending, and newly uncovered debt from his soon-to-be ex-wife Claire that left him strapped for pennies. He was a phone call away from calling his mother to move in for a month, so he could get his life together but was saved by his younger baby brother's offer to move in.

Greg sighed, tossing his black fountain pen onto the blank sheet of yellow legal pad paper. "I hope you know I'm not cheap. My retainer fee makes that clear. So, before we go forward, I want to ensure we understand what's being expected. I like to think I do my job ten times better when I know my bill gets paid on time."

Leonard held up a hand, stopping Greg from rambling further. How dramatic this man appeared in the mere minutes of conversing with him. "I wouldn't be here if I knew I couldn't afford you. I'm starting to turn it around and keep my overhead low in the meantime."

Greg's face brightened, not from the natural light spilling in from his clear, unshaded windows but from the guarantee that his bill would be paid promptly. "What do you do now?"

"Real estate still, but now I've started to flip. So far, I've sold two really fast projects. Hoping to keep the momentum going. Who knows, maybe I'll own a bunch of properties one day."

Greg shifted forward in his seat, licking his lips quickly, a move Leonard would grow to know as Greg's shark fin raising for the kill. "Well, if you ever need a real estate attorney, I practice that as well, but that's a different conversation for another day."

Leonard nodded, agreeing.

"So, tell me," said Greg. "What's your deal with your estranged wife?"

That bitch, Leonard thought already, his stomach swishing the contents of his half-eaten egg sandwich from this morning. Here he went, ready to spill—the story, not his lunch.

Greg pulled his blank yellow legal pad dead center onto his blotter with a black obsolete fountain pen in hand. Leonard stared at the pen, half a centimeter above the paper, ready to write. Suddenly, though, Leonard was unsure if he could speak. He never wanted this divorce. No, not at all. He fantasized about their forever when he proposed to Claire on the Long Beach boardwalk. Kids that led to grandkids and maybe great grandkids if time was good to him and Claire. He could still have all of that, but not with Claire and their family unit as one.

"Would you like anything to drink before we begin?" asked Greg.

"Diet Coke would be great," said Leonard, forcing out the words with a sputter.

Two minutes later, Leonard nursed a crisp diet soda as he battled the ringing in his ears. Halfway through the beverage, he was ready to start figuring out his divorce with Greg.

"What is the reason you're seeking a divorce?" said Greg.

Leonard's eyes darted about the room, searching for an answer he knew by heart. He just needed to figure out a way to articulate in a cotton candy manner. "Um... we stopped getting along, and she really started to change."

"Can you be more specific?"

Fuck it, Leonard thought. If he couldn't be honest with this guy, then why even go through a divorce. He needed to be free and refused to settle. He tossed his sugar-coated ideas out the window and decided to just say it. "Claire is bat shit fucking crazy. Like really, fucking nuts. She's a pathological liar. Spent all of my money. Faked injuries. Faked cooking our meals for us and our children when she would cry to me about how long she slaved over the oven just so I could have a hot plate of food to come home to. Meantime, it was a rotisserie store-bought chicken and frozen vegetables she tossed onto a plate."

Leonard watched the man write at a speed he never thought possible, but after observing Greg jot down every word, Leonard started to believe that this guy was the best.

"And eventually..." Leonard stopped speaking for a moment to gather his nerves. A sprinkle of sweat bloomed on his stubble-free mustache. "I started to sleep around. Not with a lot of women, but just a few. She finally went through my beeper, jotted down phone numbers, and called them." Leonard rolled his eyes. If only Claire had invested this much time into acting normal, then maybe things would have worked out for them, for their family. But she didn't cheat. Leonard did. He shouldn't have done that. He always said that if he were to cheat, he should just end the relationship. He faltered in this stance with Claire, and now he faced the hell he walked right into.

A thick stream of oxygen entered and exited through Greg's nostrils with a heavy force, his only reaction. "So, you have children. How many?"

Leonard swallowed a lump the size of a golf ball. "Millie, who's six, and Steven is four."

Greg flipped to a new page. "What's everyone's living situation right now?"

"The kids live with Claire in our house. I'm staying with my brother Robert. I'm about twenty-five minutes away from the house."

"What are your goals with pursuing the divorce? Custody? Alimony? You will need to pay alimony probably and child support. I'm assuming Claire did not work during your time together," said Greg, emotionless.

Leonard shook his head no. It was an unspoken arrangement for Claire to stop working once she became pregnant with Millie. Even before Millie, she barely worked. When Claire met Leonard, it was as if her full-time job puttered out to barely a part-time one. When Leonard attempted to recall what Claire actually did, he couldn't say.

"How would you like me to represent you? What do you want this divorce to result in?"

Leonard was confused. The only thing he thought about divorce until now was breaking away from the person you couldn't stand. He never thought about anything past that point, but he had kids. And then everything turned complicated. He stopped worrying about himself and began worrying about them. How could he forget about his children? He would get away from Claire, but not them. They would be with her. Then his mind raced. Were they safe? Would he lose them? What were his rights? What were Claire's rights to keep him from seeing his children? If he was going to be their sole provider, he better get to see his kids. At least once a week... or more.

The panic crept into his chest, spiraling down to his fingertips, triggering a numbness. He grabbed his sweating glass of soda but couldn't feel the cup. He squeezed the glass harder until he saw it slide away from his hands, smashing onto the floor. He never felt the glass leave his skin because he couldn't feel anything. His body succumbed to the numbing panic his mind triggered. He forgot what tools he had to combat the anxiety. He should have continued with therapy. He should have done a lot of things. But here he sat in a chair, losing himself to the panic and the thought of losing his kids.

It was all too much. The world threw spots in his field of vision until his head hit the floor.

He never recalled falling out or sliding from the chair, but he'd never forget the look on Greg's face hovering above Leonard's once he returned from his brief sleep.

Greg cradled Leonard's head in his hands, holding his soda to Leonard's semi-parched lips. He took a grateful sip until there was no more left to drink.

"Thank you," said Leonard, so quietly that Greg leaned in closer just to hear the words.

"Leo... can I call you Leo?"

Leonard nodded.

"Leo... in all my years of practice, you are the first client to faint on me. And I sure as heck hope you'll be the last. I'm going to take care of your case. I'm going to take care of you. And I hope you'll keep me in mind once you bounce back."

And just like that, Leonard found his magic man, Greg.

# *November 10th, 1990*

It had been about two weeks since Claire kicked Leonard quietly out of the house. The night she decided to pull the plug on their marriage, he begged Claire to let him leave discreetly and not to say anything to the children until they came up with a plan. He never challenged her decision to end their marriage, but he did beg her to let things finalize peacefully for the kids' sake. He didn't want them to get hurt, even though some hurt was inevitable in a divorce. She scoffed, reminding Leonard she owed him no favors. She was correct, Leonard agreed. Except, they owed this gentle exit to their kids. At least, that's how Leonard viewed this new chapter of their lives. The children would understand, especially Millie, who was bright and wise, possessing a heart full of love and compassion far from what it should be for a girl her tender age. Steven, only four, didn't worry Leonard too much about how his immature emotions would bend from the news. Leonard just needed to go in peace, and he did.

Last night, Claire called him frantic, saying she wouldn't live a charade any longer and that they needed to tell the kids the divorce plans immediately. Fifteen hours later, Leonard, who no longer possessed a key to a house that had been his home two weeks ago, rang the doorbell, awaiting permission to enter.

He spotted Claire's blue Volvo station wagon in the driveway, knowing both kids would be home by now from school. So, where the fuck was she? Was she trying to spite him by not answering the door or reminding him she held power over his entering the house?

He wasn't sure, but all he knew was that she had to be home, and his kids were here. If he didn't have a right to enter, surely, he held a higher right to assure his children were safe from danger.

Leonard grabbed the brass doorknob, only to find it turned like silky butter in his hand. It was unlocked. How many times did Leonard warn Claire to lock the front door every time she entered and exited, especially with the uptick in burglaries over the last few weeks? Claire always rolled her eyes whenever Leonard warned her about safety. She said they lived in a safe, affluent neighborhood, and he just panicked. Leonard said that's precisely why this area was a target for sloppy people like her.

Leonard twisted the brass knob and let the door swing open with a singular, drawn-out groan. Not one light was on, either. Thank God the sunlight flooded the house with its rays.

Leonard took not even two steps inside when he found Claire sprawled out on the floor, head turned to the side, eyes closed. The scene didn't even scare him. She was breathing in her floral yellow printed dress and red Mary Janes, clasped neatly on each foot. That's when he knew this scene on the floor was a lie. She'd done this before to him, thinking it would make him care about her, heightening his attention span directed towards her. It was before he discovered her manipulative, pathological liar ways. Except for this time, he had broken away from her toxicity, but his kids were still with her, upstairs in their rooms. His stomach flipped, thinking about how they were here with Claire and not him.

"Where are Millie and Steven?" said Leonard.

She didn't move, only breathed. Her stomach rose and fell in steady breaths. Her nose twitched, trying not to break her pathetic cover.

"Where are the kids, Claire?" Leonard's pulse quickened. Until then, he had resisted the idea of going to a psychiatrist for his anxiety, mainly his panic attacks. But whenever his heartbeat increased, the fear of another episode paused his mind. Maybe he would go to one, even though he had resisted the idea his whole life.

He allowed another ten seconds of silence before he stepped over her body and climbed the carpeted staircase, clutching onto the banister with his clammy hand, hoping it didn't slip from the wood.

"Oh, they're fine," said Claire.

Leonard stopped mid-step and turned to a perfectly fine Claire sitting on the floor. The only thing out of place was her hair from laying on the floor for God-knows-how-long.

"They're in their rooms watching television. Something educational, don't worry," said Claire, straightening her pale-yellow cardigan and flicking dust off her shoulder. She locked eyes with Leonard. Those ocean blue eyes once melted him. But now, the blood in his veins froze whenever he set his eyes upon them.

Leonard skipped down the steps he had just climbed, landing inches from Claire's face. He lost control as the heat seeped out of his every pore. "What the fuck is wrong with you?" The air exited his nose in thick, heavy streams. He didn't feel like a human. He felt like a beast as his blood boiled under his sweaty skin. If he ever desired to hurt a woman, it was now how she toyed with him and put their children's lives in danger. She deserved something.

Claire smirked, running her eyes up and down Leonard's appearance, settling on his loosened yellow power tie. "What? Are you gonna hit me, Leonard? Tough day at the office?"

He pushed his tongue on the back of his upper teeth, threatening to push them out of his mouth. He bit his tongue instead, tasting blood.

"How many times have I told you to always lock the door?" Leonard pointed to the closed, locked door behind Claire's shoulder. "You're lucky it was only me and not some intruder."

Claire crossed her arms, grinning. "Well, technically, you are an intruder. I asked you to leave, nicely and quietly, per your request. You're no longer welcome here. Remember you broke up our family because you couldn't stop fucking other women?"

Leonard shushed her. "Yeah, and now that I'm gone, you're leaving our house open for someone to enter as they please."

"Already trying to paint me as the unfit parent, are you?" Claire bit her bottom lip, failing to stop the smile spreading across her makeup-caked face. "The only way you would ever get these kids is if I abandoned them. So, don't even think about that."

Leonard clicked his jaw, swallowing the fight burning in his stomach. "Let's go talk to them."

Leonard, followed by Claire, opened the door to Millie's room. Two weeks ago, her room was spotless. Now, it was the opposite, with clothes strewn across the floor, not a single toy placed back into her engraved cherry wood toy chest. Her laundry basket spilled over with dirty and clean clothes mixed. When he was here, everything was neat. There was an order. It was only a matter of time until this variety of mess filled the entire house.

He would fight for this house. Yes, that was going to be a goal from this separation. He'd let Claire and the kids stay here until things were figured out. He would be fair, but ultimately, he wanted this house back.

After Leonard walked through the rubble, his eyes shifted to Millie, who played with a baby doll set on her full bed. She pretended to feed the baby orange juice out of one of those fake baby bottles that never spilled. She took great caution not to mess up her doll's face. After each fake sip, she wiped her doll's mouth with its bib. Leonard didn't want to ruin Millie's moment, but he was going to shatter it, and all he ever wanted to do was protect her and make his little girl happy. She was his oldest but would always be his baby.

Steven played in a chair, consumed by his Gameboy. Leonard was amazed at how well Steven mastered the toy device. Not even Leonard navigated the game on Steven's level. Then it dawned on Leonard that neither child acknowledged his presence. He had been gone for two weeks, only popping in once when they got off the bus, and this was the greeting he received. He let it slide only because no one seemed terribly bothered, except for Claire, who functioned naturally as a bothered person.

Leonard turned to her, who remained in the door frame, unmoving, with her arms crossed. She shook her head, saying she would not be the one to start this conversation.

"Look who's here," said Leonard, taking a deep breath. He was about to say home but stopped himself.

Millie lifted her eyes from her doll's care, landing them on Leonard. She dropped everything, sprinting over to him. He dropped to his knees and embraced Millie's hug. Leonard's cackle filled the room the instant Millie's weight slammed into his body. She still needed him.

Steven didn't flinch from his game.

"Hey, you. Come over here... Steven. C'mon," said Leonard.

Steven shifted his eyes away from the Gameboy, unamused. He plopped the toy onto the chair and marched into Leonard's open arms. He squeezed both children close to his chest. This was his life. They were his life. He needed to be the best father to them, needed to be his best version for them. This would break their hearts, the divorce, but Leonard would pick the pieces up and somehow make it up to them.

He led both kids to the bed, lifting Millie first, followed by Steven, onto the crumpled sheets. Leonard motioned Claire to join them. She miraculously complied, dragging her feet behind her. Leonard sat next to Millie while Claire leaned against the bookshelf that didn't hold a single book. Every book was anywhere in the room, except for the bookshelf where it belonged.

"How have you been?" asked Leonard to Millie and Steven.

"Are you coming home?" said Millie, her lip quivering.

Leonard took Millie's hand, toying with each little finger in his large palm. With his other hand, he smoothed her wavy hair, staring at her green hazel eyes, the same color as his own.

"Mommy and Daddy decided we're going to change things a little. It'll be better for everyone. Right, Claire?" Leonard searched Claire's face for any help at all.

She nodded, understanding his request. She stepped towards the bed. "This is all Daddy's idea. I'm going to let him speak," said Claire, raising an evil, penciled-in eyebrow.

Leonard's chest tightened, and his throat dried. He shook it off, clearing his senses. "Your Mom and I are going to live separately, in different houses going forward." Leonard stopped a tear streaming down Millie's cheek with his thumb. "We're still a family. We will always be a family. You'll still see me. You'll see me so much, you'll probably get sick of me." Leonard mussed Steven's hair, who hadn't said a word yet. Millie couldn't stop crying.

"Would you like a tissue, Millie?" asked Leonard.

Millie nodded, leaning in, and used Leonard's shirt as his tissue. He didn't flinch and continued to pet Millie's hair.

"It's going to be okay," Leonard rocked Millie gently on his lap. "There'll be some changes, but nothing bad."

Leonard caught Claire out of the corner of his eye. A single tear streaked Claire's face. She stared at the ceiling, refusing to look at him.

Millie lifted her head just enough to meet Leonard's gaze. "Will you forget us?"

"I would never. I love you both so much." Leonard's voice cracked. He pulled Millie into his space, never wanting to let her go. He fought back the tears. He needed to be strong. The Rosen men were strong.

"Stop crying, Millie," said Steven.

Leonard leaned over, rubbing Steven's shoulder as he consoled Millie, patting her head, not curbing any of her tears.

"You're such a cry baby," said Steven, forcing both index fingers up each of his tiny nostrils, sticking his tongue out at Millie.

"Steven, that's enough," said Leonard. He glanced in Claire's direction, hoping for some help, but was met with a blank stare.

Steven extracted both fingers from his nose, staring at his left pointer finger. He lost a shade of color in his face and jammed his finger back into his nose.

Leonard scrunched his brow, studying Steven, noticing the boy's squirming as he dug for gold.

"Is everything okay, Steven?" said Leonard.

"It's stuck!" A sweat broke out on Steven's forehead as he transformed into a beet red.

Leonard jumped off the bed, landing inches from a flailing Steven. The boy wouldn't free his finger that was jammed way up his nose.

Leonard grabbed Steven's shoulders, failing to settle his son. "What's going on, Steven? What's stuck?" Leonard tried to control the volume of his voice but failed.

"A marble!" Steven screamed.

Leonard grabbed Steven's face with one hand, stilling his head while prying open Steven's nose. Leonard let go of everything, whipping around to Claire. "You were standing in front of him the whole time, and you didn't see him shove this up his nose?"

Claire dropped her arms, rolling her eyes. "I guess I'll call the pediatrician's office to see if they have an appointment."

"Oh, screw the pediatrician. I'm taking him to the ER." Leonard couldn't even face Claire. She didn't care. This was a bother for her, that's what Leonard surmised. He grabbed Steven off the bed, almost dragging the boy out of the room.

Millie bolted off the bed, face swollen and her eyes bloodshot from the incessant tears. "Dad, wait. Can I come?"

Leonard frowned. To say no to Millie meant shattering her world or what remained. He glanced at Claire for any direction, maybe even an answer.

Claire crossed her arm, shrugging. She resumed her position of leaning on the dusty bookshelf.

"You can come," said Leonard, softening his voice and outstretched his hand for not even half a second before Millie grabbed onto it.

"I'm going to stay here. Get dinner ready for you kids when you're back. Something yummy, I promise," said Claire, smiling through the tiniest of slits in her eyes.

Of course, she wasn't going to go. With his luck, she'd probably fake another accident when Leonard returned from the hospital. To imagine she would live with his kids full-time triggered an impossible knot in his stomach. He was already tipped off by a few friends at his brokerage house over custody battles and how the courts favored the biological mothers. He would lose.

"Fine. And lock the door after we leave. Goddammit." Leonard stormed out of the house, holding each of his children's hands-free for the first time. Millie hugged his forearm, pulling him close, and for once, Leonard knew he had made the right choice.

# How It Began

**ROSEN**

MICHELLE HALL

# March 14<sup>th</sup>, 1988

It was Millie's fourth birthday, and all she wanted to do was go to the beach to pick seashells of all shapes, sizes, and colors, as she repeatedly told Leonard in the week leading up to the event. During the serene, sun-ridden car ride, she told Leonard all about her goals for her big giant day. She kept emphasizing the key detail of wanting to go to the beach with him and kept saying, "Daddy will help me." He couldn't say no. The only answer for her was yes.

He couldn't believe she was four; it only felt like five minutes ago she was born. Now she walked beautifully, spoke like an adult, picked out her clothes, and insisted on privacy when she used the potty. Time moved too quickly, and if Millie's birthday wish was to go to the beach with her daddy, he would never deny her of such a pure want.

Claire was supposed to come but at the last minute canceled because she claimed Steven didn't let her sleep at all the night prior from his latest teething spell. Steven was a bull once the sun set and the midnight blue blanketed the sky, and the one thing Claire permitted Leonard to do at night was sleep. If Claire needed some time to rest, then Leonard couldn't argue. Millie was easy to handle these days. She was fun to hang out with, actually.

Leonard pulled out his tripod and Fuji camera from his trunk. He wanted to capture every second of this day and rationalized the purchase of a super expensive camera with a built-in timer executed by a hand-held remote. It was the latest of its design on the market.

Thank goodness he planned ahead since Claire decided to skip the last minute. At first, Leonard winced at the price tag, but now Claire's absence validated the purchase.

By the time Leonard unloaded Millie and his camera equipment from his car, he could barely catch his breath. He had no idea how Claire did this with two toddlers daily, but it was a task he didn't envy. He loved being with his children but appreciated his breaks. Maybe that's why he went in for the kill with every real estate deal he chased. He loved the thrill of making money and then spending it how he pleased. Although she went overboard, especially on that diamond tennis bracelet she insisted was a must-buy, even though she wasn't athletic in the least and never played tennis, he also got a kick out of watching Claire spend it. She insisted it was a look.

The wind whipped Leonard's face and extracted a yelp from Millie as she covered her head with her tiny hands but failed to shield her face. Her pink puffer fought the bitter wind as Leonard's hair flew in all directions. He tucked his equipment under one arm while reaching for Millie with his free, ungloved hand.

"Come, baby. Grab Daddy's hand."

"I'm not a baby. I'm a big girl," said Millie, taking Leonard's hand.

"You are a big girl. Daddy was wrong." Leonard spotted something furry under Millie's arm and, for whatever reason, caused his heartbeat to falter. "What do you have under your arm there, Millie?"

"Pinky Rose!" Millie held her beloved stuffed pink bunny high in the air, showing it off to the clear blue sky.

"I didn't know you brought Pinky Rose with you." Leonard pictured that rabbit filling up with sand and inundating his car with the beach. He knew how to dust off shoes, but not a toy bunny.

Millie squeezed Pinky Rose to her chest.

"You don't think Pinky Rose will get all sandy? We want to keep Pinky Rose clean."

"Mom lets me bring Pinky Rose everywhere with me. She's my best friend."

Leonard still could not get over how well Millie spoke. Even her preschool teachers commented on his daughter's excellent speech. It was like conversing with a tiny woman. He loved it.

"Then Daddy lets you bring Pinky Rose everywhere too."

"Are you sure?"

"Of course, I am."

"You're not mad?" said Millie, staring up at Leonard with eyes bigger than the ocean.

"I could never be mad at you. Plus, it's your birthday. We can do whatever you want." Leonard squeezed her hand tighter, and she squeezed his hand back. "What would you like to do first?"

"Pick seashells by the ocean," said Millie, jumping high in the air.

Leonard spread out the dolphin-patterned beach towel and placed his camera equipment within a few feet of him and their shell-picking activity. Millie couldn't wait to start piling up the shells, and all Leonard wanted to do was set up his tripod. After failing to negotiate with her to wait while he placed the camera on the tripod, even using ice cream as a bribe, Leonard surrendered. He gathered all the black half shells, per Millie's instructions, while she picked the pretty shells, as she stated.

"What should we do with all the black shells?" said Leonard. He dumped two more handfuls of shells into a bucket, filling it to the top.

"Um... Baby Stevie can have the black ones."

"I thought you said the black shells were ugly?" Leonard cast a hand over his eyes. The sun was beyond strong today, like the brightest flashlight in the sky.

"I did." Millie smiled, catching every sun ray behind her head. She didn't squint an inch.

Millie's light compared nothing to the sun's. Everything around her seemed dim with how brightly she shined. Leonard knew he needed to capture their moment on the beach before the time slipped away. She was already four years old. The time went too quickly. It simply wasn't fair. He wanted to freeze time but knew it wasn't an option. So, he resorted to the next best idea: to take a picture.

"Millie, you stay here while Daddy sets up the camera."

"Can I still pick shells?"

"Of course, you can," said Leonard, running away from Millie, fighting off horrible visions of her being plucked away. He ran backward to quell his nerves and intrusive thoughts.

"Bring Pinky Rose!" said Millie, not looking up from her task. She knew how to order people around and had Leonard wrapped around her tiny toddler finger. Was she still a toddler at four?

Leonard grabbed Pinky Rose and what he originally came for, darting back to Millie. He fought his nerves, catching his breath, but set up the camera.

"Okay, baby girl. Are you ready to take a picture?"

"Can Pinky Rose be in it?"

"Of course, she can be." Leonard handed the bunny to Millie, who jammed it under her arm.

Leonard hoped the wind wouldn't knock over his plan. He bought a tripod with a weighted base, and the salesperson swore it was wind resistant. Leonard really didn't care what the sales kid preached. He knew the tripod was heavy, but he never expected the winds today. He palmed the pint-sized remote in his hand, scooping Millie and the bunny up in one arm.

"Okay, just look straight at the camera and smile." Leonard pushed through another bitter wind, grimacing.

"Daddy, how do you make money?"

Leonard rolled his eyes, just wanting Millie to smile.

"Just smile first, okay?"

"But I want to know."

"Let's take the picture first, Millie." Leonard hoisted Millie a drop higher, forgetting how much she weighed. She was lean but solid.

"Mommy tells the phone you make a lot of money."

Leonard frowned, knowing his beautiful moment was slipping, and he had lost control. What else did Claire say in front of their oddly alert daughter? He kept telling Claire that Millie had become a sponge, and they needed to be careful with what they said.

"Mommy said that? Do you know who she was talking to?"

Millie shrugged, casting her eyes onto Pinky Rose. "I'm not sure. She was on the phone."

"Did she say anything else? Did Mommy tell the phone anything more?" Leonard regretted trying to pry information from Millie, but there was a tug in his gut saying that there was more.

"Um... she never cooks."

Leonard cocked his head to the side. Never cooks? Whenever Leonard returned home from work, all Claire wailed to him about was how hard she cooked their dinner. Something wasn't right. This was information being rehashed by a four-year-old, except Millie was smart, and Leonard held zero doubts about the last fact. For now, he'd shake off this information and focus on getting their picture. That's what mattered right now.

"Millie, let's just smile for the picture. Can you do that for Daddy?" Leonard pointed to the wobbly camera. Weighted tripod his ass.

"Where do you work, Daddy?"

Leonard gave up. He'd answer all of Millie's questions if that was what it took to get the picture.

"I work for a real estate company selling houses and big, giant buildings. A lot of the buildings are in Manhattan."

"And that's how you make money?"

"Yes. That's how Daddy makes money."

"Can I sell houses with you?"

"If that's what you want to be when you grow up."

"Can I be a princess?"

"You can be whatever you want."

"And will you be there?" said Millie, staring at Leonard.

"Of course, I'll be there," Leonard said, squeezing Millie's hand.

Millie nodded, smiling. She hoisted Pinky Rose to her cheek, offering that toothless signature grin she always made when readying for a picture.

"Okay, ready and say cheese!"

Leonard hit the clicker and heard the popping of the camera erupt, capturing the ocean as their backdrop, serving as the perfect blanket to their future—earthy, blue, but bright, serene, and unpredictable. Anything could happen, and Leonard only hoped for positive things ahead.

# March 15th, 1984

"Leonard, my boy," said Pop. Leonard had adopted the name Pop when he was twelve. Something about the name Pop sounded more mature to Leonard's ears as he grew. He thought he knew it all.

Pop swung the door wide open, leaning on his wooden cane, ushering Leonard inside, shielding them from the March wind.

Leonard sat in the purple chair, his go-to spot whenever he saw Pop. It was hideous but a cloud of comfort. No one recalled where Pop bought the chair or how he came to inherit the piece of furniture, but it became a fixture in the Rosen family. Everyone ridiculed its appearance, yet everyone fought for its place whenever they visited Pop. Lately, visitors dwindled as the years caught up with his friends. Pop was one of the last of his generation to breathe the air. He tried to hide his sadness at more of his friends and family members passing, but Leonard recognized the hurt behind his oldest man's eyes.

"Woo! It's chilly out there," said Pop, clapping his hands together.

"It's a cold one, but I'll take it," said Leonard. He hadn't stopped smiling since yesterday. Tired as hell, but never as happy as he was sitting in the chair than he was now.

Pop hobbled over to the tanned, broken leather couch, putting extra weight on his cane, Leonard noticed. He popped down, releasing a grand sigh. "So... Dad?" said Pop, smiling.

Leonard nodded. "Yup. I guess I am officially a dad now." Leonard reached into his pocket, pulling out a polaroid he snapped of Claire and his new daughter moments after the birth.

Pop took the photo, staring at it like it was the first picture he'd ever seen. "What a beautiful baby. Name?"

Leonard had been waiting to reveal the name for months. He knew Pop would be happy. "Millie," said Leonard, raising a knowing eyebrow.

Pop froze in his seat, clapping a hand over his mouth. Leonard never saw Pop get choked up since the day that had changed everyone's lives until then. Pop wagged a finger in Leonard's face, releasing a half laugh.

"Millie," said Leonard.

"You named her after my sister." Pop trailed off, gazing out the window. He shook his head, speechless.

"I hope that's okay?" Even though he already knew the answer.

"Is it okay? Leonard. This is the greatest gift you could have ever given me." Pop raised the photo high above his head, looking at baby Millie in complete wonder. He gazed at her like the brightest star in the sky. "Millie. She's going to be special. I just have a feeling."

"I can't wait for you to meet her in person. We should be home this weekend."

"How's Claire doing?" Pop released a crippling cough, pulling out a crumpled tissue to wipe his mouth.

"She's doing great." Leonard eyed Pop, focusing on the tissue that now wore a tinge of red from Pop's mouth. "But I'm more concerned about you. Any news from the doctor?"

Pop waved a hand at the comment. "I'm old, Leonard. It is what it is. I'm eighty-six years old. So, I made it to eighty-five in fine health. These end years? It's like icing on the cake."

"You could have more years. I have a few names of doctors. I've been asking around."

"Are you happy in your marriage?"

"Of course, I am. We just had a baby," said Leonard.

"It's very important to be happy with the one you're with. A good marriage gives you the stability you'll find nowhere else. And the kids know it too. They need that stability just as much as you."

"Maybe that's why I turned out so great." Leonard slapped Pop's knee. "You and grandma always loved each other. Robby and I saw that."

"Oh, yeah, we loved each other. Having kids really shows your true colors. The first year with a new baby is hard. And it gets harder. But if you and your wife are there for each other, you have it all."

"I already feel like I have it all."

"Good, good. Then don't listen to me. I'm just a rambling old man. How about a drink?" Pop was already up and pouring a shot for himself and Leonard.

"You know I don't drink. I hate the taste."

Pop stared at Leonard like this was the first time he had heard this tidbit of information. He shook his head, registering the reminder. "Old age. It's not always fun."

Leonard reached for the shot glass.

"What are you doing?" asked Pop.

"I can make an exception. I just became a father, and you just became a great grandfather." Leonard raised the glass, ready to drink and holding his breath.

Pop wagged his arthritic finger in Leonard's face. "Give that to me." He took the glass from Leonard, slamming it on the counter. "Don't you ever change or settle. Rosen men don't change who we are for people. Not even for our wives."

"Is that so?"

"It's very so." Pop slammed his drink back and then dumped Leonard's into the sink.

"What about for our kids? Do we change for them?"

Pop considered the question for a moment, scratching his white-stubbled chin, his liver-spotted hands appeared especially browned today. "Just keep the kids healthy and happy and consider your job done. Kids are wildcards. You never know how you'll act with them until you're in the moment."

Leonard peered at his Rolex watch, the first spoil he bought himself after his fat commission check, seeing that he needed to head back to the hospital. He walked up to Pop, placing a hand on each of the old man's frail shoulders, trying to remember if Pop always felt so bony and weak, and something in Leonard's gut knew it wasn't just because of old age; it was the unnamed sickness.

"It was good seeing you, Pop."

"When did you start calling me Pop?"

"Probably around the time I became a teenager. I thought Pop sounded tougher. Thought I'd sound cooler in front of my friends."

"Sometimes I miss the other name."

Leonard hugged Pop first and kissed his cheek. It was probably the second time the men had ever hugged each other. The Rosen men didn't hug or display many signs of affection, but today was a unique occasion.

"Can I keep this?" Pop waved the polaroid back and forth. "I can't wait to meet baby Millie."

Leonard nodded. "Me too, Grandpa."

# 1968 – Career Day

"Okay, everyone! Line up. Line up." The teacher was way too perky for a Wednesday and happy for any day of the week and before lunchtime. She clapped her hands twice, summoning her students to obey her command. She rehearsed this special lineup of the children against the blackboard in height order for all the parents taking part in Career Day to enter the classroom to see. This was her pride moment, nine-year-old Leonard guessed. Her big achievement for the week. He didn't know what adults measured as triumphs. He didn't know much at all.

The teacher, Ms. Finnegan, spoke to Leonard's class ad nauseam about today's Career Day. This was your time to bring your parent in, most likely your father, to show him off like a shiny trophy. Leonard raised his hand when the event was presented to the class and asked if mothers could come too. Ms. Finnegan blinked twice at his question and then gave a slow yes. Leonard sensed she didn't mean her answer, so he let it rest and chuckled his question away. Just kidding, he said to Tommy, the incessant class nose picker. Tommy didn't care. He probably didn't hear Ms. Finnegan's announcement, either. He was the class mute and an expert at ignoring commands.

Leonard asked his mom when she returned from work if she'd be willing to go to school for Career Day. She gave him a flat no and then told Leonard how he needs to consider how much their family depends on her pay. She also didn't want to waste a vacation day on doing something for Leonard's school. She cheekily said if she was going to take a day off from work, she better find herself on a beach or a hair salon getting pampered like the queen Leonard's father married. Leonard rolled his eyes at the finale of her rant and stomped to his room that night, shutting the door. He was so upset. It was the one time he didn't say goodnight to his Grandpa.

Leonard was first in line against the chalkboard. This year, he was the tallest in his class. Stuart Rubin was all the way at the other end, the shortest and the kid with the fattest black-rimmed glasses this town ever witnessed. Stuart said his mom said the bigger the glasses, the smarter you are. Leonard told Stuart his mom lied.

Leonard wasn't a bully, but he made sure he never got picked on. He remembered his dad told him on the first day of kindergarten to find the biggest, toughest kid in the school, walk right up to him and beat the shit out of the sucker. That's exactly what Leonard achieved, and from that day forward, no one challenged Leonard. Walking through the school hallways proved a breeze and rather peaceful. Sure, he got into trouble with the teachers and hall monitors, but it had always beat being the victim of some shithead kid.

"Listen carefully, everyone," said Ms. Finnegan. "When you see your parent arrive, step out of the line gently and join him on the opposite side of the classroom." Ms. Finnegan motioned to the other side of the room, where it was a wall of windows and a line of chairs made for kids. It would look silly once the fathers sat in chairs meant for students.

Leonard glanced down the row of students, their backs plastered against the fresh blackboard. All eyes were glued to the class entrance, awaiting the parents. Leonard inhaled all the oxygen his lungs could take. He shifted his eyes from the door to the clock.

"Career Day is going to start any minute now. Eleven o'clock, to be exact. Everyone, please be on your best behavior. You wouldn't want to embarrass your parents today." Ms. Finnegan shot everyone one last warning glance before plastering a red lipstick smile on her face and staring at the door with the children.

A light, cool sweat erupted on the back of Leonard's neck. He fidgeted, wiping away the moisture when Ms. Finnegan shot him a side-eye. Leonard dropped his hand immediately back to his side. The teacher sucked in a sharp breath when the first parent, a father, entered the classroom. He wore thick black-rimmed glasses, and Leonard knew who he belonged to.

Ms. Finnegan opened her arms, welcoming the parent inside. "Mr. Rubin, please come in and welcome to Career Day. Stuart, please join your father on the other side of the room."

Mr. Rubin reached for Stuart's hand, and the two walked to the blue chairs. Of course, Stuart's dad was first, Leonard thought. It was guaranteed Leonard's parent wouldn't be one of the first to arrive. The truth was that Leonard had no idea who would show up today. He really didn't ask anyone. He couldn't ask his dad because it wasn't an option. He couldn't be here today. It was as simple as that.

By minute seven into the event, everyone's parents except for Tommy's and Leonard's had arrived and sat, cramped in the chairs with their children balanced on their legs. All fathers and students were on one side of the room while Ms. Finnegan waited with the last boys against the chalkboard.

"Tommy, do you know when your dad is coming?"

Tommy shrugged, staring straight ahead into blank space. She rolled her eyes for only Leonard to notice. "Leonard, how about you? Any idea?"

Leonard shook his head no. Ms. Finnegan sighed, twisting her body back to the door. Her pencil tweed skirt didn't allow for much movement, anyway. She was like a ballerina popping out of a jewelry box, confined to her spinning rod, rotating in a slow circle.

Ten minutes in and still no signs of the family for Leonard or Tommy, the teacher planted herself in front of the boys, bending down to their level. "We're going to have to begin. I'm sorry. If you'd like, you may go sit with the other parents. If you know any of the fathers, maybe you can link up with them." Ms. Finnegan cast her eyes downwards, a stray shadow of guilt crossing her face.

Just then, a familiar cackle, followed by a foreign laugh, filled the classroom with new life. Leonard's, Tommy's, and Ms. Finnegan's heads shot to the door. She was the first and only one out of the three to bolt over to the voices.

"Mr. Byrne and Mr. Rosen, welcome to Career Day!"

"Sorry, we're late. You have too many steps in this building," said Mr. Rosen, wiping his brow.

Leonard couldn't hide his white-toothed smile. He wasn't going to be alone today. He was going to fit in with all his other classmates. He never cared about whether he would blend in with the crowd, but something about today, he didn't want to be the outsider. Leonard realized that his grandpa would never allow that to happen.

# 1965 – Grandpa's Porch

"Always protect your queen," said Grandpa, tapping on the cherry brown wooden queen sitting at the end of the board with her army surrounding her. Today, Leonard's grandpa proclaimed that he would teach his grandson to be the chess master of the Catskills. "Without your queen, the king is set up for failure. Sometimes the king doesn't need a queen, but…." Leonard's grandpa trailed off, not offering much hope to the contrary.

Leonard drummed his fingernails on the splintered, faded wooden table, waiting for his Grandpa's next words of instruction to teach Leonard how to master the game. Grandpa's eyes shot to the source of the noise, squinting at Leonard's hand. Leonard pulled his hand into his lap, hiding it from his grandfather's sight and casting his eyes downward.

"After we finish up out here, I'm cutting your nails," said Grandpa.

"What's wrong with my nails?" asked Leonard.

"They're too damn long. Men should not have long nails. Says something about your hygiene, I always say. Don't worry. I'll fix them for ya in no time."

"But I take a bath every day. I'm clean, Grandpa. What's wrong with my nails?"

"You ask too many questions, boy. Luckily for you, I have the patience to answer them." Leonard's Grandpa resumed showing him the ropes of chess and the secret tricks to slay your opponent to triumphant defeat.

The summer heat burned into the scorched grass for the majority of August. One week remained in the month, and today, on this particular Friday, the sun battered down with an unforgivable force.

For the last ten minutes, Leonard's mother had said she was preparing ice-cold lemonade for Grandpa. Twenty minutes ago, that promise passed. The sweat dripped from Grandpa's forehead as his white rag morphed into a yellow sweat-stained cloth.

"It is a doozy out here, my boy," said Grandpa, lining up his knights as they slowly advanced the board. "Here, pay attention. Did you see what I just did?"

"It's too hot," said Leonard. He slapped a mosquito off his forearm, awaiting the pink welt that would inevitably follow. "Why can't we go inside?"

"Inside is no better than outside, my boy. The air-conditioner conked out, and I'm not paying to fix it when winter is close."

"I bet Dad could fix it."

Grandpa lifted his eyes from the board, homing in on Leonard's wide eyes. "Your father, who is my son... did you know your daddy is my son?"

Leonard nodded, fighting to swallow.

"Your daddy is off fighting a war for us. He's a lieutenant. Do you know what a lieutenant is?"

Leonard had no idea.

"That means he's high up. He fights for you and me and our country. Fixing a cheap window AC unit is not high on his list. Got it? You're lucky to be here and not where he is."

"Why?"

"Because it's dangerous!" Grandpa fought to keep his voice even. He smacked his hand over his mouth, tugging hard at his lips, extending them from his face. "I'm sorry. Sometimes it just gets to me."

"What gets to you?"

Grandpa shook his head. "Forget it. Hey, can you go inside and check on your mother? Ask her for that goddamn lemonade."

Leonard didn't think twice and bolted from his chair. He'd ask his mom for the lemonade but not include the word goddamn. He knew that was a bad word.

Leonard skipped inside, whipping around the wall into the kitchen. He found his mother staring straight ahead out the kitchen bay window, overlooking the open land and long dusty driveway. She never averted her eyes or broke her trance as she washed a bright red China platter over the half-filled, soapy sink. Ever since Leonard's father had departed for his latest assignment, Leonard's mom's mind drifted away with him. That's what Grandpa said, at least. Leonard could tell his mother was never in the best mood, but he thought it had to do with her wanting to live with her father instead of Leonard's grandfather.

The sponge dripped with an abundance of water, and it oozed white suds. The red plate never appeared to get any cleaner, it only got submerged in deeper water as the sink filled.

"Don't wake your brother. He's napping," said his mother, in a dead, muted voice. She continued her circular motions against the plate. The blood red plate.

Leonard hated the color red.

"What do you want?" asked the mother. She stopped washing the dish, turning to Leonard. There was no smile, no recognition of joy when she saw her oldest son, just a blank gaze, staring down an obligation.

"Grandpa wanted to know where the lemonade is." Leonard winced. "He's hot."

The mother blew a loose strand of black hair away from her forehead, rubbing her own sweaty forehead. She half laughed, rolled her eyes, and resumed soaking the red dish.

"Should I tell Grandpa there's no lemonade?"

"Shh! You're going to wake Robbie. He didn't sleep well last night. He kept crying for your father."

Robbie cried every night, and it wasn't always for their dad. Last night it was, but not every night, as his mom made it seem, as if Leonard was heartless for not crying out for his dad. Except he did. He did it in silence. Whenever the tears threatened to spill over his eyes, he bit his tongue or pinched his skin until it brought him back to reality. He needed to be tough, like his grandpa. Rosen men were tough. They didn't show weakness or emotion.

"When is Dad coming home?"

"For God's sakes, Leonard, go back outside to your grandpa. You never know when to stop, do you? I always tell you enough, but it's never enough for you. Go outside now."

Leonard shuffled backward, stumbling out of the kitchen. He waited a second before heading upstairs, taking two steps at a time. He tip-toed to the room he shared with his baby brother, Robbie.

Robbie lay sprawled on the bed, snoring lightly with a fan pointed at his curly head. His cheeks were rosy pink from sweating. Robbie always sweated in his sleep but never soaked his clothes. Leonard never understood the science behind the fact. Grandpa always joked that Robbie was a hothead, and that's where the heat stopped. It was the opposite. Robbie was the kindest soul in New York, Leonard's mother preached. She was right.

Leonard was the bad kid. He always thought Grandpa wanted to paint Robbie as not so pure, just to deflect some of Leonard's roughness onto someone close with blood ties. No one bought the tough Robbie persona, but Leonard appreciated his grandpa's efforts. Leonard saw his mother's favoritism, but he didn't care. All he wanted was his dad to come home.

Why did his dad have to go off and fight in wars? Across the seas? Grandpa said it was so they could be protected. That's what Leonard's father did, protect his country and the people he loved. Leonard only found himself safe when he saw his father in the morning and wished him goodnight. Didn't his father know any of this?

Leonard crept to Robbie's side, shaking his brother out of his sleep. "Robbie, wake up." Leonard's voice hissed through the blue-tinged room. A stream of daylight spilled through the parted blinds.

Robbie's eyes fluttered awake, but he was still half asleep. "Is Dad home?"

Leonard frowned, shaking his head.

"Why are you waking me?"

"I don't know. Do you want to play?" Leonard didn't want to play, though. He just wandered in without a plan.

"I'm tired, and it's hot."

And Robbie missed their dad. Everyone missed him, but no one had to say it anymore. He rolled away from Leonard, closing his eyes, and seconds later fell back asleep. Their mother would never know of this exchange. God forbid Leonard awoke precious Robbie. If he did, his mother would whip out the wooden spoon and chase Leonard until she hit her target.

Leonard dragged his feet downstairs, walking past his mother and back onto the porch. Grandpa's sweat picked up with the heat as he dabbed his drenched, red face.

"No lemonade, my boy?"

"No lemonade. I'm sorry, Grandpa." Leonard plopped down on his creaking wood chair, thinking it might just snap and land Leonard on his tailbone this time.

"Nah, don't be. It's not your fault." Grandpa cast his eyes towards the bay window, catching a glimpse of the mother. "Grandma should be home soon. She makes the best summer drinks. I'll have her whip us up something real good."

Leonard grinned, knowing his grandpa was right. Who needed his mom when Grandma was here? Leonard let the luck of the moment wash over him.

A hot breeze stung his face as he squinted down the driveway. A motor could be heard miles away as it closed in on their country house. Grandpa's country house, to be exact.

"Maybe that's Grandma heading back," said Grandpa, not lifting his head from the chess board as he reset the pieces. "Grandma is my queen. My one and only. You'll see, Leonard."

Leonard only saw a dot of a car closing in on the house in the far distance. It didn't resemble Grandma's Chevy Corvair. Her car was cream, and this vehicle was black. A lump formed in Leonard's throat, growing, stopping at the size of a golf ball.

"You'll grow up, go to college. Find a good woman to marry. And then have kids. It'll be great. Won't be easy, but it'll be a good life. You'll see."

"What does Grandma do to make her your queen?"

Grandpa rested his finger on top of the queen's crown. He raised his eyes to meet Leonard's and smiled. "I'm just very lucky."

"Is Mom Dad's queen?"

Grandpa's smile faded, and he was about to say something when his gaze shifted to the black speck of a car that came into clear view.

It wasn't a car, though. Leonard's young eyes fooled him into thinking it was just an ordinary automobile. The vehicle neared the house and cruised down the dusty driveway, leaving a tan cloud of dirt in its wake. The army green vehicle with a white-centered star on its hood closed in on the front porch. Leonard recognized these SUVs from his history books. His teacher called these vehicles Humvees.

Grandpa stood from his rickety chair, tipping it backward. He grabbed Leonard, squeezing him by the shoulder.

"Get in the house, now."

"Is that Dad?"

"Leonard," said Grandpa, hissing his name through his weathered teeth. It was the first time Leonard's grandpa shunned him away, leaving the boy standing frozen in place with his tongue glued to the roof of his mouth.

Grandpa shot back into the house, leaving Leonard alone on the breezy porch. Suddenly, the day's heat faded, leading the way to the first cool wind, setting off the chimes above the door. Leonard's head fogged from the shift in temperature, and he couldn't see without squinting his eyes.

The Humvee pulled to an abrupt stop, kicking the dirt in front of its front tires a foot away. Two men in their fifties with gray hair and in uniform, similar to his father's but with more medals and pins on their jackets, emerged from the vehicle. They reached the passenger side of the car, parallel to the porch.

One man sporting a black beard sprinkled with ample grey hairs on his chin stepped toward Leonard. "Son, is your mother home?"

His deep, rich voice, thick with comfort and warning, left Leonard speechless. His voice was lost, and so was his breath. He fought to recover any oxygen for his lungs but couldn't. His heartbeat raced, and a cold sweat started on his hands, spreading across the rest of his tanned skin.

Leonard took a stumbling step backward, grabbing the empty air for balance. A crash sputtered from the house, but Leonard never peeled his eyes from the two gentlemen standing in front of the porch. Something was amiss. Where was everyone, and who were they?

Footsteps dragged from the inside, making their way to the front door. Leonard turned around to capture his glassy-eyed mother frozen in the doorway, holding the storm door ajar. In her other hand, dangling at her side, she held a broken piece of the red China platter that was intact moments ago. Her hand dripped blood. Leonard spun around to the two gentlemen approaching the porch with cautious steps.

They removed their hats, and Leonard knew that whatever was about to be said would change their lives forever. He had two choices: to stay here, stand with his mother, and wait to hear what these men would say, or run.

The bearded man stepped ahead, bowing an inch. "Mrs. Rosen?"

"Yes?" said Leonard's mother, her voice a quivering dying heart.

"We're so sorry to deliver this news, but your husband..."

It all turned to a weeping blur as Leonard couldn't stay to listen to the rest of the sentence. All he could do and focus on doing was run into the house, yelling, "Grandpa!"

# Millie's Day

Millie sat on a wooden bench that showed signs of its fraying age. She ran her flat sweaty palm against the back of the bench, testing to see if any splinters would penetrate her skin. She wanted to feel a sting, anything other than what she experienced now. There was an unending ache in her stomach, sinuses, and head. Everything weighed on her like heavy, wet, dripping clay bricks, whatever those felt like. But she assumed it wasn't comfortable to be buried under a heap of stone. She was trapped in Georgia. Trapped in her body. Trapped in her mind. Millie was trapped.

She took a sip of her mango slushy, opting for the extra-large cup today. She didn't care to count calories anymore. Millie needed the sweetness the beverage delivered to her soul since it was the only pleasant thing going on in her life right then. Just the week before, she begged her father to come back to New York to see her family, her son Jackie, for the holidays. He said no once again, and that was it. Millie accepted the fact that she was stuck in Georgia, but it wasn't going to help her. The fight she had possessed in her body to stay clean a month ago changed. She wanted to be clean every day waking up. She wanted to quell this curse and declare this would be the minute everything changes for the better. It was her plan, except things grew worse. Yesterday she drank a beer, and last week she actually got drunk and didn't return to the halfway house until sunrise, getting into trouble with a counselor. The guilt consumed Millie because she knew her father would receive a call about the incident.

She knew staying in Georgia meant having a fighting chance of getting and remaining sober, but in exchange, she wouldn't speak to Jackie as much and not see him, period. She was damned either way she viewed it. Today she awoke, deciding that today would not be the day she stayed clean.

A guy she had met in the alleyway of a pub one afternoon three days ago slipped her a bag of stuff, as she'd like to call it. But it was the stuff that would provide comfort on a cool and lonely day in Georgia, far away from the solace and warmth of her family in New York. She viewed everyone as abandoning her. No one even visited her. She initiated all the calls to home lately, and whoever she spoke to made the conversation seem like an obligation to humor her. What was there to even fight for? How did she get to this place? She remembered that one night early into her relationship with Jesse when he offered her a Valium, and she took it. Somehow Jesse managed to stop, but she couldn't. She just couldn't. How come he pulled away from the really bad things he showed her, but she couldn't stop? She would never understand, and whenever her father pointed the finger and blamed Jesse for what she became, Millie never wanted to tell him he was right. Except, her dad wasn't always right, for he did a lot of wrong to her and Steven. If she thought about it much more, she would go crazy sitting on this lonely bench.

And then she remembered Jackie. He didn't know better, and she wondered if he thought about her? He must. They hadn't been apart that long, and Jesse was gracious enough last night to let Millie wish Jackie goodnight. It was a decent night until the phone call ended. Hearing his tiny, perfect little boy voice, she thought speaking to Jackie would remind her to stay clean and feed her strength to reach that goal, but this morning proved the opposite. It wasn't enough for the day.

All Millie had left for the afternoon was this bench, her melting mango slushy, a small bag, and a clean needle she had just found earlier. Well, not found, but a very nice stranger she met two days ago gave her a clean needle, wrapped. He worked in a medical office, always the jackpot finds for a junkie who needed accessories to aid the habit. She'd do it just once this afternoon and figure out the rest tomorrow. She'd be honest with her counselors in the morning and tell them she needed to start again. Being in the halfway house wasn't the right place for her and her path to recovery. She'd need to be sent back to the rehab facility, and her dad would have to suck it up and pay for another month or however long she needed. If Leonard wouldn't permit Millie to return to her home state, he'd have to pay to keep her down here in whatever form necessary. He had the money to lose anyway, Millie figured.

A mother and her daughter took the seat next to Millie. She thought it was strange since there were other benches vacant in the park. Millie eyed the girl and her perfectly braided pigtails. The child had to be Jackie's age or older, but not by much. She kept twirling as the mother tried to tie her own shoelaces. The mother rolled her eyes at her energetic child, grabbing her wrist to stop her.

"I have a son your age," said Millie to the girl. "How old are you?"

"Don't even bother. She only talks when she's in the mood," said the mom with a visible eye roll made to discourage further conversation.

Millie frowned, looking at the girl who continued to spin, only stopping to stare at the ground that was probably moving for her eyes only.

Millie laughed softly, remembering how Jackie had just started to go through the phase of learning to make himself dizzy and studying the aftermath of the twirling ground while trying not to fall over. Millie ached to witness those moments. She wondered what Jackie was doing now. It was almost four o'clock, getting closer to supper time for him. Maybe it would be a hot dog and tater tots night for him. She didn't know what Jesse prepared him for dinner and couldn't judge either. Whatever Jesse provided for Jackie was ten times more useful than what Millie had over the last year and a half. She failed as a parent.

"I'm Millie." She lifted her eyes from the dirt ground only to be met with silence. The mother and daughter left, unbeknownst to Millie. She had no idea when they left or what direction they ventured to. It was like they never existed, leaving her alone. Alone. She was alone in every sense of the meaning. The only thing keeping her company was this small clear plastic bag tucked away in her purse. She didn't want to use it, but the thought of leaving it unattended left a trail of chilling goosebumps all over her body. Every hair on her body stood to attention, on ultra-high alert.

She inserted a shaky hand into her bag, palming the baggie. She could do one push here, right on the bench in broad daylight. She didn't even care if she got caught. And if she did get caught, maybe it would save her from making this mistake. The bottom line was she did not care about anything. Only the idea of getting high occupied her mind. She kept repeating just one push to herself, and she would be free.

# November 25th, 2021 – The Revelation

"What the fuck am I doing?" Leonard's voice pulled him out of something he had little idea about, almost forgetting where he had stayed the entire day.

His eyes popped open from a poor, restless nap. Seeing Millie on her last day was the one thing this awful slumber cast light on. He never dreamt of what she endured during her last moments or if they were even truthful from what he just saw in his sleep. It was a moment, he saw. She didn't appear overly upset, but she was unsettled. His body ached, and he thought it was the flu coming on. He hadn't gotten his flu shot yet, and the numbers in New York were already climbing with the virus.

He sat up, straining his neck, looking over to a sleeping Jill. The final hour of daylight spilled through the drawn curtains, shining on her face. She appeared older than what he recalled about an hour ago, and suddenly Leonard realized what she wasn't. She wasn't perfect, but that was okay. She didn't owe him perfection, and he didn't owe her anything in return. They were two strangers, bonding over the grief of losing their daughters. That was all. They were buffers for each other, preventing them from going after what they needed to find. He needed to find the answer to keep Jackie here, and she needed to be in Florida with her sole grandchild and family. Today served as a big distraction from facing the larger truths that surrounded them daily but exacerbated themselves on the actual dates of death.

Leonard gazed at Jill one more time before he caught a new wrinkle drawing from the corner of her mouth he had never noticed. She was still beautiful but far from what his mind drew her up to be. He almost fell again. He almost walked into another bear trap of his own making. He almost got caught in his distraction, a woman, blinding himself from his priority: Jackie. From what he needed to do before it was too late. Before Jackie moved to Thailand and Leonard's world vanished.

Leonard bolted out of bed, throwing on clothes, making sure to not wake Jill. He wouldn't desert her, no. He would give her a proper goodbye after how she allowed him to walk through his past and indulge her in all the memories he dug up. It was the first time he had recalled everything with another individual present. This was a lonely activity that Leonard partook in every year, but today it was different, still just as dark, but not as lonely.

He studied himself in the mirror before grabbing the doorknob, ensuring his appearance was half presentable. For good measure, Leonard filled up a glass with cold bottled water, downing it in three gulps, and when he finished, he realized water didn't taste so bad after all.

Minutes later, Leonard printed what he needed in the business center with surprising ease. He hoped Jill took to his idea as much as he did. Leonard thought this would strike a chord with her. She wouldn't blame him for what he was about to present to her and only hoped she appreciated his efforts.

As he logged off all his accounts and pushed himself away from the computer, he overheard a cackle he knew, the hyena laugh unmistakable. Leonard spun around to see a former business associate in his real estate dealings inches from his face. Charles Satin, who had married a much younger and more attractive Danielle Satin.

"Son of a bitch, if it isn't Leonard himself," said Charles, half drunk, slapping Leonard's shoulder, sending a jolt of quick pain through his body.

"Charles, good to see you," said Leonard, pumping Charles's hand in a hearty shake.

"You here with the family, Leonard? I'd love to meet them. Are you here for the Thanksgiving dinner? Best I've ever tasted."

Charles's red wine breath, with purple-tinged teeth, stung Leonard's face. "No, I just stopped in for a little. Needed to get to a computer." Leonard pointed to the machine he had just abandoned.

Charles nodded, understanding. "Always business with you. How's the family? It's been years since I last saw you. Always remembered you, though. You made some of the best buys in this city."

"Family is good. Can't complain. I actually have a grandson."

"Get out. You're a grandpa? I thought you were fifty. Damn, man."

"How much did you have to drink tonight?"

"Seriously, man. How old are you?" said Charles.

"Let's just put it this way. I collect social security."

Charles took a step back, stomping an unsteady foot. "You're shitting me. You're that old? I mean, I collect social security too, but man." The spit flew out of Charles's mouth unwarranted. "Don't tell me. Are you seventy?"

Leonard scrunched his eyebrows, unsure of where this inebriated rant would land. He shook his head, no.

"I was going over my will last week, and it suddenly hit me how old I really am. Sixty-eight, can you believe that?" said Charles.

"I can believe anything. And I definitely believe I'm younger than you."

"Still the wise-ass, too." Charles punched Leonard's shoulder. "Anyway, I was going over my will with my attorney. Great guy, by the way, if you're ever looking for a new lawyer. And he says, 'Charles, you have all these properties, and you're not selling them.' And I think, shit, he's right. What am I doing with all these properties? Just holding onto them. They're not going anywhere, and I'm not in the mood to sell them. So, what am I doing? What? Will I cash in on them when I'm eighty and getting sponge baths by Danielle?"

"Nothing wrong with sponge baths." Leonard checked his watch. He needed to get back to the room, and fast.

"And with millions in the bank... if you need a great broker, I have the guy for you. He got me those millions in the bank over years of telling me to buy this stock, that stock… you know? Anyway, with money in the bank to last me two lifetimes, I asked myself, why keep all these properties? What for? Tell me, Leonard Rosen, how many properties do you own?"

"Probably thirty to thirty-five."

"And then I thought, let me gift my daughter this building. Let me put this building in my grandson's name." Charles paused, putting a flat hand to his chest, fighting testosterone tears. "I gotta tell you, I never felt so brave and powerful until I saw myself securing my family's futures in what I held under my name. It'll be because of me they'll never have to worry. God made this plan for me, and then I spun it around for my family. A real full circle moment. And I never believed in that shit until I planned my will."

The world stopped to a screeching siren. Leonard's ears burned and vibrated in a strange mixture of discovery and being handed the answer, the offer. Give the property away. Give the biggest property away and hope it sticks.

"So, you just divided up your properties?" said Leonard.

"I secured my family's futures by doing that. It was the best damn will anyone could have concocted, and it's all mine." Charles jabbed a crooked finger into his chest.

"Charles. It was great seeing you. Give my best to Danielle, and have a very happy Thanksgiving." Leonard slapped the big man's back and jogged to the elevator bank with new vigor in his step. He knew what to do and hoped it would work. But first, he needed to speak to Jill.

# November 25th, 2021 – The Goodbye

Leonard crept into the darkened room, turning his phone flashlight on to find his way to the bed where a sleeping Jill lay peacefully. The only sign that she was alive was the small swell of her stomach rising with each breath. He sat beside her on the bed, turning on the bedside lamp.

The orange light hit Jill's eyes, causing her to scrunch them awake. She searched the room before landing on Leonard's hovering, fully-clothed body. She peered once more to ensure nothing else occurred and steadied her gaze on Leonard.

"What are you doing?" said Jill.

A wave of hesitation washed over Leonard, making him rethink what he was about to do. He peered out the drawn curtains he had opened a few moments before awaking Jill. A large building in the distance caught his eye, solidifying his reason for the upcoming words he was about to exchange.

"I got you something." Leonard pulled out a white sealed envelope from his back pocket, holding it in front of Jill's face.

She was about to reach for it, the blanket exposing her bare chest, when Leonard grabbed her bathrobe, insisting she cover herself. She raised an eyebrow and opened the envelope at a snail's pace. She pulled out its contents and read it over. "A plane ticket to Florida?" Jill locked eyes with Leonard.

"You should be with your granddaughter as much as I should be with Jackie."

Jill rolled her eyes, covering half her face with her hand. "Oh, my God. I can't believe you're breaking up with me."

Leonard's pulse skipped two beats. "Breaking up? We barely know each other."

"I learned your entire life's story today in this room."

"It was a good day for the both of us. But it's ending now. Not because I want it to end, but... I can't get distracted. I can't make the same mistakes I did in the past. I realized it just now, speaking to you. You're a pretty good therapist."

Jill laughed, palming the plane ticket in her hand, rereading its fine print. "Wow, first class. You do know how to treat your women."

"It's the right thing for us to do. Go our separate ways, concentrate on our families. This has nothing to do with the idea of us not being able to work out."

Jill sat up, pulling the bathrobe tight, closing off Leonard's last glimpses of her nude body. "You really are something. Do you think it would have led to marriage if we lasted beyond this room?"

"Knowing my track record, I probably could've convinced you." Leonard served a wicked wink to Jill, but she didn't budge. "Or at least to an engagement. I've had a handful of broken engagements."

"Oof. It sounds like the only thing I dodged is a bullet with you."

Leonard slapped his chest, feigning a fatal gunshot wound. This was the best and fastest breakup ever. If only it was always like this, but it wasn't. Ever.

"I have news for you. We would have never worked," said Jill.

"No one ever works with me."

"I mean beyond this room. I've realized something. We're too similar."

"I'm one of a kind, baby. Not sure if you realized that."

"No, no. It's true. We see someone and think they're perfect, almost too quickly. But then it all crumbles."

Leonard straightened his posture, pushing off her comment as it drilled into his heart. She was right, but it took Leonard decades to realize the flawed patterns of his ways. Things could have been different; Millie could be here today, enjoying one of the biggest family holidays of the year with him, with Jackie, with everyone. The simple gift of being alive she was robbed of at such a young age, and Leonard couldn't save her. He was always too busy with his own bullshit, distractions, and life. And while he may have his own life and was entitled to one, he should have realized who the priorities were and what was most important each time. Some might have said he did nothing wrong, but his heart said otherwise. He always knew the marriages weren't his number one priority, even though at the specific moment, he believed they were, except they never lasted. Millie and Steven were the constants who deserved his full and undivided attention, and yes, Leonard did try the best he knew how to at the time, but now it was different. He knew now he would be at his best with Jackie. He didn't need the love of another woman to fill the void his mother left vacant; he didn't need that at all. Leonard needed Jackie because Jackie needed Leonard. They needed each other.

"What kind of therapist are you?"

Jill's face adopted a shade of red. "A marriage counselor, mainly."

Leonard threw his head backward, letting it all make sense now. "I should have known. You talk like a therapist."

"You know nothing, Rosen." She flashed a smile before staring down at the plane ticket. "I don't need your money. I could have easily bought a ticket there myself."

Leonard pushed the ticket into her hand. "Consider this a little push. Sometimes we need that to get to the right place. You should know that, especially if we're that similar."

Jill dropped her eyelids, shielding her pupils from Leonard. She closed them completely, leaning forward as she pulled his head towards her body, planting the final goodbye kiss on his forehead.

# November 25<sup>th</sup>, 2021 – Revisiting

Leonard zoomed into the midtown tunnel. The sound of his engine growl roared to life as he accelerated through the empty tunnel lanes, and the reverberations of his exhaust bouncing off the walls signaled to Leonard that he was free. Nothing stood between his determination to get Jackie and his life back on track. This would be the last year he dwelled on the day Millie passed. Instead, he would celebrate her life.

He pulled into the cemetery parking lot with a fresh bouquet of sunflowers. The sun would set in less than fifteen minutes, and the garden lights already illuminated the parking lot and empty grounds.

Leonard jogged to Millie's plot, at odds with the dying sunlight. Losing his breath, he only caught it when he spotted another figure bowing over Millie's grave. It was Steven.

Leonard approached his son from behind, careful not to startle him, who hadn't shared a moment with his deceased sister for years. Steven sniffed a few times, jamming his hands into his black trench coat.

Lifting his head, Steven turned to meet Leonard, who half hid behind the sunflowers. Steven chuckled, shrugging his shoulders, as if saying 'you caught me'.'

"Millie loved sunflowers." Steven pointed to the bouquet.

Leonard pulled one from the bunch, handing Steven a lone stem with a giant yellow sunflower head. He accepted it silently from Leonard, placing it at the foot of Millie's stone.

Steven shook his head back and forth, stomping his foot twice. Leonard slapped his hand onto his son's shoulder, trying to calm whatever brewed.

"I should've been here every year. I'm an asshole," said Steven.

"Don't do that to yourself. You're here now. She knows."

"Sometimes I feel like I just float in life. Do you know what I mean? Just go through the motions. Go to work. Go home. Go home to Theresa because she misses me, and I guess I miss her when I'm not there... I'm going to change. I'm going to visit Millie and try with Jackie. I promise." Steven's eyes glassed over, but he fought away the tears. "Any breakthrough with Jackie?"

Leonard kicked some loose dirt from his shoe, biting the inside of his cheek. He only thought of getting Jackie but didn't actually think it aloud. "I'm going to bribe Jesse."

"Oh, wow. You know I was only half joking when I said it earlier." Steven shifted from foot to foot. "Is it going to be a lot?"

"Don't worry. There's plenty to go around. But I'll tell you this: I'm done with getting married. I'm going to stay focused this time. No more being pulled in the wrong direction."

"Don't punish yourself. Or change. I don't know." Steven avoided eye contact with Leonard, staring at his feet. "I don't know if I want to get married."

Leonard shot a glance at Steven. He offered to pay for their wedding but not shell out money when doubts were in the equation.

"Well, right now, you're only engaged. Make sure it's really something you want to do. Not that I'm the expert. But don't be like me."

"Ha! I don't think I'll ever have the energy to be you. It's just that I'm not sure if I want to marry her..." Steven wanted to talk more, but he shook away his words and released a heavy sigh.

"What's wrong? Are the two of you fighting? Talk to me. I'm here."

"No, it's not that. I just don't feel it... with her," said Steven, swallowing his words.

Silence fell between the two men, father and son, like a cold winter's edge. They shivered in unison. Leonard's ungloved hand holding the sunflowers felt iced over, his skin ready to crack from the frigid pending night's chill.

"I gotta go. Good luck with the plan, Dad." Steven engulfed Leonard in a hug, a rare action between the two.

Leonard paused, not knowing how to respond until he remembered the right thing to do. He hugged Steven back with his free arm, and as the seconds passed, Leonard pulled closer to his son, his only child here. He couldn't let this moment pass them by, and Leonard needed to make sure Steven knew. Leonard leaned into Steven's ear, putting his hand behind his son's neck, ensuring there was no way to escape. "You have made me so proud all these years, and I couldn't ask more from a son or be prouder of you. I hope you know that. And I am and always will be there for you whatever decision you make."

"I know." Steven's voice barely escaped his mouth.

"I know you know, but I needed to make sure you heard it."

Steven nodded, broke the embrace without a single word, and marched away, morphing into a tiny speck, jamming a black beanie onto his head. When Leonard saw him disappear, he exhaled, letting his breath fog in front of his face.

Leonard took two steps towards Millie's grave, breathing in, readying his body to carry on living. "I got you a fresh bouquet of sunflowers. They smell great... Here. I'll let you see for yourself." Leonard placed all the sunflowers at the base of Millie's stone. He propped them up, only to watch them tumble over seconds later. Clearing the rattle from his throat, he continued. "I met a woman today, but it's not going to work out for the best. I'm hoping she goes to Florida to see her granddaughter. I think she will. But anyway, I broke it off, even though we really didn't have much of a start. It lasted for five hours but felt much longer. Did you ever have anything like that with a boyfriend?" He stared at the stone, of course not waiting for an answer, but in the back of his mind, he yearned for a sign she was listening.

He knew what he needed to say, but the idea of opening his mouth threatened to release years of buried regret, hurt, and mistakes, except he owed all of it and more to Millie if it was going to happen at all. He owed her his sheer and brutal honesty about everything he chose to do until now.

"I am so sorry, Millie. I am so sorry if you never felt like my priority. You and Steven were always my one. Always. I always thought I was doing the right thing by you, but I see now it wasn't enough. I'm not saying I blame myself completely, but I have a lifetime of regrets." A tear ran down Leonard's face. He flicked it away, trying to stop the parade of tears threatening to spill from the rims of his eyes, but it was a losing battle.

"I should have fought harder for you when you were little and when you were older and said you needed me for the summer camp rides, for everything… for anything. My biggest regret was when I decided not to fight for you when I was figuring out the divorce from your mother. It's something I never admitted to you and Steven. I didn't want either of you to think I didn't choose you, even though that day I really thought I made the right choice, even though I knew it was the wrong one that day, sitting in Greg's office. I gave in too fast. It was a selfish move on my part. And we all suffered. I hope you'll forgive me."

A sudden brisk wind slapped his face. He palmed his wet, wind-whipped cheek, stifling a laugh. If that was Millie's answer to his partial confession, then he deserved it. He cleared away some loose debris that blew across Millie Rosen's plot. More tears fell off his face that he didn't bother to wipe away anymore. He was sick of fighting his emotions and putting up the Rosen tough façade. He just wanted to live and not prove anything to anyone, especially to himself. He just wanted to feel.

"Steven always said to me he had two lives. One with your mother and then the second life once you guys moved in with me." The quiver in his voice quickly won over Leonard's ability to speak. He thumped his foot on the ground, hoping the pain halted the free-falling tears. "Maybe Steven was right. But Steven was still growing up. But you had already grown up by the time you moved in. So, I guess it was too late. Anyway, I'm going to make things right. I'm going to make sure Jackie is safe and give him the best life possible. I'll figure this out, Millie, for you. Well, I love you. And I'll talk to you soon."

Leonard kissed his wet tear-filled hand and placed it onto her headstone, holding it there for six seconds before letting go, leaving the outline of his fingers on her grave.

Leonard pulled into the driveway of a handsome black and white colonial house, assessing the property as he exited his car. The house was an easy four thousand square feet. Leonard could tell that real estate is what he breathed. He carried a thick manila envelope filled with papers up the driveway. Several cars were parked in the driveway and on the street, typical for this time during the Thanksgiving festivities. The night was still young for a holiday, especially in those households without younger children. It was just about six o'clock when Leonard rang the grandiose chime doorbell.

He held his breath, knowing his presence was unwelcome, but Leonard was used to that by now. With many burned bridges from disintegrated marriages, Leonard grew used to being the semi-villain. Not that he was the bad guy tonight, but crashing someone's holiday meal thrust him under a negative spotlight.

The oversized wooden front door swung open.

"Oh, for fuck's sake," said Greg, who wore a green checkered belt and suspenders.

Leonard could only push through a smile without words backing up its presence.

Greg's bulged eyes shot from Leonard's face to the manila envelope tucked under Leonard's arm.

"No," said Greg, waving a singular finger back and forth.

"It'll only be five minutes," said Leonard, stepping onto the front porch, closer to the entryway.

"You're unhinged."

"I don't have time to be anything but unhinged," said Leonard.

"My wife is going to kill you," said Greg.

"Does that mean I can come in?"

Greg frowned, looking over his shoulder to see if anyone spied the intruder. "I'll give you five minutes, and this better be good, Leo."

Leonard beamed, showing every perfect white tooth in his mouth while holding up the folder. "It is going to be great. Maybe a little crazy, but great."

Greg motioned Leonard to step inside with the flick of his two fingers, signaling the beginning of their night.

# *November 25th, 2021 – The Plan*

The contents of the folder were sprawled across Greg's at-home office mahogany desk. The meeting, so far, had lasted well beyond the promised five minutes, but both men didn't care. Greg loved lawyering, and Leonard loved being told what to do by his attorney. They were the perfect match.

Greg's reading glasses balanced on the thick bridge of his nose. He tossed a pile of papers back into the folder. "I can't believe you want to do this. I know I said buy Jesse out, but wow. This is really wild."

"That's why I wanted to get your opinion first. If something like this can even be done?" said Leonard.

"Of course, it can be done. But it'll cost a lot in taxes for everyone. Gift tax for you, and taxes made on the sale for Jesse."

"Oh, screw that. He'll walk away with millions." Leonard fanned the air. "But will he give up Jackie for it?"

"This is more money than he'll ever get his hands on, ten times over." Greg shook his head, widening his eyes. "I mean, if he turns down this offer, then you'll know for sure he'd never give Jackie up. I can't believe you want to give up this one. This is the property with the Knicks tickets, right? The night you found out about the pickup truck?" Greg snorted.

"He has to take the offer, Greg." Leonard couldn't control the volume of his voice as it bounced off every wall in the room. His gestures went wild in all directions. "He has to fucking take it."

Greg shot a finger to his lips. "If my wife hears you're here, we're both dead men."

"If Jesse doesn't take this, I'll want to die."

Greg scrunched his face. "Just relax. You're getting ahead of yourself." Greg leaned back in his red leather chair, crushing the fabric under his hefty frame. "I just can't believe you'll give up this property. After how long you've held onto it. Why this one?"

"I'm not holding back or taking any chances. If Jesse doesn't want this one, then I know what I have to do."

Leonard's heart ached and picked up a few beats, admitting to the idea of really losing Jackie. He came to terms with what everyone kept saying. Pay Jesse off, bribe the guy, he had a number, as Jill said. Leonard just hoped it was the right number and if Jesse could really be bought.

"If Jesse won't accept my offer, then I'll let it go. He'll put up an ugly fight in court. I know it. And I don't want to put Jackie through that. The difference between what happened with my kids and Jesse here is that there would be an ugly fight. With my kids, money stopped me because I really couldn't afford to do it. And by the time I did recoup everything I lost, we were in a routine. I thought everything was fine. I mean, not great, but good enough, you know?" Leonard ran a shaky hand through his hair. It contained a wiry texture, older than what he remembered. "I was wrong. Very, very wrong. This time I have the money to fight, but I don't want there to be a fight, for Jackie's sake. If Jesse is willing to turn down millions of dollars, then I know there's nothing he won't do to keep Jackie as his."

"Hold on. Hold on." Greg held up a rigid, tanned finger. "Aren't you dating someone new? Where is she? The woman from today."

Leonard nodded to the air. "I literally sent her away."

Greg already started laughing before Leonard had a chance to elaborate.

"It's not what you think, Greg." Leonard shifted in his seat, his face burning up but unsure why. "It's not like the other times. We agreed to end whatever it was we had going today. We were too similar. And I need to focus now."

"So, where did you send her to?" Greg wiped the tears from the corners of his heavy eyes from the red wine he had consumed throughout the day.

"Florida..." said Leonard, waiting for a further reaction.

Greg grabbed his bloated turkey-filled stomach, wailing at the top of his lungs. If there were any concerns about Greg's wife hearing them from this room, Greg's laugh would alert her attention. Leonard shot his head in the door's direction and back to Greg.

"Someone will hear us if you know who I mean..." said Leonard.

Greg gasped for breath, clutching at the empty air and space in the room. "Don't worry. This room is soundproof."

"Then why did you warn me about someone hearing us earlier?"

Greg shrugged, and for the first time, he didn't have an answer.

Leonard checked the time and wondered if Jackie would be asleep by now. It was still early, so he shouldn't be, but Leonard could never figure out what exactly went on at Jesse's house. If only they would let him in, just once, he could see where Jackie lived.

"My apologies, Leo." Greg sniffed in a juiciness that warranted a tissue. "So, you're really ready to switch the grandpa hat for a full-time dad hat? At your age?"

"Another thing…" said Leonard, ignoring Greg's last question. "If you have the name of a good psychiatrist, I'd like to go see the person for myself. I don't know if I ever told you, but I suffer from panic attacks. If I'm going to do this, I need to be at my best for Jackie."

"Of course, I knew. Don't you remember you had one in my office and fainted the first time we met?" said Greg. "Wow, Leo. You really are changing, and yes, I have the name of someone great for you."

Leonard half laughed, and suddenly his eyes turned heavy, filling with water, as Leonard blinked the tears away, staring up into the Tiffany lamp hanging over their heads.

Leonard cleared his throat, picking at the nail of his thumb. "In answer to your question about being a dad again at my age… not many people know this, but uh…" Leonard readjusted his seat again, accepting he'll never feel comfortable in this spot. "My grandfather actually raised my brother and me. Sure, my mom was there, in the same house. But she wasn't there for me. She favored my brother, but she just didn't like me. I was annoying, according to her. I always asked questions because I wanted answers. Robert was always so happy and agreeable. She liked Robert more, but that's where it ended. My grandfather was always there for us."

"You never liked your mother. I remember you telling me."

"Hated her," said Leonard.

The air hung over the men like thick cobwebs that were impossible to abate. Neither one made eye contact with the other. Leonard rarely spoke to anyone about his upbringing. Only Robert knew what happened, and Steven heard sprinkles of Leonard's childhood, but it wasn't spoken about in depth.

"My father died when I was very young, so his dad, my grandfather, stepped up to fill that role. He did a pretty great job, I have to say."

"What was he like?" said Greg.

Leonard smiled. "Nothing like me. I mean, we both held the family man values but executed them differently... obviously. He was a very loyal man. He was cut from good stock. And I miss him every day."

Greg neatly lined up the strewn real estate papers into a singular pile, placing them into the manila folder and pushing it towards Leonard. He accepted the file and put it back on his lap. Understanding their meeting had approached its end caused Leonard's stomach to stir. He leaned forward and grabbed the glass of water, downing it in three gulps. He couldn't recall ingesting this much water in his lifetime, and he didn't want to stop this new habit either. Leonard was changing, and he felt the adjustment washing over him each minute he grew closer to laying out his offer to Jesse.

"Will you, um... draw up whatever papers needed for this? I don't even know what to call it," said Leonard. He almost combatted a strange sensation of guilt pressing into his gut. Here, Leonard was accustomed to making business deals that usually went his way after his blip, nearly leaving him destitute when he divorced Claire. Yet there he was, attempting to make the deal of his life. But it wasn't business. It was all personal, and Leonard steered an impossibly large ship in the smallest and darkest rooms. At any moment, Leonard could crash.

"I'll draw up the papers; don't you worry about that. Now go get 'em, Grandpa," said Greg, downing the last of his neat Scotch. He slammed the empty tumbler down onto the glass coaster, releasing a stream of air.

Leonard reached into his back pocket, extracting a lone folded check, and grabbed a fountain pen. "For your time, good sir." He began scribbling an unknown amount. Whatever left the tip of his pen onto the paper would be Greg's fee for this evening. Leonard wouldn't disappoint.

"Oh, stop," said Greg, protesting the fee. "Seriously, stop. Save your money. You're going to need it." He snorted, not making eye contact with Leonard.

Leonard completed his signature and folded the check in half, offering it to Greg, who didn't budge. "Take it. Come on. You know you're going to." Leonard flicked his wrist for Greg's taking. The heaviness in Leonard's arm produced a battle to keep his limb afloat with the check. He slid it across to Greg, who didn't touch the paper.

"You know, you don't always have to write me a check whenever we see each other. We're friends, Leonard. I've always considered you a friend."

Leonard offered a small smile, the day catching up with him, despite it not being over yet. "I always said that people who get paid to do their job do a better job." Leonard loved money and only assumed others who made a lot of money shared his sentiment. The thought of just how much money he was about to part with theoretically produced an instant clamminess consuming his hands and legs. He wanted to stand up, but his limbs morphed into jelly.

He slumped backward, taking a minute for himself. He breathed in and out, allowing each second to process through his body and recharge his battery.

"Let me get you something to drink," said Greg, going over to the black mini-fridge in the room's corner. "Diet Coke, okay?"

"Make that water."

Greg paused a moment, considering the odd request, before unscrewing a fresh bottle of Poland Spring.

"I don't think this will be as complicated as you think. I feel it in my gut."

Leonard raised a lone eyebrow as he chugged the water, already embracing its cooling effect deep in his stomach. "What makes you so sure Jesse won't drag me through hell?"

"I just have a sixth sense for these things. I'm usually right."

Leonard's phone vibrated wildly on the table, half spinning around as friction fought the silent ringtone. He tipped the phone forward, revealing Jesse's illuminated name splashed across the black screen.

"It's Jesse," said Leonard, locking eyes with a brightening Greg.

"Answer," said Greg.

# *November 25ᵗʰ, 2021 – Jesse's Porch*

"Leonard, the kid is hysterical," said Jesse, unsteady on his feet.

Leonard got the call at Greg's house. Jackie was a mess over moving to Thailand and had a pre-teen tantrum during Thanksgiving dinner. No one told Jackie that Leonard was uninvited. Instead, they told Jackie that Leonard simply was not going to show for dessert, per the original plan, and Jackie snapped. The truth about Thailand spilled from Jackie's mouth like a geyser, and he morphed into an inconsolable beast as Margot described her stepson to Leonard over the frantic phone call.

So now Leonard stood on the damn front porch under the yellow buzzing light, hearing Jesse vent and awaiting what came next because Leonard had no fucking clue.

"He totally ruined the night and the surprise. We were going to tell our family about the big move to Thailand right before dessert," said Jesse, chasing down the rest of his beer. It certainly was not his first one for the night.

"So, this is really happening? You guys moving and all that?"

"Well, yeah. We have a broker listing our house next week. She says this place should sell fast with the market and all."

Leonard shook the crazy out of his head, trying not to collapse from the whirs of dizziness flashing across his eyes. "This is just so insane. I can't believe it."

"Well, how am I supposed to move a hysterical kid halfway across the world? I can't have this ruined. Tell me, Leonard. If you were in my position, what would you do?"

"Not move. Stay here. Move to another state if you're unhappy in New York. I get it's become a rat race here, but there are plenty of other states where life is better."

"That's not gonna work. This is Margot's dream. It's all she's talked about for the last year."

He'd never know just how long Jesse and Margot concocted this plan, but Leonard had a strange sensation in his gut that maybe this wouldn't be as difficult as he once thought, keeping Jackie here with him. Something approached Leonard's horizon of flickering hope. Maybe Greg and Jill were right all along. Jesse had a number. But it all seemed too easy. Where was the fight?

"What about the kids? I know you said Margot's kids were excited, but then reality starts to set in. It's going to be a huge change for everyone."

Jesse shook his head through every syllable out of Leonard's mouth. It was like speaking to a dumb wall that breathed. Leonard had no idea where this conversation was going or what Jesse wanted, but no one had asked him to leave yet. They asked Leonard to come here and fast. They wanted something from him.

"I just don't know what to do, Leonard." Jesse threw his arms in the air, landing against his skinny thighs with a slap. "It's like Jackie's trying to ruin the plan."

"He's twelve and confused."

"Hold on," said Jesse, holding up a finger. He disappeared into the house for a second to return with a fresh, open can of beer. "I'd offer you one, but you hate alcohol, right?"

"You remembered."

Jesse tapped his skull, taking a sloppy swig. "Not many men I've met turn down a real drink like you."

They both forced fake chuckles, squinting at one another in a queer showdown of visuals.

"Can I see him?" asked Leonard.

Jesse waved a finger in Leonard's face, not confirming or denying the request.

"That's the thing. Look, no one expected Jackie's breakdown today, let's call it. Margot and I were talking, and maybe you should take him."

Leonard's eye widened as he swallowed his pulse, ready to jump out of his throat. Yes, yes, *yes*... Leonard's mind screamed. His heart thumped against his chest, threatening to break free any second. This couldn't be happening. It couldn't be this easy... but could it? Leonard's mind raced, yet he needed to remain placid. He couldn't let Jesse see this was the plan, the hope all along.

"Take Jackie? What exactly do you mean?" Leonard could only hope he thought what Jesse meant was correct. Now was not the time to assume poorly. He would not be the fool this time.

"You know, take him. Jackie loves you. I mean, sometimes I think he likes you more than me."

"Oh, that's impossible," said Leonard.

It was so fucking possible.

"You have a way with Jackie. It's a good thing, Leonard. And I'm almost thankful for it because here we are. Margot and I have to go to Thailand. It's our calling. I can't break Margot's heart over this. I haven't seen her this excited about something in a long, long time. And she made a lot of sacrifices here. She's a mother to her kids, to Jackie. A lot of giving there, you know? I can't let her sacrifice Thailand because someone in the bunch doesn't want to go."

Leonard fought through the thick saliva in his mouth, begging for a drink, but he didn't want to push his luck. He watched Jesse take another chug of the cheap beer from the dented blue and white can. He was ready. He wanted to hear Jesse say why Leonard was beckoned to a house where he's never been welcomed.

"So, yeah, Margot and I were wondering if it would be a good idea for you to take Jackie while we make the big move to Thailand. He could live with you."

Leonard's ears scorched with the news he had wanted since day one without Millie, and it was finally here.

"If it's too much, just tell me to shut up now. Margot's got her hopes up," said Jesse, leaning into Leonard's personal space. "I kind of told her you'd probably do it."

Do it? Leonard wanted to yell, consider it done.

"And then once we're settled and have things up and running, we'll arrange to have Jackie come to Thailand. Of course, that might be months, maybe even a year. But we'll be ready for him eventually, and vice versa."

"So, this wouldn't be a permanent thing?" Leonard's heart lurched as the contents of his stomach swirled. He didn't know which emotion he needed to cater to first.

"Nah, Leonard. I couldn't ask you to do something like that. Plus, Jackie knows where he belongs. Despite what he said today, he knows." Jesse's voice cracked, trailing off while he chased a stray fly with his eyes to the center of the yellow porch light.

"What did Jackie say today?"

Jesse smacked the air with a hand. "Oh, he was yelling some crazy shit. Excuse my language. He kept saying how he hates it here. If he hates it here, he'll definitely hate it in Thailand. He wants to live with you... blah, blah, blah." Jesse rolled his eyes. "Like if he really feels this way, how long has he kept this inside? That boy has the greatest restraint I've ever seen if you ask me... if any of that is true."

Leonard knew it was true. It had to be. He needed it to be the truth. But he also needed to play the role of the sympathetic ear. The grandparent who wanted to make everything work in the sweetest way possible.

"Ah, jeez, Jesse. That must have been very hard to hear."

"You should have seen how pissed Margot got when she heard Jackie rattling off his mouth like that. And I don't blame her. I know we don't talk about it often, and I know what today is, but sometimes I think Millie's passing messed Jackie up more than we know."

It was a punch to Leonard's gut. Something he didn't want to hear, but it was still important to acknowledge. Today, Jackie should be with his real mother rather than remembering her... if he truly remembered her at all. It was something Leonard couldn't recall ever speaking about with Jackie. Maybe he traded words once, twice at most, with Jesse when figuring out logistics for Jackie. But that was it. Millie was a ghost who haunted everyone.

"Maybe he needs therapy. Sometimes it can be very beneficial with the right therapist," said Leonard.

"Maybe that's something you can work on with him while we get things straight in Thailand."

Whenever Jesse uttered the word Thailand, Leonard bit his tongue. The whole idea sounded ludicrous, fake, and ignorant. Like Thailand would serve everyone better. The extreme of the situation didn't make anything sound real. But the reality of Leonard's life proved stranger than any fictional story. Leonard sucked in a sharp breath, ready to answer Jesse's proposal.

"You make it sound like I've said yes to your request," said Leonard.

Jesse did a double take of Leonard's bold statement. Of course, Jesse assumed Leonard had said yes already. Upon reflecting on his past, Leonard always played into Jesse's palm somehow. Tonight would be different. Jesse stopped blinking. He shifted back and forth before planting both feet on the splintered floor.

"You sound upset, Leonard. Have I asked too much? I never actually said it, but you have been generous with Jackie and the help you've given me over the years. Margot appreciates it too." Jesse dropped his voice to an almost whisper. "We both know she can be crabby sometimes. But this is why the move to Thailand is so important to her. To us. She's not happy here anymore, and I want her back."

Leonard now understood. It was about making his woman happy. Leonard could relate because that's how he functioned and ultimately failed so many times over, never learning and always repeating. He saw the wrong of his ways, but seeing it and embracing it, he knew how to make things right.

"I hear you. It's very important to be happy in life. Why settle is what I always say."

"Exactly. So... can you help us out here?"

Leonard inhaled all the breath he could before bursting. "I can help you. But I need more."

Jesse cocked his head to the side, waiting for clarification.

"I have no problem caring for Jackie. In fact, it would be an honor," said Leonard.

Jesse's smile broke free before Leonard could finish.

"But if you'd like my help caring for Jackie while you're in Thailand, then I want him full-time."

"Oh. What do you mean full-time?"

"I want Jackie to live with me permanently. As in, he stays here... with me. For good."

Silence by more silence by even more silence fell between the two men. Night dust particles danced in the struggling yellow light, the only signs of life between Leonard and Jesse. Jesse wasn't mad; he just didn't move. Leonard surmised shock blanketed the father. Leonard had plenty of time to wait for him to come back into the conversation. He had all the time in the world.

"What makes you even think you have the right to ask me something like that? To give up Jackie like that? For good," said Jesse, pushing the words out through his closed teeth.

"I have no rights. That's why I'm asking you for them."

"Give up my parenting rights? Like full rights? Like what happened with Millie before everything fell apart?"

"Yes. But you wouldn't need to worry about anything with me. I can provide a stable home for Jackie. He'll be happy. You'll be able to have your peaceful move to Thailand. Get your family back with

Margot. This could work out really well for everyone. Jackie would visit at least once a year with me, guaranteed."

Jesse crossed his arms, unleashing his snake eyes, scanning Leonard like a pest that needed to be flicked away. He shook his head, unsure of what to say. He tugged at his greasy hair, smacking his lips together.

"You really think I'd just give Jackie away like that? I'm very insulted, quite frankly."

"I don't take you as a fool, and I don't think you take me as one, either. I don't expect you to give up so easily. But I have something to keep you thinking for a little. Give me a minute." Leonard held up a fast finger and bolted to his car. He pulled out the legal-sized folder that held the answer, hopefully.

Jesse's eyes burned into the back of Leonard's head. He knew what people thought of his track record and never cared. But now, walking back to Jesse, he felt like a wobbly boy walking over hot fiery red coals with no barrier protecting his skin.

Leonard held the folder to his chest as his armor, ready to strip it away. He tapped the folder twice with his sweat-soaked hand. "I want to offer you something in return for full custody of Jackie. It's a property, and you'll become a wealthy man from it. You'll never have to worry again," said Leonard through heavy huffs of struggling breath. "You'll live the life you never dreamed possible in Thailand, or anywhere, for that matter."

"Is this a joke?" Jesse never tore his eyes away from the folder.

"I'm serious. This property is my prized possession. My greatest buy. It's matured in value like no other property I ever bought, and I'm offering to gift it to you." Leonard opened the folder for Jesse to show him the stack of papers that existed, but not with the intent for Jesse to actually read anything.

"What's the catch?"

"I told you. Jackie lives with me permanently. We'll have to draw up some paperwork and go to the courts. Don't worry. No one will get into trouble, and it will cost you nothing. What do you say?"

Jesse whipped his head back and forth, trying to absorb these words, this offer that would change both their lives. Leonard believed in the best, but he didn't know if Jesse agreed.

"It can't be this simple. How can it sound so simple?" asked Jesse, his voice threatening to break. "How much money are you talking about?"

"The building is worth eighteen to twenty million. Now you will need to pay taxes on the gain from the sale price, but you'll easily walk away with over ten million dollars in your pocket. That should guarantee a very comfortable life in Thailand or wherever you'd like to be."

Jesse stumbled backward, clutching onto the siding's peeling paint. "Holy shit. I wasn't even expecting a million dollars. Ten million dollars?" Jesse finished his beer in one long gulp. He wiped the back of his mouth with his stained shirt sleeve. "Let me talk to Margot. You wait here." Jesse turned his back to head inside when he stopped. He covered his eyes with a single hand as his shoulders shuddered. He turned around to face Leonard with tears in his eyes.

Leonard's pulse lurched in his throat, preparing himself for anything because he honestly had no idea how this whole proposal would end.

"Whatever I decide, I'm not a bad father," said Jesse.

"I know you're not. And that's why I completely trust you'll make the right decision for Jackie. He's all that matters, despite what you and I may want."

Jesse's eyes darted about the dark night until he nodded and disappeared into the house.

Leonard closed his eyes, letting a long hiss of oxygen leave his body. Whatever was meant to be would happen; he laid it all out to Jesse. He handed over control to a guy who didn't deserve anything, let alone this much money, but that's all it was to Leonard at this point. Just some green rectangular paper with a matte texture. He didn't care about losing anything anymore, except for Jackie, and he couldn't lose Jackie because to lose Jackie meant losing Millie all over again.

Jesse emerged, but with Margot this time, who dressed up for Thanksgiving, Leonard mused. Her hair was pinned up with too many bobby pins, her face flushed from too many cocktails, and of course, ample cleavage to round out her red house dress. She and Jesse leaned on the doorframe for support.

"What's this Jesse is rambling about some property?"

"It's true. The property is worth about twenty million dollars. It's yours once you sign over full custody rights to me for Jackie."

Margot snorted. That's all she did, snort.

"It's a real offer. I already told Jesse before that I'd cover all legal costs to draw up the paperwork from gifting over the property and arranging the custody rights transfer. But this offer won't be on the table forever. I need an answer tonight."

"Tonight?" asked Jesse and Margot.

"If you don't accept this now, then you never will. While the two of you do think about it, can I say hello to Jackie?"

"I'm not sure if he's awake," said Margot, crossing and then uncrossing her fat arms, only to cross them again.

Jesse shot Margot the first dagger glance of a warning Leonard had ever witnessed. His eyes triggered her to drop her arms to her sides instantly.

"Can I please go see Jackie? I won't ask again."

Jesse and Margot glanced at one another before locking eyes with Leonard.

They inhaled together and said, "Yes."

# *November 25ᵗʰ, 2021 – Jackie*

The house was a wrecked space with beer cans, empty chip bags, and crumbs strewn on the floor to decorate the place, and it wasn't a mess from the Thanksgiving festivities either. Leonard took shallow breaths, hoping not to catch the true odor of this house, Jackie's home. How can anyone call it a home? But anything was possible. He thought about how his children lived with their mother before moving in with him later in their lives. Complete gruel they lived off before shifting into Leonard's world. People survived somehow, like his children, if this was all they knew. This was what Jackie knew, but Leonard could give Jackie much better. More of everything in every way imaginable. This wasn't to show up Jesse or anyone. This wasn't to prove anything or make Leonard out to be a better person. It had nothing to do with money, for once. He wanted Jackie to know and experience the fullest life possible. He wanted his boy to know he had an unconditional support system waiting for him every day he awoke.

Leonard stepped on something sticky. Maybe gum? Or maybe beer-stained floors. At least the floors were hardwood. They needed to be refinished, but that was the least of what this house needed. It was a gut job. Leonard didn't even want to imagine if the house had wall-to-wall carpeting and the stench it would emit. He cringed, thinking about it as he took cautious steps every inch of the way to Jackie's room. His pulse throbbed in his ears, afraid to see what Jackie's room resembled.

He climbed the aching staircase. That was carpeted at least, safer for a house with children. The railing wobbled beneath his light touch. He shivered to imagine a child falling down the steps or pushing too hard on this unstable barrier and toppling over the side, breaking his neck. He shook off the image and fought the tingling in his fingertips. He was so close to Jackie, only inches away.

Jesse and Margot echoed to Leonard how Jackie was in the first room on the left, right off the staircase. When Leonard reached the top, his eyes scanned the tiny upstairs. It wasn't even a hallway. It was a pocket of a corridor with one room. The door was slightly ajar. This had to be Jackie's room, all alone on the floor.

Leonard entered Jackie's room and stopped when he spotted the boy slumped back to him. The room was perfect. Immaculate. Not a particle of dust. He was like Leonard. Amid complete rubble, Leonard always found his spot of solace, of cleanliness. He was neat by nature, and so was Jackie. His room was the opposite of the house. The dichotomy produced a dull ache in Leonard's chest. This small room was all Jackie had amidst the noise here.

Leonard tapped on the door. Jackie didn't budge. He probably didn't realize Leonard's presence. Leonard knocked again with two knuckles.

"Jackie?"

Jackie spun at the sound of Leonard's voice. He did a double take, not believing Leonard was standing a few feet away from him. Jackie jumped from the floor and ran into Leonard's gut, wrapping his skinny arms around Leonard's torso.

The cackle escaped from Leonard's mouth. "Hey, kiddo. Happy Thanksgiving."

They hugged and squeezed each other until it was impossible to apply more pressure on their bodies without causing harm. Leonard finally pried Jackie's hands off his back and pushed him away. He needed to see his grandson's face. There were tears in Jackie's eyes.

Leonard fought back his own tears before giving up and letting them flow. "What's wrong, my boy?"

"I don't want to go to Thailand."

"Then what do you want to do?"

"I want to stay here with you."

Leonard's world froze only to allow it to thaw and welcome the warmth standing in front of him. This was love. The pure love he should have embraced with his own children before he permitted his own distractions, his own vices, and all the women to cloud his judgment.

Leonard knelt to Jackie's level. They were eye to eye. He wiped a lone tear sliding down Jackie's face. Jackie's eyes were identical to Millie's and, in turn, identical to Leonard's. Jackie pulled a tissue from a box underneath his bed, offering a single sheet to Leonard, and took one for himself. They wiped their eyes until not a trace of liquid remained.

"Do you think Dad will let me stay here with you?" Jackie wiped both eyes, followed by his nose.

"I think there's a very good chance we can work something out. Would you like to live in my house? You might need to start a new school and make new friends. Not to say you won't keep your current friends now. Would you be okay with starting fresh?"

"I remember talking to Uncle Steven and he told me how he lived with his mom before moving in with you. He said it was like he had two lives. He said the second was better."

Leonard could count on his hand when he witnessed Steven speak to Jackie after Millie's death. He must have missed this interaction.

"I want to feel like I'm home. I know I live here, but that's it. When I'm with you, I feel... home. When I'm with my dad, Margot, and my stepbrothers and sisters, sometimes I really feel like I don't belong here. But when I'm with you, it's different, Grandpa. I know we don't talk about my mom. I only remember a little bit about her, but maybe we can start to talk about her more?"

"Of course, we can," said Leonard, taking Jackie's hand in his. "That's something we can work on, any way you want to. And just so you know, I feel the same way when we're together, too."

"Even though I don't remember my mom that much, I do miss her. I know missing her won't go away, but missing her doesn't feel the same when I'm with you. It's like I have other things to think about. Good things. Things to look forward to."

Leonard wiped his face, and his hand came away wet with tears. He didn't know when he started crying again but wasn't ashamed. Maybe the saying about Rosen men needing to appear tough was wrong all along. To be tough, Rosen men needed to feel and show their emotions, like his own grandfather. His grandfather wept the day he found out Leonard's father died in battle, he wept at the funeral, and he wept when Millie was born. No one ever saw Leonard cry until now.

Jackie held a white tissue out for Leonard. First, Leonard wiped Jackie's face and then his own.

"If I come live with you, can I change my name to Rosen?"

Leonard waved his hand. "It's just a name."

"Grandpa. Will I need to move to Thailand?"

Leonard smiled. He wanted to say no, but as Greg said, there were no guarantees in life. "I have a feeling everything will work out just the way we want them to."

"So, can I come live with you?"

Leonard ruffled Jackie's dirty blond hair. He looked at Jackie, his boy. Leonard draped his arm around his shoulders, pulling him close to his side. "First things first. How about we go out and get some dessert? And then after we eat, I've been wanting to give you something for a long time, but you must promise it won't interfere with your homework."

The boy's eyes lit up, leaning his face inches from Leonard's nose. "What is it?"

Leonard couldn't suppress a smile as he opened his mouth. "The latest PlayStation console."

Jackie's jaw dropped. "Do you think Dad and Margot will say it's okay?" Jackie's jaw dropped.

"Jackie, my boy. Things are going to be very different for us from now on."

Leonard led Jackie out of the bedroom and down the steps. Leonard knew they walked closer to a new home with each step forward. Closer to a new life together. He never felt so sure of a decision, even if it cost him everything. At least everyone he loved would be in a safe and loved place. A home. Full of Rosen family or not, it was time to head into a new day through the night, and Leonard had no doubts that somehow, in the most perfect style, they would manage.

*THE END.*